CHASING DEMONS

Melissa M. Garcia

Cover designed by BWNO Design http://www.bwnodesign.com

Acknowledgements

I'm grateful to my family and friends for all their love and support, especially my parents Ray and Lisa. For helping with the rough edges in the early drafts, a special thank you to Amy Olson and Melinda Norman. Thank you to my editor, Bob Greenleaf for his keen eye and helpful suggestions.

Above all, thank you to Neri Garcia for everything.

"What causes fights and quarrels among you? Don't they come from your desires that battle within you? You want something but don't get it. You kill and covet, but you cannot have what you want. You quarrel and fight. You do not have, because you do not ask God. When you ask, you do not receive, because you ask with wrong motives, that you may spend what you get on your pleasures."

-- James 4:1-3

Chapter 1

The first body washed ashore Saturday morning. It was discovered in Abalone Cove in Rancho Palos Verdes by a group of fishermen who had thought the decomposing corpse was a marine animal. The Los Angeles County sheriff's deputies responsible for protecting the citizens of Palos Verdes spent their entire weekend scouring the beach for clues to the man's identity and why he'd been sliced and dumped on such a beautiful Southern California beach.

I didn't hear about the body for a few days. That happens a lot in Los Angeles. With more than one hundred fifty people dying every day in LA, the news gets old and stale.

It was early May, and I was just settling back into the LA lifestyle after being away for three years. I was back working at the *Crime Reporter*, a small rag of a newspaper where I had gotten my first legitimate start years earlier. I had joined the *Crime Reporter* crew with the sole purpose of uncovering police corruption in Southern California. Between the Los Angeles Police Department, which handles the city of LA, and the Los Angeles County Sheriff's Department, which attends to the unincorporated areas in the county, someone is always screwing up.

It was a fun job, and they actually paid me to do something I would do for free. They gave me a steady paycheck and kept me so busy I had little time to resort to my old lifestyle of stealing cars.

I also had acquired a new ride: an original green 1966 Porsche 911. If I was going to live in Malibu and drive into LA every day for work to piss off law enforcement, I needed a ride that would draw attention. I wanted to be seen.

I normally didn't work on Saturdays, but I hadn't been in the office all week and was annoyed at the text messages and e-mails from my editor. He was quite impatient waiting for my next big story. Unfortunately, I had spent the entire week digging into several LAPD officers, with no luck finding any dirt. I was starting to think the chief was doing something right.

I had missed the Saturday story run. For the first time since returning to the *Crime Reporter*, my name wouldn't be on the front page. I didn't care too much about that, but as the only Pulitzer Prize–winning writer on staff, I knew my name sold papers. So did the editors. Missing a deadline would upset them. Apparently the newspaper business wasn't doing so well in the age of the Internet, and that was somehow my fault.

I woke Saturday morning feeling on top of the world. Mattie Hardwin was sleeping next to me with a satisfied smile on her face. I wasn't hungry. I skipped the coffee, but grabbed a shiny red apple from the clean, spacious kitchen. I looked around at Mattie's place, a far cry from where I had grown up. My life was finally on the upswing. I decided to drive to the office for a few hours to catch up on the crime reports and be a responsible working stiff.

I was driving to the *Crime Reporter*'s offices on Sepulveda Boulevard when Orin McKay, my only real friend at the paper, called me on my cell phone.

Orin is a funny little old Irishman whom I allow to follow me around because he listens to me and because he's a hell of a writer. He's kind of like a leprechaun, except he surprises people by being very street smart. He follows the obituaries closely, always looking for leads. Unfortunately, he wasn't calling me with a story.

"Luc, there are two deputies waiting for you in your office," Orin said.

I smiled as I slowed my Porsche at a red light along Pacific Coast Highway. I had done something right this week after all. I pitched the remains of my apple out the window.

"Did they say what they wanted?" I asked.

"No, but they mentioned that John Carliss was on his way, too."

John Carliss was an old high school rival. We had shared a jail cell together once after a bitter fight. His father, still a cop at the time, was able to get us both released. Since the fight, John had joined the LA County Sheriff's Department as a deputy and over the years worked his way up the ranks. He had recently been promoted to assistant sheriff, but Sheriff Bernie Maclay had four such assistants, so I didn't actually know what John did for a living. John was always concerned about my stories.

If I had to put a face to my enemy, it would be John. He stood up for the organization I was trying to take down. He was a good, honest cop and the only one who had no problem going head to head with me. He had nothing to hide, and I knew I'd never find dirt on him. When writing my stories, I discovered that John did as much investigating as I did. If he found one of my targets to be innocent, he'd present me proof before I could get the story in the paper. If he found my target to be guilty, he would undermine my story by putting the deputy on administrative leave. It was a clever response that somehow always made the department look good and me look like a vindictive reporter out to ruin someone's life.

I decided a confrontation with John wasn't what I needed this morning, so I told Orin I wouldn't make it into the office after all, and if John showed up to tell him to make an appointment.

I pulled a U-turn at the next light and followed the highway back up the coast past Santa Monica and into Pacific Palisades. My cell phone rang again. I ignored it, figuring it was either John or my editor, and tried to enjoy the drive.

The weather was cool for May, but the overcast skies most Southern Californians knew as "June gloom" had crept in early this year. With the offshore marine layer hanging on, the inland areas wouldn't see sun until late in the afternoon. At the coast, we would be lucky to see the sun at all.

Pacific Palisades is known as the place where the sea meets the mountains. Palm trees and multi-million-dollar homes line the highway. On one side, the Pacific shoreline stretches out to the abyss. On the other, the high cliffs and bluffs look ready to fall on top of you. I drove past the beautiful beaches toward Malibu, where I was currently living with Mattie.

I had moved in with her just a few months earlier when her divorce to my best friend, Spencer Hardwin, was finalized. It was a difficult transition for all of us, but we were making it work. I would do anything for Mattie. She was the reason I had the life I had.

I was so close to paradise, but a glance to my right, up the steep cliffs, reminded me I was still living on the edge. One wrong step, and it could all come crashing down.

When I turned the corner toward Mattie's house, I felt the first stumble. Two black-and-white LAPD patrol cars were parked in the long driveway. The front door stood wide open. Panic gripped me as I slammed the car into park.

Running toward the door, I saw two uniformed police officers standing in the doorway. They jumped as I came in, and one of them spilled coffee down his arm. It dripped onto the red Spanish tile. Mattie's dog was raising hell from the back yard, which scared me more than the officers did.

"What the hell is going on?" I yelled.

Mattie walked in, and I felt myself relax just a bit. She was alive, safe.

I don't think she actually knows how much she commands a room when she walks into it. Every head turned in her direction, yet her eyes were on me. She looked like an angel, soft and fragile next to the men with uniforms and guns. Her chocolate hair hung to her shoulders.

Her small face was soft, and although it hinted at sadness, I knew she was okay.

"Luc, I'm sorry. I tried to reach you on your cell."

I grabbed her hand, mostly to keep her at my side and away from the officers.

Two other men appeared from the living room. They wore suits, stood stiffly, and had serious looks on their faces. They had their badges already out, offering me a look.

"Get the hell out of here," I yelled, ignoring the badges.

"Luc—" Mattie said, her voice soft. The protest stopped when I held up my hand.

Taking the cue, one of the officers wearing an expensive black suit stepped forward and offered his hand to me. I didn't bother to shake it. I was looking for an arrest warrant, or at the very least a search warrant. I didn't see either.

"My name is—"

"It doesn't matter," I interrupted. "You're all the same. You've been harassing me my entire life. If you think I've done something illegal, you can discuss it with my lawyer."

"Mr. Actar, we'd just like a few words with you."

"No." I looked at Mattie. "Did they give you anything?"

She shook her head. My fear turned to anger as I tried to figure out why these men were in Mattie's house.

"Do you know who I am?" I asked.

The officer who had offered his hand smirked. "Yeah, we know your whole story. You felt harassed by law enforcement as a punk kid, and now as an annoying adult you write stories attacking anyone wearing a badge."

"What's your name?" I asked, wondering if I had written anything about him lately.

"David Marquez. Do you want me to spell it for you? Try as you might, you won't find anything dirty on me."

Marquez was in his late thirties, but I could still see enough of the cocky attitude new officers often display right out of the academy. I immediately dismissed him and focused on the older man who was obviously in charge.

The man waved to the uniforms at the door. "Wait by the car," he said, taking the mug from the one who had spilled coffee on himself. He turned and handed the mug to Marquez. Finally he broadened his shoulders and looked me straight in the eye, as if daring me to confront him. He was older than Marquez, with gray sprinkled through his thinning hair and mustache. He held himself like a lifelong cop, and his demeanor told me he was used to controlling the room. I knew that if I was going to start trouble, I should stay away from him. It wasn't cockiness oozing from him like his younger partner; it was confidence.

"My name is Evan Carter," he said, pulling out a business card. "We just need a minute of your time. We can discuss this anywhere you'd like."

I knew the threat was coming. He would suggest talking here or at the police station. I didn't like the threat, and I didn't like the options.

"Luc, please just listen to them," Mattie said.

"I'm not answering any of your questions. This is Mattie's house. You don't belong here."

"When was the last time you spoke to your father?" Marquez asked.

I grabbed the coffee mug from Marquez and pointed at the door. "Out!"

Carter turned and waved Marquez ahead of him toward the door. Once Carter was across the threshold, he turned around and faced me, squaring himself for anything.

"Mr. Actar," Carter began again, "I'm sorry to tell you that your father is dead."

I stepped forward. "Get out of Mattie's house."

Marquez took a step toward me. "You don't need to be hostile. Mrs. Hardwin let us in."

I didn't like him. I could tell in his eyes that he was smug and enjoyed messing with me, but he made a mistake by mentioning Mattie.

So I threw the coffee in his face.

I smiled at his pain and confusion, but his older partner was faster than I had anticipated. As the smirk disappeared from Marquez's face, Carter grabbed my arm, spun me around, and shoved my hands toward my shoulder blades. Pain shot up my arm as he twisted my wrists, and my forehead crashed into the wall. Bells rang in my head, and black spots appeared. I heard the handcuffs click as they tightened around my wrists.

I was handcuffed before the mug shattered on the Spanish tile, the coffee spreading toward Mattie.

Carter pulled me away from the wall. "Down," he instructed before kicking the backs of my knees. I fell, and intense pain engulfed my bad knee.

"You're an asshole," I muttered.

"Mr. Actar, I'll forgive you for your rudeness and your misdirected anger and pain over your father's death, but you're going to have to ask the judge for forgiveness for assaulting an officer."

I looked over at Marquez. He was still wiping coffee from his face. The other two officers were watching, shocked, but with a glint of humor in their eyes.

"Luc Actar, you're under arrest," Carter said.

Chapter 2

They didn't transport me to the county jail. Instead they led me back to the living room and sat me on the couch. Mattie sat silently next to me. She looked furious, but she knew better than to say anything. I wasn't sure if her anger was for me or the officers who had barged into her home.

"Are you going to book me?" I asked Carter. He appeared to be the one in charge, but I had no idea of his rank. He ignored me and continued talking on his cell phone in the entryway.

"Shut up, Luc," Mattie said, her eyes watching Carter.

I had a great view of the open front door and watched as the two officers wiped up the spilled coffee and broken mug. Charlie, Mattie's German shepherd, sat on the other side of the sliding glass door, quiet now, staring at me. I could tell he was confused as he waited for a sign from me. I leaned back on the couch to relax as much as I could with my hands tucked in the crook of my back.

"Did you invite them in?" I asked Mattie.

Her eyes met mine, and I could see the anger was directed at me. We aren't a perfect couple. We fight. She wins most of our fights, but that doesn't stop me from trying every now and then.

"Do you have to make a case out of everything?" Her voice was just a bit too high.

"What the hell are you doing letting cops into this house?" I asked.

"Not everyone is your enemy, Luc."

I resisted the urge to roll my eyes. "What did they ask you?"

"They didn't ask me anything. They were waiting for you."

I pushed. "Tell me exactly what they said."

She sighed, rolled her eyes. "They wanted to know when you would be home and when the last time was that you saw your father. Okay?"

"What did you tell them?"

"Nothing. I told them they would have to wait for you."

"Did they ask where I was?"

"No, and I didn't offer the information."

I saw the officers at the door straighten. Then John Carliss walked through the door. He wore a gray suit with a thin green tie and looked like he had just walked off Wall Street. He had a square jaw and a tight mouth.

Something about his stance made people respect him and bow to him. He had the ability to control a room without using fear and intimidation.

His face was all cop. His stance was all cop. His angry and distrustful dark eyes were all cop. Which meant we weren't friends and never could be.

I smiled at him. He didn't smile back. John looked at me like I was a little brother who had disappointed him, and he shook his head. I shrugged. It was all I could do with my hands cuffed behind my back.

"My knight in shining armor," I said.

"More like the first horseman of the apocalypse. You really know how to ruin my Saturday afternoons."

Apparently, John wasn't in the mood for my humor. He looked at Carter. "Take the handcuffs off."

I smiled and tried hard not to snicker like a little girl.

"Can't do that, sir," Carter said. "He's going to be charged with assault on an officer."

John looked at me, then waved Carter and Marquez outside. I was disappointed. I wanted to see the fight. Mattie stood up.

"Where are you going?" I asked.

"I'm going to get John a cup of coffee."

"Why do you have to be so nice to the cops?"

She gave me a look. "How the hell can I listen to what they're saying about you from in here?"

I smiled and let her leave. My stomach grumbled, and I realized the apple hadn't been enough of a breakfast. I tried to remember what food Mattie had in the kitchen. After ten minutes, I decided I would have to get some fast food somewhere. After twenty minutes, John returned alone. The front door closed behind him. I heard Charlie whimper from the sliding glass door.

"You screwed up, Luc," John said.

"Remove these handcuffs."

"I can't. LAPD has a case against you. It doesn't involve the Sheriff's. I can only do so much."

I knew he had worked out something with the officers. It was only a matter of time before he offered it to me. I leaned back and decided to wait it out.

"Fine," I said. "Let them book me. What are we waiting for? If they keep me in these cuffs any longer, I can add kidnapping to my suit against the LAPD."

"Kidnapping requires them to take you somewhere."

I rolled my eyes.

"Do you know why the officers came here?"

"Someone's always trying to pull this shit on me. Anything to keep me from writing my stories."

John smirked. "You didn't have one this week. What's up with that?"

I didn't answer. "Why were you looking for me?"

He shifted, and then sat down across from me. "Your father passed away last night. I know you didn't like the man, but I wanted to see if there was anything I could do."

I was surprised by the gesture. I was also a little confused. "The LAPD sent cops to my house and office to tell me my asshole father, who I haven't seen or spoken to in over fifteen years, is dead? And you come out to make sure everything is okay. I don't understand."

"Luc, when your name comes up around a badge, they panic. No one wants to get in your crosshairs."

I laughed, thinking how I could really mess with the four cops who had walked into Mattie's house. They would regret it.

"Here's the deal." John slapped a business card on the table. I only glanced at it. White card with red and black writing.

"No," I said. I was hoping for a better offer.

"That's the best I can do. Agree to anger management, and the LAPD will drop the arrest right now. No paperwork, no booking, no night in jail."

I shook my head. "That's bullshit, Johnny. I don't need therapy. I don't have an anger problem."

"You assaulted an officer. The prosecutor is going to suggest the same thing after you spend a night in jail."

"I threw coffee on a cop. I didn't hit him." I shook my head. "I'll take my chances in front of the judge."

"After spending a night in jail?" he asked.

"Have you had Mattie's cooking? The jail serves much better food."

John laughed. "You might be right. You probably won't even miss Mattie tonight. I hear the sex isn't half bad in there, either. If you like it that way."

I dropped the smile. John was right. I didn't want to spend the night in jail. I may have been a criminal once, but I wasn't affiliated with any gangs. In fact, there were a few gangs that didn't like me very much.

"Five sessions, an hour each day this week. It's not that bad. And I'll even throw in my help with your father."

"What help?" I asked.

"I'll deal with the coroner's office and have the department take care of his remains. I know you don't want to take on the cost of your father's burial."

"Dump his body in the first hole you find. Or leave him out for the coyotes to eat. It's better than he deserves and costs a whole lot less."

"I'll take care of it. Will you go to the damn therapy, or do I need to go out there and tell Mattie you're leaving with the LAPD tonight?"

I cringed. "Deal. I just want you to know that I hate you for dragging Mattie into this."

He smiled and produced the key to the handcuffs. "It works every time. You know Mattie is your Achilles' heel. You should be careful not to let other cops see that."

Chapter 3

John left me alone in the living room. I heard the cars leave and still hadn't seen Mattie. I slipped the business card in my pocket and went in search of her. I didn't want to have the fight, but it was better to get it over with.

We'd only been together six months, since my return to Los Angeles, but I'd known her most of my life. She was my best friend, and despite my upbringing and my knack for criminal endeavors, she had always encouraged me and shoved me in the right direction. I would never have graduated high school without her help, would never have considered college without her insistence. I had always thought stealing cars and robbing drug dealers was much more profitable. But looking around the house I now lived in, I knew I had done the right thing in listening to her. She would always be the sane one in our relationship.

I found her in the kitchen, rummaging through the pantry.

"What are you looking for?" I asked.

"Alcohol," she said.

I folded my arms over my chest and leaned against the counter. This wasn't how I expected the fight to start. She was always surprising me.

"How come we have no alcohol in this house?" she asked.

I stared at her ass as she kept digging. "Because you don't drink, and I'm an alcoholic who gave it up when I moved in here with you."

"You're not an alcoholic, and I do drink. Ah, found it."

"Found what?"

She produced a bottle of wine. "Orin gave this to me when you moved in."

I cocked my head. "Why?"

She smiled. "He said something about you driving me to drink."

"Is that what this charade is about? I'm driving you to drink?" I hadn't expected that angle. I tried to reorganize my defenses.

"No, we're celebrating." She pointed to the cabinet behind me. "Grab some glasses."

I didn't bother with the glasses. "You're celebrating that I didn't get arrested?"

She laughed. Her laugh always made me smile. "If I celebrated every time you weren't arrested, *I'd* be the alcoholic. We're celebrating your father's death."

I straightened. "We're not celebrating my father's death."

Her smile faded at my tone. "Why not? You hated that man. Aren't you glad he's dead? After what he did—"

"I don't care about my father. He could have died years ago, and I wouldn't have cared. He's not important enough for me to acknowledge now. I've moved on."

Ignoring me, she reached behind me and grabbed two glasses. "I'm celebrating his death with or without you. I hated that man, and I've been waiting years to hear this good news."

I watched as she opened the bottle and wondered about the rich Catholic upbringing of hers.

"Do you think this changes something?" I asked.

"Sure. That part of your life is over now, right? We can move on."

I grabbed the bottle. "Mattie, the second I moved in here, I moved on from that life. I'm not a criminal anymore. I have an honest job, and it pays me well. You don't have to worry about me."

She smiled, but I could tell something was wrong. "And yet you were sitting in my living room with handcuffs on."

"Slight disagreement. Johnny cleared it up for me." I pulled out the business card and handed it to her. "Unfortunately, I have to go see a shrink."

She read the card. "Dr. Holstein. Anger management?"

I looked at the bottle. "This is cheap wine. You're not going to feel well tomorrow if you drink this."

She handed me the card back. "You could use the therapy."

"Why? I don't have an anger problem. Have you ever been afraid of me?"

She drank and handed me a glass. I wondered if the delayed response was important. I waited for an answer.

"You could use someone to talk to."

I took the glass. "I have you. That's all I need."

"When was the last time you saw him?"

"My father?"

She nodded. She had locked onto me, and I knew she was digging for something. I wasn't too thrilled to be having this conversation, but it was better than turning and walking away from her.

"Do you think I killed him?" I asked.

She didn't answer.

I put my glass down. "Honestly, he wasn't worth going to prison for."

"How did he die?"

I shrugged. "I didn't ask. I don't care."

She downed the remainder of her glass and poured herself more.

"I'm not that person anymore, Mattie. My past is my past. I'm not going back."

I had no idea how wrong I was.

I woke with a start early Sunday morning. I was used to the nightmares and weird dreams that came when I was stressed, but I had gone to bed happy. Figuring it was the bad wine, I sat up and found Mattie missing from my side.

She wasn't on the balcony, but I looked outside anyway. The fog had rolled in, hiding the ocean view and the moonlight. Making my way down the stairs, I could see the light from the alarm system still on. There were no lights on in the house. I checked the kitchen, but it was empty. I considered starting a pot of coffee, then decided it was too early for that.

I found Mattie in the office, sitting quietly at the desk in the dark. Her loyal dog, Charlie, was stretched out asleep at her feet. The computer wasn't on, and there was no light coming through the window.

"What's wrong, Mattie?"

"Why is the desk locked?" she asked. "You have something that shouldn't be there?"

I rubbed my eyes and stared at her through the darkness. "I wouldn't put you in danger."

"That's not what I asked."

"But that's the answer you're getting. I told you I left that life behind. Don't you trust me?" I wasn't quite sure why I was snapping at her, but I wasn't in the mood to deal with an interrogation, nor did I feel like sharing.

"Why were you so worried to have the cops in the house?"

I shook my head, trying to make sense of the situation. She was changing topics just like an experienced detective. I wondered who had put the questions in her head. Who was really attacking me?

"Mattie, I don't want cops in the house because I don't want them near you."

"Not all cops are bad, Luc."

"Just because you were raised rich doesn't mean you should be naïve."

"They weren't here to arrest you. They didn't even have a warrant to search the house."

I laughed. "They wouldn't need one—you invited them right in!"

She stood. "So what happened yesterday was my fault?"

I shook my head. I was too tired to fight fair with her, and I obviously wasn't prepared for her sneak attack.

"It was my fault," I said. "I screwed up and let my emotions control my actions. I'm sorry. Can we go back to bed?"

"Are you going to see the doctor?"

"The anger management guy?" I hadn't had time to figure out a way out of it yet. "If you want me to go, I'll go."

"I think it would be good for both of us if you go." She walked past me, and I could see from her puffy, red-rimmed eyes that she had been crying.

Chapter 4

On Monday morning, I headed to work late after sleeping in. Mattie was gone when I woke, but she had left me a copy of the *Crime Reporter* on the kitchen table. It was a simple gesture to let me know we were okay again.

It was another beautiful day in Los Angeles. The weather was expected to be in the eighties inland, and even the marine layer that had hung on strong the last few weeks was expected to disappear by the lunchtime rush.

As I pulled the Porsche into the parking lot of the *Crime Reporter,* I felt the car's engine stutter. I had acquired the Porsche three weeks earlier. It was a great find from an old man who no longer had the energy to take care of it. It was in good shape, and I've always been a sucker for fast cars. Unfortunately, since the only thing I knew about cars was stealing them, I would have to have a mechanic look at it soon.

From the outside, the offices of the *Crime Reporter* looked much like those of your local tax accountant. Maybe that was why I avoided it whenever possible. I opted out of the elevator and took the stairs up to the third floor. I had the Monday edition under my arm and a smile on my face.

I reached my office out of breath. My lung capacity was just starting to improve since I had given up smoking three months earlier. Soon I could start training for a marathon, or at least outrun the cops looking to send me to Pelican Bay.

I opened the door to the *Crime Reporter* and found Natalie, the receptionist, on the phone. I signaled I needed coffee. She responded by pointing to her wrist. I ignored her look of displeasure and headed for the kitchen myself.

It wasn't much of a kitchen, but it worked for me. I've never been used to large kitchens. This one had room for only a sink, a fridge, and a small table with two metal chairs no one used. It was dirty and often smelled of stale food, but I didn't mind.

As I looked for a clean mug, Natalie walked in. Only fifty-five, she resembled a sweet old grandmother, but I knew she wasn't that sweet. She had a mean streak in her that matched my own. She'd been living with an older woman for the past thirty years, and I never understood how she had been able to pull that off.

"You're late," she said.

I smiled and winked. "I need coffee before I can argue with you. Where's my mug?"

"You don't have one. You just steal mugs from the other reporters and then forget to wash them."

"Isn't that your job?"

"Why do you insist on being an asshole?" She pushed me aside and handed me a clean mug. "Callahan is pissed at you."

"And you're here now to warn me or annoy me? I don't care if Callahan has a whole herd of buffalo up his ass. He can wait. I need coffee. Where the hell is my lemon?" I rummaged through the fridge and pushed past the stacks of rotten food. Reporters aren't just lazy, they're slobs.

"Why do you have to yell at everyone?"

"The same reason Callahan insists on hiring people that annoy me." I slammed the fridge hard enough to shake the room. My good mood was diminishing quickly as I tried to determine the possible culprit who had taken my lemons. "Someone stole my fucking lemons again! God damn it. I swear I'm going to bring a gun in here tomorrow and take everyone out."

Natalie shook her head and reached for the step stool. "I believe the *Reporter* has a no-tolerance policy on workplace violence."

"Oh yeah, a policy, that'll stop me. What are you doing?" I watched as she stepped on the stool and reached above the refrigerator.

"I bought you a few lemons yesterday and hid them up here."

"What?"

She turned to me with a smile. It wasn't the sweet smile she gave to everyone else. This was the disapproving one she reserved only for me.

"I don't like you when you don't have your morning coffee," she said. "You're mean."

I helped her off the stool and kissed her on the lips. I tasted nicotine. "You're an angel. Will you marry me?"

She laughed and handed me the lemons. She always forgave me for my bad attitude. I wondered if her partner did the same for her.

"If I thought for a second you would leave Mattie," she replied, "I would have to remind you the *Reporter* has a no-tolerance policy on sexual harassment, as well."

"Okay, I promise never to have sex with you, Natalie."

I pulled a lemon out and sliced it. She watched as I squeezed it into my coffee.

"I don't understand why you like that."

I drank the coffee and smiled at her.

"Callahan's waiting for your story ideas from Saturday," she said. "He wants to see you in his office."

I walked out of the kitchen. "He'll have to wait until I come up with something."

Most of the reporters had cubicles in a large, open space outside the editors' offices, but I had negotiated—or threatened, depending on your point of view—for my own office near the front reception. It made it easy to come and go without most of the staff seeing me. The room was small, but I didn't need a lot of space. The tired and worn red carpet needed to be replaced, and the paint had been peeling off the walls for some time. The desk was old and rickety, but I knew the space was temporary so I didn't care.

I had a laptop I used only for e-mail, and a phone I used even less. The drawers in the desk were almost always empty, except for a spare bottle of tequila and emergency cigarettes. There may have been a paper clip left over from the editor who had previously occupied the space.

The only object of any real value was a framed photo Mattie had given me when I got the job. It was a photo her father had taken of the two of us as children. I put it out only when I knew she was coming by. The rest of the time it was stuffed in a drawer. She thought it was a great photo. It only reminded me of a beating I had received the next day for not being home on time.

Today my desk was buried in mail that had sat for almost a week. I tried to remember the last time I had gotten anything of importance, then gave up. I turned on my laptop and quickly deleted the e-mails from Callahan. I flipped through the mail and tossed most of it in the trash. At this rate, I would be out within the hour.

I stopped at a US Postal Service Priority Mail envelope which was addressed to me. There was no return address. I ripped it open and slid out a gray folder

The phone on my desk rang. I knew it could only be Callahan. He had obviously heard I was in, but was too scared to confront me face to face. He hated confrontation and enjoyed yelling at me over the phone. I picked up anyway.

"Luc, the Monday story meeting is not optional."

"Good morning to you too, Callahan."

"It's almost noon. The story meeting—"

"You seem to forget that stories aren't discovered in a conference room. The best stories come from working the streets."

I opened the gray folder and read the top page. It was a police report. A missing person's report. I closed the folder and looked for a note. Not finding one, I looked in the envelope and pulled a small piece of paper from inside. *Thought you might want this.* There was no name, and the handwriting didn't look familiar.

"So you have a story?" Callahan asked.

"Not yet, but I'll have something for you by Friday." I looked back at the missing person's report, hoping for some clue as to why someone would think this would interest me. Then I saw the name, the city, the year.

"Luc, I run a daily newspaper. You can't hold stories for Saturday."

"No one buys your paper during the week." I turned the page and picked up a photo.

I hung up the phone as Callahan's voice continued to rise. My only thought was about the photo in my hands.

It was clearly a crime scene photo. The alley behind the Torrance Liquor Store, a store I knew all too well. I had stolen food from that store when I was a kid. Sold dope inside as a teenager. And I had killed a man in that alley.

Blood covered the brick wall and the rusted green dumpster. A label on the bottom of the photo identified it as the crime scene. The next picture was of Carl Palfy, the no-longer-missing person. His eyes were vacant, his face covered in dried blood.

I reached into a drawer and pulled out my cigarettes. I lit one without taking my eyes away from the picture.

"Thought you gave up smoking."

I jerked my head up and slammed the file closed. Orin stood in the doorway, looking even older than usual. His white hair was a mess on top of his head, and he had bags under his red eyes.

"You okay?" he asked, his slight Boston accent slipping in.

I grabbed the folder and the envelope and yanked open a drawer. "I'm fine." I dropped everything into the empty drawer and locked it.

Orin studied me. I considered asking what was wrong with him, just to change the subject, but I didn't want to hear the story, whatever it was.

"I thought you had an agreement with Mattie about the smoking," he said.

"Shut up, Orin."

He sat down across from me. I rarely snapped at him, and even I knew I wasn't acting normal. I turned and opened a window to allow some fresh air into the cramped room.

"Don't screw this up, Luc."

"It's one fucking cigarette. Let it go." I threw the cigarette out the window.

"I'm not talking about the cigarette. You have a tendency to self-destruct when left to your own vices. Mattie's officially divorced. You have a good job. Don't do anything stupid."

"This time around, I know what's important."

"Good." He studied me a moment longer, then asked, "You have a story?"

I shook my head. "Anything popping for you?"

"LA Sheriff's has a dead body that washed ashore this weekend in PV. No ID yet, but I've heard the body was cut up."

Palos Verdes wasn't a hot spot for crime. A body in the water there was probably due to an accidental drowning. Just being in the water could result in the body being cut up. I wasn't interested, so I waved it off.

Orin shrugged. "What's with the cops showing up here on Saturday?"

"Just bullshit. They claim they just came to tell me my father died."

"Sorry to hear that."

"You wouldn't be if you knew the man. I think it was just a ploy to put handcuffs on me."

Orin's interest piqued. "Yeah? What happened?"

"I threw coffee on one of the guys. His partner wasn't happy about it. Johnny mediated and got me stuck in anger management therapy."

"Sounds like fun," Orin said. "Better fifty enemies outside the house than one within."

"I don't know what that means."

"Just don't let the doctor get into your head."

"I have my first session this afternoon, and it's all the way in Irvine. I have to clean off my desk and get moving soon."

"What about your story idea for Callahan?"

I waved my hand. "I'll make some calls and see if I can come up with something."

After Orin left, I took the empty envelope out to Natalie and asked if she knew when it had come in.

"Saturday," she answered. "I remember because it was the only thing in the mailbox when I checked it."

"Any way to tell where it came from?"

She looked at it. "No return label . . ."

"Can we call someone and find out where it came from?" I asked.

"It's standard USPS packaging. It could have come from any post office in the country. The envelope is free." She examined it more closely. "The only thing you can tell for sure is it was processed in LA. The stamp shows 90001 as the ZIP code. That's the downtown LA area."

I thanked her, even though she hadn't been much help in narrowing down who had sent the envelope. I decided my time was best spent making calls to try to dig up some dirt for a story, but the picture of Carl Palfy stayed on my mind.

Chapter 5

I wasn't too pleased to find out that Dr. Holstein's office was in Orange County in the city of Irvine, nor that I was going to have to make the commute at the worst possible time of the day.

Situated near the decommissioned Marine Corps air station, Irvine was developed by the Irvine Company in the sixties and was now home to numerous technological corporations. It was becoming a very popular place for large businesses, and the commute was wreaking havoc on the 405 and 5 freeways.

On the drive to my appointment, the air conditioning in the car started blowing hot air at me. I called LB Motors. Mac managed the chop shop for me in Long Beach to supplement my income at the paper. To the outside world it was just a simple mechanic's shop, but I had spent numerous summers working at the shop when I was a teenager. I learned how to steal cars and how to sell hot cars, but I never learned how to fix cars.

"Mac, I need you to take a look at my car. I'm having some problems, and I don't know what to do about it."

"The Porsche? That baby should be purring."

"If I'm calling you, it isn't. It's losing power."

"You gotta bring that into a dealer, *homie*. I don't know shit about a Porsche's engine."

"I don't want anyone looking at this car except you. I'm having problems with the air, too. And it's too damn hot to live in California without air in my car."

"Roll down the window."

"How does that help the air conditioner?" I asked.

"I don't know what the problem is with the air, unless I look at it. For now the problem is you're hot. Rolling down the window fixes that problem."

I shook my head at his logic. "When can I bring it to you?"

"Anytime. We're pretty slow right now."

I told him I'd try to bring it around by the end of the week, as I stared at the brake lights ahead of me.

After two hours in brutal stop-and-go traffic on the south 405 freeway, I arrived thirty minutes late to Dr. Holstein's cushy office. I tried not to let the enormous traffic jam affect my mood as I walked in and met Dr. Mary Holstein.

She was a thin woman with small eyes and a pointy nose. She seemed younger than I had expected. I guessed her to be in her early forties, but she could have been older. She wore tan slacks and a light blue shirt with just a hint of makeup. Her blond hair was pulled back in some sort of clip.

She had a firm handshake and soft, manicured nails. She glanced at her watch while still gripping my hand. I tightened, she released.

The office was homey, decorated similarly to Mattie's house, by a professional designer. It made me uncomfortable, despite the obvious intention to put me at ease. The carpet was a dark green and the walls were painted beige. Expensive-looking artwork hung on the walls, and a tray with china sat between the couch and her stiff, old-fashioned chair.

"Relax, Mr. Actar. Sit down. Would you like some tea or coffee?"

I thought she'd be annoyed with my late arrival, but there was no sign of it. Her lips pulled into a smile as she reached for the tea, a subtle smile probably used to calm her patients, to make them feel welcome or at peace. I didn't like it any more than I liked the room.

"You think I'm going to jump over the desk and attack you?" I asked.

Her hand stopped on the teakettle as her small eyes looked up at me like a doe caught in the headlights. Her smile disappeared, replaced with an obvious look of concern.

It was my turn to calm her. "Relax, Mary. I'm not crazy, nor am I angry."

"You can call me Dr. Holstein," she said. She poured herself some tea, forgetting her offer to me, and sat down.

"I don't like titles," I said, staring down at her.

She pointed to the chair. I didn't sit. She didn't seem bothered that I didn't follow directions. She picked up her notebook and read to herself.

"I thought you volunteered for the sessions," she said, looking up from her notes.

"'Persuaded' is a nice way to say it."

"Under what threat?"

I relented and sat on the overstuffed couch. I was surprised to find it quite comfortable. "A night in jail."

"I think this is a fair trade-off. Did it take some arm-twisting?"

I smiled. "My arm was twisted, but unfortunately, there was no excessive force, if that's what you're asking. Still, it wasn't an easy decision."

"I wasn't asking whether the police hurt you. I'm concerned with why the decision over therapy was something you had to consider."

"I don't need therapy, especially anger management."

She grunted. A small smirk crossed her lips.

"What?" I asked. "You have something to say?" I leaned toward her.

The smirk disappeared. She closed the notebook. "No need to say it. You don't want therapy, so I'm done here." She stood and grabbed her tea.

"That's it? We're done?"

"I am. I can't help someone who doesn't want . . . someone who doesn't *think* they need help. My time is valuable. I'd rather help people than waste my time with you."

"You're scared of me?"

"From the second you walked in here, you've been trying to intimidate me. Well, it worked. You're an intimidating person. I can see how people in your life could mistake that for anger. You use your emotions very effectively to control your environment. If you don't see how that can affect your relationships, then there's nothing I can do to help."

I thought about Mattie and wondered if she had ever mistaken my behavior for anger. Had she felt intimidated by me? I thought of her tears as she sat in the dark office, and I wondered what I had done that could move such a strong woman to tears.

"Sit down, Mary," I said.

She cocked an eye at me.

I leaned back. "I may intimidate you, *Doctor*, but you're not scared of me. I'd see it in your eyes. Sit down. Please."

She sat down and blew on her tea. "Anger is a normal, healthy emotion, but when it gets out of control it can become destructive. I'm not going to tell you not to get angry, but I'd like to see if your anger may be affecting your relationships or your quality of life. Tell me about the incident that brought you here."

I recalled my return to Mattie's Malibu home, my decisions with the coffee, and John making the deal.

"Why were the officers there to begin with?" she asked.

"They claimed they came to tell me about my father's death."

"I'm sorry. Were you two close?"

I shook my head. I didn't want to talk about my father, and I knew that as a therapist, Mary would pounce on a dead parent.

She waited for me to say something. I responded by just staring at her. She finally re-opened her notebook and made a note.

"Claim?" she asked. "Why didn't you believe the officers?"

"Cops enjoy hassling me as much as possible."

"You don't trust law enforcement?"

"I don't trust anyone who thinks they have more power than I do."

"Thus your dislike for titles. What's your earliest memory of the police?"

I folded my arms over my chest. "We're going to analyze my childhood now?"

She shrugged. "My goal today is to figure out what triggered your anger and violent outburst. Then we can develop strategies for keeping those triggers from tipping you over the edge. I'd like to know where the distrust of the police first came into play. I'd like to see the world as you do."

"You'll never see the world as I see it. You didn't grow up on the streets hungry. You didn't have to steal to survive or watch good friends die beside you. You lived in a sheltered world with fancy furniture and china to drink your tea in."

She made another note, but didn't look at me. "What part of that makes you angry? The fact that I was sheltered or the fact that you weren't?"

I felt the burning in my stomach and settled myself. I didn't want her to see my anger. I decided short answers were probably the way to go here as I thought of Orin's message about letting people get in my head.

"It didn't make me angry. It made me determined."

She nodded. "You lived on the streets?"

"Yes."

"How long were you homeless?"

I considered her question. "A long time. We didn't have a permanent home until we moved to the Torrance apartment. I was eight, I think."

"When you were living on the streets, where did you go? Did you have a shelter to go to at night?"

"No. We slept on the street with the other drunks and junkies. If I was lucky, I was left alone for the night."

"That must have been scary for a child."

I said nothing. She was a smart woman, and I figured she could answer that one on her own.

"Where did you eat?"

"I ate where I found food, which was hard to do back then. I stole from the liquor stores or I broke into homes to find food. I used to steal fruit from the trees in people's back yards. You'd be amazed how many rich people ignore their fruit trees."

She had stopped writing in the notebook, and I thought she actually looked interested. She probably didn't have a lot of homeless people sitting on her couch.

"You were stealing food before you were even eight?" she asked.

I smirked. "People don't normally suspect a five-year-old with good hands. Besides, my father was a great distraction."

"How long did this go on?"

"Stealing food?" I shrugged the question off. "Doesn't matter. I got a roof over my head now."

"Did you ever get caught?"

I thought of the first time I had been caught by a little girl staring down at me from her tree house as I stole lemons from her tree. I almost smiled as I thought of how young and innocent Mattie had been.

"Rarely. I'm good at blending in, and most people ignore the homeless on their streets."

"Living on the streets is dangerous. Did you join a gang?"

I looked at her, confused. "A gang? No, why?"

"Some people living on the streets turn to gangs for money or protection."

"No," I said, shaking my head. "People turn to gangs for protection from other ethnicities that insist on putting people down to make themselves feel better. I was poor and homeless. I was ignored, not discriminated against. I didn't need a gang to steal what I needed."

"And the cops ignored you, too?"

"Not always. They enjoyed hassling all of us."

"So why not join a gang to protect yourself from the cops?"

"Look, I wasn't into the gang lifestyle. You have to be willing to die for others. I wasn't into that shit. Besides, joining a gang only brings more attention from the cops. I wanted less. I could steal better when they weren't looking at me. I could deal with their harassment now and then as long as I could feed myself every day."

"So, is that why you didn't believe the cops when they told you why they were there? You thought they were just harassing you?"

"Yeah. They don't send four cops for a next-of-kin notification. It's overkill."

I glanced at my watch. Since I had arrived late, our time was almost up, and I knew I'd hit traffic on the way back to Malibu. I couldn't wait to see Mattie. I couldn't wait to put this day behind me and move on.

"I'm curious," she said. "How many cops usually come for next-of-kin notification?"

She seemed intrigued. Her interest kicked something loose in my head. I cursed and pulled out my cell phone.

"It depends," I said. "If it's a natural death, the LA coroner's office will send one of their investigators. No cops necessary. If it's murder, suicide, or otherwise suspicious, you'll probably be visited by a couple of homicide detectives."

I dialed Orin's number at the *Reporter* and listened to it ring.

"What's wrong?" Dr. Holstein asked.

"Marquez and Carter weren't in uniform. They were suits. Homicide detectives."

I had assumed they had sent four cops to harass me. Now I had to wonder if there was another reason. If my father's death was being investigated as a murder, was I a suspect? And was the police report I had just received that morning somehow connected to his death?

I tried to ignore the sense of impending doom as Orin picked up. I told him to look into Detectives Marquez and Carter. He didn't ask why, but promised to dig up as much dirt as he could find by morning.

"Why is that important?" the doctor asked me as I closed the phone.

"It means my gut was right. The cops were lying. They're trying to keep me away from my father's death."

She tapped the pen on her pad. "What's your proof?"

"An hour of therapy every day? Let me ask you something, Doc. Do you know John Carliss? He works at the LA Sheriff's Department."

She shook her head.

"Have you taken a lot of referral cases from LAPD or LASD?"

"Not really. I do take a few, though."

"Do you know of any anger management doctors in LA?"

"Quite a few. Why?"

"John wanted me out of reach and way out of town. That's my proof." I stood. "Time's up. I gotta get back."

Chapter 6

I drove to West Los Angeles to the In-N-Out Burger on Venice Boulevard. A patrol car sat in the parking lot. I parked next to it and found Officer Patrick Golla at a booth inside, reading the *LA Times*. A large burger sat half-eaten in front of him, and his hand was stuck in a container of french fries.

Patrick was one of the few LAPD patrol officers I was still in good standing with. He was fairly new to the force and wanted everyone to like him. He had just switched partners, from his training officer to a veteran who wouldn't stop talking about how horrible the city had become. Patrick liked the community and the people in it. He had joined the force with the belief that he could change the course of things. But in the past few months, he'd had too many reminders that he wasn't in control. No matter the training, no matter the hope, it would never be enough to change reality.

He was already getting discouraged by the lack of respect officers got on the street. He had first put on the uniform expecting to be seen as a hero. Instead, he faced fear and hatred every day.

I could see the job tearing him up already. He had packed on at least forty pounds in the last few months. The shoes were no longer shiny, and I often found him searching the classifieds for jobs.

"Those double-doubles will kill you," I said as I sat down across from him.

I saw him jerk as he put the paper down.

"What the hell are you doing here?" he asked, looking around at everyone else but me. He wanted me to like him, but he also knew other officers wouldn't be too thrilled with him talking to me.

"Your leads last week were bullshit. I looked into Lieutenant Melina and found nothing."

He shifted in his seat and wiped his hands. "Then you didn't look hard enough. The guy's dirty."

"Bullshit, Patty. If there was something to find, I would have found it. I don't like looking into clean cops. It makes me look untrustworthy."

"You *are* untrustworthy. You're a journalist."

"You made me waste a week of digging, and the only thing I found was Melina dating your ex-girlfriend. Are you trying to use me to get dirt on him?"

He leaned back. "Believe what you want. That guy's gotta be dirty."

"I thought we had a deal. You help me, I help you. You gave me shit, so you owe me."

"I don't owe you anything, Luc."

I smiled. "She dumped Melina. You're back in. So you owe me."

He looked over at me now. "How'd you do that?"

I didn't answer. He pushed the tray of fries toward me. I shook my head.

"I need some information on some fellow officers," I said. "Detectives Marquez and Carter. They're probably homicide."

"Oh yeah. RHD. The A-team."

"What's that mean?" I asked.

"They work Robbery-Homicide. They're considered the A-team because they're the best the city has. If Britney Spears takes a bullet coming out of the Viper Room, the A-Team is on it. If the mayor's daughter is a suspect in a drive-by in Carson, they're the ones called in. They've both received the medal."

I knew he was referring to the silver-and-blue medallion the LAPD handed out for valor. It was impressive, but didn't mean the cops weren't dirty.

"So they handle high-profile cases?"

"Sure, but not just high-profile cases. They handle the favor cases. If someone comes to the chief or the mayor and asks for a favor, those boys are called in. And it doesn't matter where in Southern California. They can take over just about any investigation in any jurisdiction." He shook his head. "Whatever reason you're looking at them, forget it. They're clean. You don't get picked for the A-team if you can't handle every part of the job. The chief can't afford to be embarrassed in the courtroom or on the six o'clock news."

I thanked Golla and left him to finish his lunch. He had a smile on his face now, and I hoped his love life would make him happy for a bit longer.

I needed to know why the LAPD was putting the A-team on my father's death. I didn't believe for a second that it was because of me. Since I didn't trust John to tell me the truth, and I didn't have anyone else in the LAPD who trusted me, I decided to try a homicide detective in the Sheriff's Department.

Chapter 7

I called the LA Sheriff's Industry Station and asked for Detective Ward. I was told he was off duty, and they wouldn't give me any more information. I drove to the Last Call Bar in La Puente, frequented by many of the officers and detectives, hoping to run into someone I could persuade to give me information about where I could find Ward.

The bar was clean and busy, unlike my usual hangouts. A baseball game was playing on the big screen, and the bartender looked young, pretty, and friendly. The place was decorated for Cinco de Mayo, with sombreros and tequila bottles everywhere.

I spotted several uniformed deputies wearing the normal tan shirts with dark green pants, sitting at a large table with a few others in dark suits. Detectives, I hoped. I was about to make my way to the party when I spotted Detective Ward alone at the bar.

Ward is one of the few cops in this city I would come close to calling a friend. If he didn't have a badge, I could see us hanging out. He's actually too good at his job. He's good at reading people and even better at bluffing. I have to be careful around him. One look, and he can detect my bullshit. He knew I had secrets to hide from law enforcement, so he never trusted me.

He looked unusually unhappy as he stared into his beer. I sat down on the stool next to his. He glanced up, cringed, and returned his gaze to his beer. He said nothing, so it was up to me to break the ice.

"Whatcha working on?" I asked.

"Move on, asshole."

I was only slightly upset with the reception. I knew he didn't really like me much. We had met a few months earlier when I returned to LA to help Mattie find her soon-to-be ex-husband, Spencer, after he had suddenly disappeared. Detective Ward had appeared to lend his assistance, but in reality he was investigating a murder Mattie's husband was suspected of being involved in before his disappearance.

Ward and I had started on the wrong foot and never really got to a better footing, but we had spent some time working together looking for Spencer, and I realized we were both looking for the truth. I had found Spencer first, which irritated Ward further, but I had helped him close his case. In the end, another lawyer was behind bars for the murder, and Ward had helped me bring Spencer home.

We had learned a lot about each other despite the constant fighting. We had both grown up with lousy childhoods and messed-up families. I looked up to him because he had survived despite the difficulties. And he had done it legally. I knew he looked down on me because I hadn't. He still had a long way to come before liking me.

"Come on, Ward. I need your help. I have a boss crawling up my ass for another story on police misconduct. You work with it every day. Give me something."

"Do you notice the table full of law enforcement over there?"

I looked. A Hispanic woman at the table, dressed way too sharply, was staring back at me. She looked out of place with the uniforms. She was beautiful in an understated way. Her straight black hair was parted down the center and fell just past her shoulders. Her large, dark eyes took in everything in a matter of seconds and made you feel like they had never left your face. She was thin, and she wore a long, dark green skirt, either meant to hide her figure or demand that you focus on her stern face. Either way, she seemed to have given no thought to the fact that she was a beautiful woman. No makeup, no nonsense, and no vanity. She was too beautiful to be the normal badge bunny.

Not noticing my stare, Ward continued, "Those are excellent individuals who protect and serve Southern California. They deserve respect for their service. They don't deserve you barging in here on their turf and waging a war."

"I'm not starting a fight," I said, returning my eyes back to Ward. I pulled the beer away from him and drank. "And this is not your turf."

"I'm not assisting you, Luc. Find another snitch."

"Ward, you know I can make your life a living hell. Don't make me go there."

He turned to look at me now. He was about to speak, when he suddenly closed his mouth. I could see something change on his face. Fear? Panic?

"Detective, did this man just threaten you?" It was the woman from the table. She had asked the question of Ward, but her eyes were locked on me. The tone wasn't friendly and was just loud enough for everyone in the area to hear. I knew all the uniformed officers were now looking in my direction, but I kept my eyes on her. It didn't matter to me that I was clearly outnumbered. I was only thinking how I could turn this into front-page glory.

Definitely not a badge bunny, she was more beautiful up close, and I found myself smiling at her. She smelled like Dentyne gum. I heard Ward fidget, but he didn't answer.

I stood and offered my hand. Smiling back at me, she offered her hand in response. She'd be a perfect politician: threatening one second, and kissing babies the next. Then I realized who she was.

I introduced myself. Ward groaned, but my eyes stayed on the beautiful woman. I watched the smile fade as she tugged her hand away. Back to cold bitch. It was such a lovely transition.

"So I finally meet the infamous Mr. Actar," she said. "Are you still working at the *Crime Reporter*?"

I ignored her question. "Please, call me Luc." I looked at Ward and noticed his face had turned a brilliant red. I'd never seen Ward this uncomfortable before. I had only heard rumors of Ward's questionable past in the department. Now I wanted the juicy details. "You must be Maria, right?"

"Sergeant Ramirez," she corrected. "What can we do for you, Mr. Actar?"

"I'm just harassing Ward here. He doesn't like me much."

Ward cleared his throat and continued to pretend we weren't standing right next to him. He raised his hand to the bartender to bring him another drink.

"We don't have the time to fight with the media," Maria was saying. "I must ask you to stop harassing our detectives. If you have questions on a particular case, you need to go through the media liaison like everyone else and leave Ward to his job."

"Hey, everyone's got a job to do. I just hate when people with a badge abuse it."

"Are you accusing the Sheriff's Department of breaking the law?" Her back straightened, ready for the fight.

I smiled. She had passion behind her eyes. I knew I would enjoy this. "There's lots of crime to report. You should read the *Crime Reporter* sometime. The innocent people you arrest read it religiously."

"We do not arrest innocent people. We arrest criminals." She was beautiful even when angry. I could see why Ward was attracted to her.

"Oh, but you're wrong, Maria. And I think Ward here would agree with me."

She turned her angry glare toward Ward, but he was already interested in his new beer.

"See, this is your problem," I continued. "You seem to forget that the people you arrest are innocent." She opened her mouth to argue, but I interrupted. "Innocent until proven guilty. Those carrying a badge not only ignore the fact that a court and jury are needed to prove guilt, but they tend to hand out their own sentencing. I have firsthand experience, so I'm here to make sure you stay in line."

This time Ward did look up for a split second to throw an angry glare, but he remained silent.

"My detectives are above reproach. And for you to—"

"Oh, yeah. I can see that. Would you like me to list the names of those investigated by your own department for misconduct both on and off the job?" I pulled out my notebook. I heard a chair scrape the floor in the direction of the uniformed officers. I grinned at Ramirez. "I always keep the list handy."

This time when she tried to speak, Ward interrupted her. "Sergeant, you're not going to win this argument, and your comments will only end up on the front page of the *Crime Reporter*. I'd suggest you leave it alone."

I realized my game was over as her lovely mouth dropped open. She stared at Ward, considering her next move. Deciding it probably wasn't worth it, she spun around and stormed back to her party. I received some stares from her fellow officers.

"She's gorgeous and fun to play with," I said. "I like her, but she is very dangerous."

Ward looked up at me with curious eyes. "Why do you say that?"

"I would never have pegged her as a cop."

Ward shrugged, his interest gone. "Luc, don't ever categorize the rogues as 'those carrying a badge.' I'll admit there are some flawed seeds. I don't want you clumping me in with them. And listen to your own preaching and toss the list. They're innocent until proven guilty, too."

"Sure. So she's the one you slept with to get the gold badge?"

Ward cringed. "Can you say that louder so the entire department can hear?"

"I would, but I'm pretty sure everyone already knows."

It was common knowledge that Detective Ward and his boss had hooked up a few years ago. He had just passed the detective test and had been assigned to the homicide division when Internal Affairs started their investigation. Both were cleared, but he was branded with a scarlet letter even though it was Maria who was bound by marriage.

Now it appeared their relationship was more than strained.

"What do you want, Luc?"

"Let's go grab a drink, and we can chat."

"I have a cold beverage right here, thank you very much. Besides, I really don't want to be seen socializing with the reporter trying to bury everyone who carries a shield. That won't improve my popularity."

"You would think fucking the boss would help."

"Not when you're investigated by Internal Affairs. The closest I've been to hanging out with other deputies is when IAB stakes out my gym."

I didn't want to feel bad for him, but I knew what it was like to be the outsider. We had both grown up with no one to care for us, forgotten and ignored by the system. I understood him and the pain he tried to hide because of it.

"Besides, she's not my boss anymore. She's patrol sergeant now. Those boys over there report to her."

I looked over the crowd of uniformed officers and wondered if I could dig up some dirt on them. It would be fun to annoy the patrol sergeant. I made a mental note to look into her team. In the meantime, I needed to see what Ward could find out about my father's death.

"I need a favor, Ward."

He looked at me now. "Again, *why* would I help you?"

"I'll leave you alone for the rest of the year. No stories, no quotes, no anonymous sources."

"I have a feeling this isn't going to be a fair trade."

"My father died." I whispered it, hoping it would evoke whatever sense of sadness I could muster.

"I heard the news. So what? You despised the man."

I wondered how the news had spread. Did the LASD have daily meetings about me?

"I need to know how," I answered. "I don't want to deal with the LAPD. Those guys hate me. Did you know they have RHD working my father's death?"

He looked at me. He seemed interested now, but said nothing.

"Can you help me out? I just need the basics. Where and when and how."

"Why do you care?"

"He was my father. I deserve to know. Wouldn't you want to know if it was your family?"

He eventually nodded. "I'll ask a few questions, but that's all I can promise. Now leave me alone with my beer."

I noticed Patrol Sergeant Ramirez watching me as I left.

Chapter 8

When I pulled up to Mattie's house, there was no black-and-white patrol car sitting in the drive, but the blue sedan screamed "cop" all the way. The front door was closed this time, and I saw John Carliss sitting on the porch. He wore his usual expensive suit, but now was sporting aviator sunglasses and a stupid grin.

When I approached, he called out, "Mattie wouldn't let me in. She wouldn't even offer me lemonade. In this heat, that's cruel and unusual punishment. How was therapy?"

I didn't answer. "What do you want?"

He stood, and the grin disappeared. "Due to your obvious disinterest Saturday, I didn't go into the details of your father's death. It has come to my attention that you now want information. First, your father's death is LAPD business, not Sheriff's. I was doing you a favor coming here on Saturday."

I started to interrupt, but he held up his hand.

"I'm not finished. You need to leave my detectives alone. The department isn't at your disposal."

"You're mad because I asked about my father's death?" I wondered how long Ward had waited after I left to call John.

"I'm mad because you're pulling Detective Ward away from real work. Tell me what you want to know, and I'll tell you. I never said it was a secret."

"Let's start with Marquez and Carter. Why were two detectives from RHD asked to tell me my father had died? Was it murder?"

"No," John said. "Your father died from liver cancer. He'd been sick a long time. The detectives came because they wanted to talk to you about your father."

"Why? Why is the A-Team interested in my father's death?"

John shifted, and I knew he felt uncomfortable with the fact that I knew more than he had expected. John had never been one of those cops who held back information from me. He didn't believe in cover-ups. I had to wonder what had changed.

He sat back down and took off the sunglasses. "Before his death, your father was a suspect in a burglary."

"Bullshit."

John looked up.

"My father isn't a thief," I said.

"He was a drunk, degenerate criminal. His jacket is longer than my arm. I knew him when we were kids, and I've seen his crimes as a cop. Don't bother trying to protect him now. He's dead, remember?"

I said nothing and wondered if he knew more about my father than I did.

"The detectives were investigating the burglary when they heard about his death. That's why they came to talk to you. No other reason."

"Why did you send me all the way to Irvine for counseling? Were you trying to get me out of the way?"

He laughed. "Do you think I set up that whole incident Saturday so I could entrap you into anger management?"

"It wasn't a bad plan."

"Yeah, and I carry anger management cards with me all the time just in case I bump into you. The card came from Detective Carter. He had the card, and he made the deal with me. There was no covert operation here. I'm sorry it's all the way in Orange County, but then again, you assaulted a police officer. It's not our responsibility to make this convenient for you."

"I threw coffee—"

"Luc, don't try to find something here that isn't." He stood. "I don't know if this is because of the shock of your father's death or if it's because you need a story, but there's nothing sinister going on here. Your father passed away. He lost his battle with cancer like millions of other people. Even if you don't care, it'll do you some good to talk about him to someone who will listen." John stuck a finger in my chest. "If you want to know anything else about your father's death, contact me. Stay away from Detective Ward and the rest of the LASD. And stay away from Marquez and Carter, too. If you approach them, they may request restraining orders on you, and that won't look good for anyone."

I watched John walk back to his car and wondered why the LAPD detectives were also off limits. The questions they had come with on Saturday hadn't been answered. Why weren't they interested in talking to me anymore? Why did John not want me talking to anyone in law enforcement except him?

I had a bad feeling in my gut. I looked back at the house and saw Mattie staring out the window at me. I wasn't sure what she had heard.

~~~

After Mattie fell asleep, I called Mac at LB Motors. I knew he'd be working late. He picked up on the first ring, but didn't identify himself.

"Mac, it's me. I need a favor."

"Yeah, yeah. Bring the car by *mañana*. I'll take a look at it. I got a few things I gotta move tonight."

"It's not about the Porsche. I need you to clean up the records there. Make it spotless. It's time to clean house and run a clean ship."

He knew what I was saying. The shop had always appeared legit, but under close police scrutiny, there were problems. The only way to look legit to a cop who was really looking was to go legit.
~~~

"How long we talkin'?" he asked. He sounded just a bit annoyed with me, but I let it go.

"As long as it takes. Something's not right, and I'm getting a weird feeling I'm being shut out."

"What does your buddy Johnny say?"

"He's the one shutting me out. Ward's off limits, too. Everyone's extending their distance like I'm kryptonite."

"Maybe your Johnny-boy is involved in a cover-up. Guess you can finally get some dirt on him. Don't worry about the shop. I got you covered on this end. Clean up the other areas."

I wasn't sure what he was talking about. Everything else in my life had gone legit when I moved back to LA and in with Mattie.

Then I remembered the file sitting in my desk.

Only two people alive knew I had killed Carl Palfy in that Torrance alley ten years ago. The cops had nothing. I had beaten Carl in a fit of rage, leaving him in that alley with his blood all over me. After, I had slept for days in the abandoned apartment I used to call home, hoping death would take me. I wasn't so lucky.

A few months earlier, I had confessed to Mattie what I had done. She was disappointed, but she knew why I had done it. Carl Palfy had been her boyfriend, one I had never approved of. When she called to tell me the relationship was over, I knew she was upset about more than the breakup. Turns out he had hit her. I got drunk and decided it was best to teach the boy some manners. I hadn't expected it to go as far as it had, but years' worth of pent-up rage was released in just a few minutes, and I left the alley drained and defeated. Carl Palfy never left.

Someone else knew about Carl Palfy. Someone else had known enough to send me a file on his death. That someone would be coming for me. I needed help, and I knew that meant confessing to someone else what I had done, someone I could trust with this type of information. Only one person I knew came to mind.

Chapter 9

I met Big Jim when I was in college. He had been our starting center for half a season before dropping out when he was convicted of assault and sent to prison. He had been a gang member since he was eight years old, just like his father and two uncles. Now that he was approaching forty, with two convictions for assault and having been suspected in numerous other incidents, he was what law enforcement called a career criminal. Tired of the gangs, he had struck out on his own and started a business—one of murder.

During his last visit to the slammer, I had kept an eye on his younger sister, Genie, to prevent her from spiraling into drugs and prostitution. I donated time and money to keep her focused on her dream of opening her own business.

The Paradise Club, a dance club and bar that teetered dangerously close to topless, had been her creation. She had brought in friends she knew from the street to help out, and she kept a close eye on everything that happened there. So far she was succeeding and staying out of trouble.

I knew Big Jim hung out there in the evenings between jobs. That way they could both keep an eye on each other.

The club was quiet, even for a Monday night. There were no dancers on the stage. The guys there looked to be regulars, the kind who came in alone, minded their own business, and kept their mouths closed and eyes down, unless one of the scantily-clad waitresses wandered by. They came to be left alone, have a drink in peace, then wander to their poor home or family a little drunker than when they arrived.

I found Genie tending bar and sat down at an empty stool. I was glad to see she seemed happy. Her dark skin appeared to glow in the low light. The bar showcased the bottles of exotic alcohol that sparkled like gems. I stared at them for a while, entranced by the beauty.

"Hey, beautiful," I said when she spotted me.

"Luc," she said, smiling. She came over to the bar and gave me a bear hug. "It's been a long time. What are you doing in here?"

"I wanted to stare at the forbidden fruit," I said, pointing at the bottles. "Jim here?"

She pointed to the hallway where the office was located. A waitress called her away, so I waved and headed toward the hallway.

I recognized the man standing at the closed door as Jim's bodyguard, a Samoan named Pioa. He wasn't as big as Big Jim, but for some reason, he scared people much more. His head was shaved, and his dark eyes peered through small slits.

He didn't look too pleased to be guarding a door.

"I need to see Jim," I said.

"We all have needs, friend." He didn't even look at me, but continued to stare down the empty hallway.

"I'm a friend of his. He'll want to see me."

Now he looked at me. "Does it look like I care?"

"You know, I'm beginning to not like you."

"I'm devastated." He returned his stare down the hallway.

"Can you please just tell him I need to talk to him? Tell him it's Luc."

"I know who you are, and that's why you're not going in there."

"What's your problem with me?" I asked.

"I have lots of problems with you, Actar. First, you draw a lot of attention from the boys in uniform. And second, you've become quite chummy with a few of them. I got a job to do. Go away and let me do it."

"You're a real asshole," I said.

When Pioa made a move toward me, I backed up. I knew I could hold my own against him, but I wasn't stupid. I also knew Mattie would be upset if I came home bruised and battered.

"Tell him I'll pay him for his time."

He grunted. "He doesn't need your money."

"I wasn't offering money." I could see I had finally intrigued him, but he still didn't budge. "Fine. I'll go talk to Genie." I turned to walk back down the hall.

"Sit."

I turned back.

"Sit down," he repeated and pointed to the dirty floor at his feet.

"On the floor?" I didn't want to know what was down there.

"Sit, and I'll go talk to Jim and see if he wants to talk to you. Otherwise, you can get the hell out of here."

I sat because I had no choice. I felt like an idiot. Pioa disappeared behind the door. I got up to try the door and found it locked.

Pioa returned and was not pleased to find I had gotten up.

"Up against the wall," he growled.

"Why?" I asked.

"Weapons stay here."

"Bullshit." I wasn't carrying anything, but I didn't want him to know that. It was an ego thing. "My piece stays with me if your piece stays with you."

"That's my policy. If you want in, you leave it here."

"Then I guess Jim will be the disappointed one."

I turned to walk down the hallway, hoping he would stop me again. He didn't. Genie smiled at me from behind the bar. So I stopped and stared at the bottles, thinking of my father. He had introduced me to alcohol as a child. It kept the cold away. It kept the hunger pains away. It kept reality away.

"I have something for you." Genie disappeared behind a door. She returned with a brown bag and handed it to me.

"What's this?" I put the bag in my lap, knowing I probably didn't want to open it in public.

"It's the money you loaned me to open this place. I made it back and promised to settle."

"You don't have to, Genie."

"I want to. It's bad enough I borrowed the money without Jim knowing. If he found out I owed anyone money, I would never hear the end of it."

"I hate to tell you this, but I think Jim knows."

She sighed. "I should have figured. Does he know about you bailing me out of jail and having Mr. Connor defend me?"

"I don't think so. And I'm not telling."

She smiled. "What can I get you?"

I looked back at the bottles. "Whatever burns."

I begged a bottle of Patrón off her and headed for the parking lot. At least Jim knew I was there. His interest would have him coming to me. I hoped.

I hid the bag of money under the passenger seat and wondered what I would do with it. I sat in my car for over an hour, drinking straight from the bottle. That feeling of impending doom was still sitting over me, and I didn't have the strength to figure a way out of it. I didn't want to think of my father or how he was about to screw up my life again. The alcohol took my problems away, even if it was only for the night.

Just as I began to feel a buzz, the passenger door opened, and Big Jim sat down. The car tilted under his weight.

Jim's arms were covered in delicately pinned tattoos. Some came from prison needles and some from real tattoo artists, but all depicted death. He was only a year older than I was, but I couldn't imagine what he'd already seen in his life.

Jim had a way of making his victims disappear. Completely. So he didn't worry too much about being arrested. Prison didn't scare him, anyway. He worried only about retaliation from those on the street. I had no idea how many people he'd killed, but I knew he wasn't well liked among the criminal element.

"Nice ride. Who'd you steal it from?" he asked.

I didn't answer. I looked around and saw his guard dog standing behind the car.

"I don't like your security," I told him.

"You know, Luc, when I became an entrepreneur I had a lot of things to think about. I'm very skilled at killing, but I realized I needed more manpower. I needed a team focused on my security. It's become like a corporation."

"And he's your head of security?"

He nodded. "Exactly. I can protect myself. But I need someone to concentrate on protecting the company and the personnel. My employees expect the best, and I want them to feel secure. Secure employees can be trusted employees. The security protects all of us, and I don't take it for granted."

"But it's bullshit if I can't get to you."

Dimples pierced his cheeks as he smiled. "It's people like you that scare Pioa the most. Those that can get to me."

"You know I can't hurt you, Jim."

He shrugged his large shoulders. "We all have our weaknesses." He offered a cigarette, and I was too weak to refuse. "What's wrong, Luc?"

I didn't want to talk about my father or the file sitting in my desk drawer. But both were bothering me. I handed him the bottle. "I've got a strange feeling someone's coming for me."

"Good guys or bad guys?" he asked.

"Not exactly sure. Do you remember in college, when I disappeared for a couple weeks?"

He nodded. "You went after that ex-boyfriend of Mattie's. The one that hit her."

I looked at him now. I wasn't sure how much he knew of that time. I had never mentioned Mattie's boyfriend. In fact, I was pretty sure I had never mentioned Mattie to him until after she had hooked up with Spencer.

"Carl Palfy." I sucked on the cigarette, but kept my eyes on him. "How'd you know about that?"

Jim took a swig from the bottle. I watched him and thought about the nights I had spent passed out in that abandoned apartment. The smell of dried blood and vomit returned. So did the deep pain in my gut. I had been shut up for three days, spiraling out of control, until Spencer had rescued me and brought me back to reality.

"Who do you think found you?" he said.

"You told Spencer where to find me?"

"I couldn't let you drown in your own pity and vomit."

"I killed him. I killed Palfy in an alley."

I watched his reaction. He shook his head, but didn't look surprised. "He killed himself when he raised his hand to her. It was his choice. He chose wrong."

I liked his logic, even if I knew it was just his way of washing guilt away. "Someone knows. They're going to use it against me."

"And you're afraid you won't be prepared?"

"I'll be prepared. I'm just worried Mattie might be caught in the middle. I need someone to keep an eye on her. I'll pay you if I have to."

He waved his hand and shook his head.

"I promise to throw some business your way when I can," I added.

"No worries, my friend. Anything for you." He smiled and drank. "I'll handle it myself."

Chapter 10

The next morning, I was up early and made breakfast for Mattie. I was unable to sleep, thinking about Carl Palfy and the bloody alley I had left him in. I couldn't think of any reason for someone to send me the file unless they knew I had killed him. I would find out soon enough how much it was going to cost me to make it disappear.

I was on my second serving of coffee and had yet to touch the eggs I'd made, when Mattie walked in. She was a breath of fresh air.

She was working at a private Catholic school a few blocks away. I had to pull a few strings to get her hired, but I felt it was important for Mattie to be doing what she loved.

"You came in pretty late last night," Mattie said, reaching for the eggs. She smelled of sweet tangerines. "And you cooked. You must have felt guilty."

"You're looking too thin."

"And I believe that was a compliment. You must have done something *really* bad."

She sat across from me and ate. I got up to pour her some coffee.

"It wasn't meant as a compliment, but a complaint," I said. "You should eat. Don't you have a lunch break at school?"

"I'm usually too busy during the day. Some students need extra attention, but you didn't answer my question. What happened last night?"

"Nothing."

"You didn't drive home drunk, did you?" she asked.

"No." I stared into my coffee, as if it would hide my face.

I wasn't sure when I had switched from trying to distract her from her questions to handing out lies in response. I knew she could tell when I was lying, but it hadn't stopped me. I only hoped it would save me from an argument I knew I would lose.

When I looked up, she was studying me. I got up to grab another lemon.

"What did you find out about your father?" she asked.

"I'm not looking into his death."

"Luc, it might help you to put it behind you."

"I don't know anything, Mattie. I tried Ward, but he's now off limits."

She smiled, and I realized I had just admitted I was looking into it. I watched her finish her eggs. I didn't want to talk about my father, especially with Mattie.

"I gotta go," she said and stood, taking her breakfast plate with her.

Concerned that I had said something wrong, I got up and stopped her at the sink. "I'll drive you."

"That's okay. I'll take my car." She let me take the dish from her hands, but didn't look at me. She side-stepped me and walked to the window. "You've got company." She turned, kissed me quickly, and patted my face. "Play nice, and don't throw sand," she teased as she walked out.

Intrigued, I followed.

Detective Ward waited in the driveway. In fact, he was leaning against my car. More intriguing was the smile on his face.

I watched Ward say goodbye to Mattie and waited for her car to pull out of the drive before I walked outside.

I stopped on the porch. "What's up, Ward?"

He glanced at the Porsche. "Nice ride."

I didn't respond.

"I thought you'd like to take a ride to your father's apartment."

"You tattled to your daddy, and I was told not to play with you anymore."

"Carliss?" Ward shook his head. "I have a chain of command, Luc. There is a specific protocol when dealing with you. I had to report it."

"So do your job. I'm not stopping you, but you can't play both sides now."

He laughed. "And you're not playing both sides? How many cops did you talk to yesterday in hopes of getting information on your father's death? How many are offering you information today? We're taking my vehicle." He pointed to the patrol car parked on the street.

I groaned. I had spent my entire childhood avoiding squad cars. I had no intention of getting in one voluntarily.

"I'm not going anywhere in a black-and-white. Where the hell is your car?"

"In the shop." His smirk told me he was probably lying and enjoying my discomfort.

"And what happens when we go to dear ol' Daddy's place? Are we being followed, or are you recording everything I say?"

He shook his head. "If you don't want to go, then forget it, but you came to me for answers. I'm willing to share what I learned and assist you in finding the answers to the rest. No one else needs to know about this. Trust me, I'm not divulging this excursion to anyone."

I knew he wasn't supposed to be here, but Ward knew how to bluff, so I was still hesitant. I also knew he didn't like me much, so I wasn't sure why he was willing to help me, especially after being told to stay away.

"Let's take my car," I suggested.

"I'm not riding in a stolen vehicle."

"You obviously have no proof of that, or I'd be in cuffs." I set the alarm on the house. "Tell me where we're going, and I'll drive. You'll enjoy the Porsche. Believe me."

He looked at the car. "You're missing front license plates."

"It's a Porsche."

"California requires front license plates," he said.

"The car's on private property, so save your fix-it ticket, Ward."

He smiled and walked to his car. "Make sure it remains there," he called back.

I groaned and looked again at the police cruiser. I gambled it had been a while since he'd written a ticket.

"Fine, write the ticket. I'll wait."

He looked back at me. I could tell he was considering calling me on it, but the thought of paperwork wasn't looking appealing.

"Here's the deal. You come with me, and I tell you what you want to know about your father. Or you can wait here while I call a cruiser to sit on the house until you drive off in your fancy overpriced vehicle. Maybe I'll select the perfect officer who will discover probable cause to search it, too."

~~~

I sat uncomfortably in the front seat of the cruiser and kept my eyes on the road, trying not to breathe since the car reeked of sweat and piss. The stench didn't seem to bother Ward.

I was a bit surprised when he drove to Lakewood. Before World War II, Lakewood was an unincorporated part of Los Angeles County on the border of Long Beach. Many of the Navy sailors who went to sea at Long Beach liked the climate and settled in Lakewood after the war. During the war, Southern California had spent its resources building ships and aircraft, not houses, but during the 1950s, Lakewood built close to fifty homes a day.

The fast growth caused Long Beach officials to take notice. Newspapers pushed for Long Beach to take over Lakewood in 1953. A larger city would mean more advertising dollars to the paper, but as
~~~

threats of annexation began to circulate, Lakewood residents started a movement to incorporate themselves. By March of 1954, Lakewood voted to incorporate and forever separate from Long Beach.

As Ward pulled the car over in front of a series of duplex and triplex apartments, I looked down the street and spotted a church. Farther down was an elementary school with a large playground. It was a quiet neighborhood town, where people walked their dogs and spent Friday nights at the high school football game. I would never have guessed my father lived here.

Ward pointed to a triplex. "Your father lived in apartment B. We may not have a lot of time, but let's just talk to the neighbors and get a feel for your old man."

The apartment building was small and worn down, with dying grass and a cracked sidewalk. My father's apartment was in the middle. A young girl sat on the front porch of the back apartment. I hoped she was older than she looked as she flicked the ashes of her cigarette into a potted plant.

"You take the front house," I said. "I'll take the girl."

"Why do you want the female neighbor?"

"I'm better with women," I said and opened the car door. I pointed to the *Trespassers will be shot* sign posted on the front apartment. "Besides, I think I would be considered a trespasser."

Ward knocked on the screen door. A second later, the door opened and a large Hispanic man wearing nothing but boxer shorts faced him. Ward flashed his badge.

As I headed toward the girl, I knew I had drawn the better hand.

The smoking girl smiled as I approached. Her brunette hair was pulled back into a ponytail. Bobby pins kept the flyaway strands from her face. Her shirt was cut off just below her breasts. In bright red letters, it warned, *I help good guys finish first*. Classy.

"It sure is hot out here," I said.

"So are you," she said with a smile. Her confident demeanor made me guess she was in her early twenties, but her eyes looked younger.

She'd probably been on her own for quite a while. As she sucked on the cigarette in one hand, she fanned herself with the other.

I asked, "What's your name?"

"Georgia."

"Like the state?"

"Like the peach." Her smile turned sweet and innocent. She smelled flowery, despite the cigarette smoke. I found myself intrigued by her.

"How old are you?" I asked.

The sexy smirk returned. "How old you want me to be?"

I rubbed the sweat off my brow. She was a working girl, but my original age estimate dropped considerably. "At least old enough to be doing what you're doing."

She took a pull from the cigarette and raised her hand to cut the sun from her face. "You're cute."

"I was hoping you could help me out. How well do you know your neighbor?"

She shook her head. "Don't know him."

"When was the last time you saw him?"

She shrugged and looked away.

"Ever see anyone else around?"

She shook her head and looked out to the street. "Nope. Never see anyone here."

I turned to check on Ward and found him still talking to the man in the boxers. He wrote in his notebook, which I found a positive sign. I wondered if the man would have more information than the hooker and suddenly regretted my impulse to interview her.

"Did you see me step from that patrol car?"

She looked at the car as if seeing it for the first time. "You don't look like a cop."

"Thank you. You have no idea how happy that makes me. You see that guy up there, Georgia? He's a detective."

"Does he want the cop discount?"

I laughed and couldn't help but wonder why cops got discounts on everything. "Has anyone stopped by looking for your neighbor? Friends? Cops? Anyone?"

She shook her head again, but I had the distinct impression she knew more than she was offering.

I glanced back at Ward. He looked like he was finishing up with the neighbor. I didn't like losing to a cop. I needed to see the inside of my father's apartment, and I needed to do it without the detective.

"You should probably go back inside before the cop finishes." I pulled out my wallet and palmed two twenty-dollar bills. I offered my hand.

She smiled and grabbed the money. She looked like she might be reconsidering talking to me, then said, "I knew you'd come around."

I shook my head. "I'd rather have a cigarette and a bobby pin."

She shrugged and pulled a pin from her hair. She lit another cigarette, and after taking a long pull, handed it to me. "You know where I live."

I sucked on the cigarette and waited for her to go inside. My father's front door was old, and it didn't take me long to pick the flimsy lock. It's amazing what some people think security is. The lock released just as Ward turned toward me. I was inside before he could stop me.

The first thing I noticed was the stench: cigarettes and trash. It brought me right back to the place I had left so many years ago. Fear and confusion flipped through me, then were replaced by anger. The stench made me want to vomit, but the memories made me want to scream.

The second thing I noticed was the amount of furniture. When I was little we had a couch and a couple of mattresses. Later I had stolen a TV and VCR, and both sat on an old box I had found in the alley behind our apartment. My father had done nothing to make the house livable.

This place was full of furniture. It wasn't Mattie's house, but I was surprised nonetheless. A small television sat on a beat-up dresser. I walked past the couch and coffee table piled with music magazines.

A cockroach scurried past a pile of trash in the kitchen. Okay, so it reminded me a little of home. I opened the cupboard and found it empty. I pulled the water on. He had running water. That would have been convenient when I was a kid.

"Luc, what the hell are you doing in there?" Ward yelled from the front door.

"The door was open," I replied.

I walked into the bedroom and found another television, an unmade bed, and bottles of alcohol stashed in the corner. The bottles were nearly full. I shook my head and looked around. I riffled quickly through his dresser. Finding nothing but trash, I searched the closet next, knowing my time was limited with Ward breathing down my neck. My father had clothes, which surprised me. And they hung neatly in the closet, which impressed me even more.

I glanced into the bathroom. Toothbrush. Hair brush. I wondered if I had the right apartment. My father had given up on personal hygiene sometime in the seventies. I found two prescription bottles on the sink, both for pain management. The labels bore my father's name and a Dr. Rimini as the prescribing doctor. I put the bottles back and moved on.

My father used to be constantly worried about theft. In our old apartment in Torrance, he had hidden his bottles of alcohol from me. He'd also hide any money. He would cut a hole in his mattress and stuff his few valuables in there. After I found out about the hiding spot, I would pull out the bottles and empty most of the alcohol so he'd think he had drunk it. I would also steal the money so I could buy food.

I searched his mattress now, having to push aside the sheets. He hadn't had sheets in our apartment. I found the hole almost immediately. I reached in and found a stack of credit cards, all made out in different names. I also pulled out a large envelope containing a folder, a patient file with the name Henry Dillon. I couldn't read most of the scribbled writing, but each entry was signed by a Dr. Stedman, PhD. I closed the folder and put it back in the mattress. I wouldn't be able to sneak the folder out without Ward noticing. I decided to have Orin check the names, and if it popped anything of interest, I'd return for the folder.

I continued my search and inspected the wooden nightstand. It was old and falling apart. The drawer wouldn't open. The only thing on top was a clock radio that flashed *12:00*.

I crossed the hall and discovered another, smaller bedroom. Why did he need a second bedroom? I walked in. A bed and a desk, but no television here. The desk, covered with stacks of newspapers, looked to be over a hundred years old and barely stood steady when I shoved the papers aside. Buried in one drawer I found a stash of pot, though not enough to draw attention from the cops. My father hadn't really bothered with pot. He'd stuck with tried-and-true whiskey and crack cocaine. I grabbed the bags, dumped the pot in the toilet, and flushed.

"I can arrest you for breaking and entering," Ward called in.

"We both know that's not an official penal code violation."

"I can arrest you for burglary."

"I don't think you can prove intent to steal any of this crap. Besides, the court will probably give me ownership of it since my father's dead."

I found an envelope with fifty dollars, and out of habit I pocketed it and continued looking. I walked back out to the living room and searched the dresser that held the television. I heard Ward enter and waited to see if he was going to pull out his handcuffs.

"What did you find?" he asked. He didn't look happy to be standing in an apartment he had no right to be in. In fact, he looked almost ill. It made me wonder if his change in attitude was from more than just my influence.

"I'm proud of you," I said. "Putting someone's life ahead of the rules."

"Luc, the rules are meant to protect our citizens. I don't want to be one of those officers."

I agreed with him. I didn't want him to be one of those cops, either. "So get out."

"You're an asshole."

"Yeah, I know. You've told me. None of this shit fits with him."

Ward looked around. "This place is a dump."

"Not according to his standards. He's got a roof over his head. He's got running water. Furniture."

"Probably stolen."

I shook my head. It still didn't make sense. "He wasn't a thief, Ward. This stuff"—I waved my hands—"this would have been gone long ago. Tell me what I should be looking for."

"Papers, folders." Ward made his way to the desk and poked around in the drawers.

"I got bills," I offered.

"Anything without his name on it?"

I shook my head. I couldn't imagine him paying bills.

Ward's cell phone rang, making him jump. He rushed out the door to answer it. I glanced around the room once more, hoping to find something that told me why my father had lived here. Feeling depressed, I gave up the search. Ward was just hanging up when I walked out.

"Time's up. We need to go." He looked upset, and not just at me. He was about to say something, looked at me, then stopped. "Are you okay?"

I wiped the sweat from my head. "Yeah. It's just hot in there."

"You sure?"

I didn't understand the concern. I was about to drop the cigarette on the sidewalk, but he held up his hand to stop me.

"Are you going to write me a citation for littering?" I asked, amused.

"LAPD is on their way to search this apartment. Do you really want them to find a cigarette with your DNA on it?"

I smirked and wondered why he appeared to be on my side. "Good point. Let's grab a drink, and you can explain what the hell is going on."

He surprised me again by agreeing.

Chapter 11

I picked the restaurant, since I was somewhat familiar with the Long Beach area. We took the 605 freeway south and exited at Seventh Street. Following the street, we drove past California State University and farther into the seedier part of Long Beach. We drove past my auto shop, but didn't stop. I stole a glance to make sure it looked quiet before pointing to a brown building on the corner across from a liquor store.

The food was below par and the county health inspector had rated it a C, which meant it was empty. I never ate there, but I did frequent it enough to know it would be quiet.

"Nice," Ward muttered as he got out of the car. "What's the name of this place?"

I pointed to the *For Lease* sign. "For the right price, you can call it whatever you want." I grabbed the door handle. "It's always pleasant since the cops steer clear of it."

"There's probably a very good reason for that."

The restaurant was small, with only a few tables, a few booths around the left side, and a long bar on the right. The décor was mixed, from music posters on the wall to Ireland photos above the bar, indicating the multiple owners the place had had over its short lifetime.

Chuck, the bartender, nodded to me when we entered. I knew he didn't like me, but he tolerated me because I paid him to. "Hey, Luc. You want a seat at the bar?"

"No, my friend and I are taking a booth." I pointed Ward toward the far booth. The place was empty, but I still wanted the privacy.

Ward sat down, watching me. I felt a headache coming. It was either the nicotine or the heat. Or the intense struggle to keep my past behind me.

Chuck walked over and dropped a bowl of peanuts on the table, which was scarred with divots and crayon markings. He was a tall, thin man with a graying beard and brilliant blue eyes. A skull tattoo was partially hidden by his blue polo shirt.

"I'll take a whiskey," I said. "You got a cigarette?"

"Bottle?" Chuck handed me a cigarette from his pack. "Smoke it outside."

"Glass. On the rocks." I pulled out my lighter.

"You can't smoke in here, Luc. This is California." Chuck wasn't a friendly guy, probably another reason the place was always empty.

"Those laws suck." I watched Ward. He remained silent, observing the exchange. I wanted to see how far he'd let me go. He was being way too accommodating to me, and I needed to know why.

"I'm serious," Chuck said. "I can't have you smoking in here. I could lose my license."

"Let it go, Chuck. The place is empty," I said, lighting up. "No one's going to give a shit. What do you want, Ward?"

"Water's fine for me," Ward said, still staring at me. He looked annoyed.

Chuck kept his eyes on me. "Luc, put it out or I'll throw you and your pal outta here."

"I'd like to see you try," I said. I tossed the lighter on the table and rose. I felt like a good fight. I wanted to hit something. "But leave my friend out of it."

Ward pulled out his badge and slapped it on the table. "Let it go,

Chuck. If anyone complains, let me know."

Chuck glanced at the badge, then back to me. He shook his head and walked off.

I sat back down and smiled at Ward. I hadn't expected him to take my side. My little test told me more than I had expected. "I gotta get me one of those."

"That's twice now you've called me a friend. Are you just trying to annoy me?"

I sucked on the cigarette and watched him through the smoke. Pain continued to pierce my head, but I was more focused on my gut telling me something was off here. I decided to play the nice guy to see if he'd give in.

"I've been a dick. So have you. We have our differences. It doesn't mean we can't be friends now."

He nodded. "I didn't know you were smoking again."

"Yeah, well, living with a perfect angel, I've had to give up most of my vices. Until yesterday, I'd gone three weeks without a cigarette. I'm having a bad week."

Ward laughed. That was rare. "I can't believe Mattie hasn't thrown you out yet. She's too good for you."

Chuck dropped off the drinks, grunted, and walked off.

"Don't I know it. I've told her a million times. She seemed to stop listening sometime around high school."

Ward ignored his water and instead studied me. "How's Spencer doing?"

Spencer Hardwin and I weren't the likeliest of friends. He was rich and came from a highly respected family of lawyers. I was poor, and my father hated me for stealing from him. Our paths had crossed in college when he became my roommate. A freshman college jock with little else going for him met up with an intelligent, up-and-coming law student. We didn't exactly hit it off from the beginning, but we realized we were stuck with each other and decided to watch each other's back. I saved him from getting his ass kicked, and he saved me from killing myself. I thought the trade-off was fair, and he's one of the few people in the world I called a friend.

He was a genuinely good guy, so I had set him up with Mattie. I thought they were perfect for each other. He was definitely more right for her than I would ever be. I thought the match had worked when they got married, but it started falling apart when Spencer realized Mattie had always been in love with me. The divorce was still fresh, and the fact that I had quickly moved in wasn't sitting well with Spencer.

I sighed. "He's having a rough time with the divorce, but he'll survive. He's stronger than I am." I didn't want to talk about Spencer. I took a drink and waited for Ward to talk.

He leaned forward. "Tell me about your father."

"No." There was still a moat between our friendship, and I wasn't about to cross it. I also needed him to talk first. I needed to know how close to the line he was.

"I need to know the basics if I'm going to help."

I knew Ward was putting himself out on a limb here to help me. I also knew he wouldn't put his job on the line unless there was something he needed. His job was everything to him.

"How about you start with why you're so interested? If Johnny told me to keep away from you, I'm sure you were warned to stay away from me. You have a lot to lose by helping me. I need to know what's worth the risk."

He looked away, as if searching for someone or something in the empty room. Finally he said, "This is not for an article, right? You're not digging into your father's death because you need a story for Saturday's paper?"

"I'm not writing about that asshole. I'm interested only because everyone wants me to not be interested."

Ward smiled. "I knew Johnny's plan to make your father's death seem boring wouldn't work for you."

"Was his death boring?" I asked.

"I don't know. It could be, but I couldn't obtain the hospital records without a warrant. His death is officially not a homicide. The Torrance Medical Clinic told me he died of cancer. That's all they'll say. The gold shield won't help me at the clinic. You might be able to learn more if you ask the questions."

"If the badge won't work, my press credentials won't either."

"You can ask as the man's son. You're family. Go talk to the hospital. Find out what the doctors say. Make sure it's legit."

I studied him. Something told me he was still playing with me. "You don't think it is?"

"Honestly, I don't know. I think it's strange that he's a suspect in a burglary and then he dies before he can be arrested or questioned."

Back to the burglary thing. It didn't fit with the man I knew. "What's he accused of stealing?"

"Files. Almost two weeks ago, he apparently broke into an office and stole some files and a laptop."

"LAPD is wasting their time. My father doesn't steal paper unless someone promised he could drain it for alcohol. Even the laptop wouldn't be worth it to him. What office?"

"The administrative offices for the Torrance Treatment Center. Have you ever heard of the Guardian Home?"

I was confused by the quick change of subject. I wanted to know more about the treatment center and what could possibly have been stolen in the administrative offices, but the Guardian Home intrigued me.

I nodded, remembering the homeless shelter. "In Torrance? I used to get coffee there." I had spent some time in the neighborhood around the shelter, but my father had refused to enter. Something about thieves stealing from you when you slept. I decided to keep this information to myself.

"It's where your father was when he died."

"Why would he be at a homeless shelter when he had a perfectly good apartment?" I asked.

"Good question. They won't answer my questions, either."

I drank. Too many questions were circling, but the one question I had come in with still hadn't been answered.

"Why are you interested in this, Ward? I can go ask the questions, but I need to know what your involvement is."

"The office is in Sheriff's jurisdiction, but we aren't working the burglary. LAPD Robbery-Homicide Division took it over."

I already knew LAPD was working the case. I still didn't see a reason Ward, a detective at the Los Angeles Sheriff's Department, would care.

"The office belonged to Mr. Ernesto Ramirez."

I dropped my head in my hand. I couldn't hide the smile. "The patrol sergeant's husband?"

"Ernesto Ramirez is the CEO of the Torrance Treatment Center. He's a very powerful man in Los Angeles."

I knew a little bit about him. I knew he had ties to both LAPD and LASD and had pulled many of those strings in trying to take Ward's badge after he learned of his wife's affair. I was starting to see the picture.

"You're interested in my father's death because of Ramirez? Is this your way of getting back at him?"

He shook his head. "No. Ernesto Ramirez is doing everything he can to find out who broke into his office, and he's been all over the chief to locate his files. He's furious, and he's causing waves. Whatever your father stole was important."

"You think it's sensitive information?"

He looked away. I thought of the file I had seen in the mattress, but couldn't see how a single patient file would be worth this much fuss.

I laughed. "You want to bury him with it? You know you could have just asked. I'd be more than happy to help you take him down."

"This isn't revenge, Luc, but I wouldn't mind looking at what he's so adamant about finding. I don't trust the guy. He's got his hand in everyone's pocket. It's not personal. I just want to find out what he's hiding. I'm not asking you to take him down. I just want a look at the files your father stole. Do you think you can find them?"

I didn't believe Ward. I knew it was personal, but I respected him for it. I would want my revenge on the man, too.

I offered my hand. "I'll do what I can."

He hesitated, then shook my hand. "This is just between us, right? If you locate the files, you'll contact me right away?"

"Of course."

Chapter 12

I decided to look into Ernesto Ramirez as a personal favor for Detective Ward. He'd helped me out in the past, so it was time I returned the favor. I had no intention of keeping it out of the *Crime Reporter*, though. Ramirez was pretty well known in the political realm, and a story of his corruption would sell a lot of papers and get the editors off my back for awhile.

Unfortunately, learning about Ramirez would have to start with my father's death and his supposed theft.

As I drove to Torrance Medical Clinic, I called Orin and asked him to find out what he could on a Dr. Stedman and a patient of his named Henry Dillon. If my father stole anything, he would have needed help, and I hoped one of them would be the key. Orin agreed to help only after I explained the search of my father's apartment and my discovery of the hidden file for Henry Dillon.

Orin wasn't convinced Ward was only helping out of the kindness of his heart, and thus I had to listen to a lecture about working with the police. I decided to keep the Ramirez part of the investigation to myself.

"What if it's the file on Henry Dillon that your father stole?"

"It's possible, although I can't believe one file would get everyone up in arms. LAPD is probably searching my father's apartment right now. If they look hard enough, they'll find it. If not, I can always go back and pick it up and see if there's any value in it. Let's find out who Henry Dillon is and why he's so important."

I hung up on him as I pulled into the parking lot of the Torrance Medical Clinic. I decided Ward was right. The direct approach was the best way to find out about my father's death. I waited twenty minutes before someone could help me.

"Mr. Actar, I'm so sorry for your loss." Ms. Eugenia was a tall, thin woman with a soft smile. She was an administrator in a tan suit and uncomfortable shoes, clearly separate from the nurses running around us. She showed me into a small conference room. She held a folder in her arms, but it was too thin to contain anything of importance. I had a feeling I was about to be turned away with nothing.

"I was hoping to get my father's medical records. I understand he died of cancer."

She nodded and leaned against the door. "I have put in a request to have the records released to you. We didn't have you listed as next of kin, so it's going to take a little longer than I had hoped. I'll need you to complete the attached form, and I can start the process." Opening the folder, she offered me the paperwork.

"Who was listed as next of kin?" I asked, looking over the form she handed me.

"Your brother Chris."

I looked up at her. "What brother?"

"Tony's son. The child who was with him. I assume that would make him your brother."

I was confused and wondered if she was thinking of someone else. "Are you sure?"

"I remember talking to him when Tony was here last time. He told me his name was Chris Actar and Tony was his father. You don't know him?"

I felt embarrassed and stupid at the same time. Leave it to my father to still be able to do that even after he was dead. "I haven't seen my father in many years," I explained. "I didn't know him."

"I'm sorry to hear that. He was a nice man. I got to know him and Chris. They were both very kind to the staff, and they used to enjoy watching the basketball games on TV together. I'd let Chris stay past visiting hours, because I wasn't sure who he was staying with while your father was here."

I wondered why John had failed to mention a kid who was with my father. A boy claiming to be my father's other son.

"How many times was my father here?" I asked.

"Three times. I wasn't here when he was treated the first time."

"What was he treated for?"

She hesitated, deciding what she could tell me. "When I saw him, he was treated for dehydration. He refused all of the cancer treatments that were offered when he was diagnosed. He was prescribed some pain pills, but that was it."

"When was he diagnosed with cancer?"

She paused again. "I can send you the file once it's been released." In other words, I wasn't going to get much information today.

I tried one more tactic. "Was Dr. Stedman his doctor?"

She looked confused. "No. We don't have a Dr. Stedman here. We have an Emily Stedman on staff downstairs in admitting, but she's not a doctor." She looked through the file.

I rubbed my head as if I was confused, too. "His friend Henry Dillon told me it was Dr. Stedman. He must have been confused."

"Oh, I met Henry when he was here with your father. They shared a room a few months ago. He seemed like such a nice man. It was nice to see those two reconnect after so many years. I don't know why he'd be confused."

"I must have misheard him. What's his doctor's name?"

"Tony was seen by Dr. Rimini."

That matched the prescription bottles I'd seen in the apartment. At least I could cross Henry Dillon off the list of importance, but something still nagged me. Stedman couldn't be that popular of a name, and I wondered if Emily Stedman was related to Dr. Stedman. Seeing as he was Dillon's doctor and not my father's, I decided the medical records on my father were the only thing to gain here.

"Are all his records kept here in the hospital?"

"All patient records are kept on site, but as I said, I can't release anything to you without a review process. It's a legal requirement by the hospital."

I smiled at her. "I understand. I'll wait for your call and come back when you can release the files to me."

"I'll try to have it signed off as quickly as I can, and I'll send you a copy of all the files we have on him. By the way, your father loved the chocolate pudding and always called the nurses 'darling.'"

"What?" I asked, wondering why she was telling me this.

"You said you didn't know him, and I find the littlest details will help get a better picture of the person. Again, I'm sorry for your loss, and I hope you find what you're looking for."

I put the sad face back on and thanked her. Since it sounded like the process was going to take too long, I decided to involve a lawyer. As I left, I glanced down the alley toward Guardian Home. The sidewalk was filled with homeless men queuing up for the lunch service. A man wearing a purple dress and a dirty blonde wig walked past me toward the line and winked. I decided I really didn't want to fit into that crowd, so I put off my visit.

~~~

When Mattie's ex-husband Spencer disappeared the previous year, I had returned to Los Angeles to find him. I had hoped my return would only reconnect me with them, but it had ended up ripping apart their marriage in the process. Spencer had moved out prior to the divorce and focused all his attention on his growing legal career. I moved in with Mattie shortly afterward, and had seen very little of my old college roommate since.

Spencer's receptionist told me he was still at lunch. I didn't believe her, because Spencer isn't the type to take a break. I asked if I could wait for him. She agreed, but she still tried to stop me when I headed for his office.
~~~

"He's not here," she repeated. She was a mean, ugly old lady who seemed more interested in her computer screen than helping me.

"You said that. I'm just going to wait in his office. You can tell him I'm here." I figured wherever he was, she'd get word to him that I was waiting for him.

I opened his door and found his office empty. I walked around his desk and saw that his screen saver was up on his computer monitor. It showed a picture of Mattie. I wondered if he was still in love with her. It made me uncomfortable, so I moved the mouse and the picture disappeared.

Spencer's e-mail program was open, and being nosy, I skimmed the subject lines. Nothing looked interesting, and I was about to sit down and wait patiently when I noticed his calendar icon. I clicked on it and saw he did have a lunch scheduled for noon. I opened the meeting notice and saw Mattie's name. I stared at it for a few minutes before finally closing it.

She hadn't mentioned she was meeting Spencer for lunch. Maybe she had scheduled it this morning after I had left. Maybe she'd tell me all about it tonight. Or maybe not.

I sat down in Spencer's chair and thought about what I had done to their marriage. I hadn't planned on ruining his life. I hadn't planned on breaking up her marriage. It had just happened. I liked to believe that, but the reality was that I should have stayed out of Los Angeles. I knew if I had stayed in Washington, D.C., where I had fled after their wedding, they might still be together. I wondered if any of us would have been happier.

Mattie and Spencer were the two closest people in my life. I cared for both of them, and destroying their marriage still bothered me. Mattie had told me she had tried to make it work with Spencer, but she couldn't ignore the fact she was in love with me. Spencer had told me he couldn't continue to live a lie. He knew she was in love with me, and he had to let her go.

But I couldn't stop thinking about where that left Spencer. He started working longer and harder, and I rarely saw him now. I knew it was his way of moving on, but I still felt responsible for his pain.

Spencer walked in fifteen minutes later. He looked tired and annoyed, but he smiled when he saw me.

"Luc, how are you?"

I rose and offered him his seat. He thanked me and immediately sat down.

"What brings you out here?" he asked.

"I need some legal assistance. My father died."

His smile faded. "I'm so sorry. That's horrible."

"You forget I hated that man."

He looked confused. "You never really talked about him."

"Not much to say. Anyway, I'm trying to get his medical records from Torrance Medical Clinic. I'm hoping you can push them to hand it over faster."

"They were treating your father?"

"I guess. He apparently died of cancer. I don't know why it would take so long to photocopy some papers and hand them over to me. I can prove I'm next of kin, so I don't know what the holdup is."

"They probably just want their lawyers to look over the files. They want to protect themselves from a malpractice lawsuit. They're right, it'll probably take a few days."

"Any way to speed things up? Can I sign something that says I promise not to sue?"

"Are you sure you want to give up that right? What if you find out they were responsible?" He made a note on a pad of paper.

"If they killed him, I'd shake their hands. Hell, I'd probably donate to their hospital. I don't care what they did. I just need copies of everything so Ward can look it over."

Spencer leaned back and looked at me. "Why is Detective Ward looking into your father's death?"

"It's complicated. Essentially, we just need to make sure my father died the way the hospital says he died."

"I can put something together. Send me the contact information at the hospital, and I'll work with their lawyers."

I rose. "Thanks. I appreciate it." I considered asking him how his lunch was, but since he hadn't offered the information that he'd been with Mattie, I decided not to push. If he wanted to tell me, he would. I also considered inviting him over for dinner, but thought the invitation to his old home would be rubbing the divorce in his nose, so I said nothing.

"Anything else?" he asked.

"No, I think that's it. I'll touch base with you later and see how it's going."

"Luc, one more question. Why is Detective Ward helping you?"

It was a good question. "He wants to help," I said.

"I don't buy it. Are you sure he's not using you? In fact, I think maybe this whole thing is a bad idea. You should just let sleeping dogs lie."

I wondered where he was going with this. I wondered if Mattie had said something to him. "Mattie said it's a good idea to deal with my father's death. This is my way of dealing with it."

"Mattie can be naïve. Sometimes when you look back, you fall into old habits and patterns. You can't afford to screw up now."

I wasn't sure what he was getting at.

"Luc, you're not just risking yourself here. You take the wrong step, and you could lose her. You could lose everything."

Chapter 13

Reggie Voss lived in his mother's old house a few blocks from the apartment I'd lived in with my father. My father knew Reggie through his father, who'd found his way to the streets alongside us.

Reggie's mother was black and his father was white, and both had fallen victim to drug use when Reggie was a young boy. Reggie's mother was a schoolteacher, his father a bus driver for the city. They didn't have much money, and whatever they earned went straight to drugs. The only thing of real value was the home. Reggie's mother had grown up in the small, two-bedroom house, and when her mother passed, it was the only thing she held on to.

When the jobs no longer brought in enough money for the drugs, Reggie's mother refused to sell the house. She promised Reggie she would die sober in the house and leave it for him. She did, but Reggie's father couldn't break away from the drugs as easily and found himself alone on the streets, always looking for his next score. Reggie had never touched drugs, but like me, he had turned to crime as a way to survive a life of poverty and pain.

I had met Reggie not long after my father and I moved into the Torrance apartment. I was spending most of my time stealing at that point, and Reggie had a network of moving things fast. To those he trusted, he was known as Shadow.

I drove past the abandoned apartment building where I had spent my youth, giving it little more than a glance as I headed over to Reggie's house. He had always been reliable, and I knew he would still be there.

The house hadn't changed much. It needed paint, and the sound of crying babies and fighting children reverberated in the alley. By nightfall, the sounds of children would be replaced with the sounds of sirens and gunshots.

His front door was wide open. With the heat and his obvious lack of central air, it didn't surprise me. My plan was to walk right in, but I stopped short when I heard yelling.

"Get the hell outta here." Gruff voice. Reggie. He hadn't changed much.

"I just want my fair share. This is bullshit. It's worth twice that." Young voice. I could hear the innocence and knew the kid would be an easy mark for Reggie.

"You have no idea what it's worth, 'cuz it's stolen. And 'cuz it's stolen, it's worth less."

I peered in the door, but could see only one man. African-American. Cornrows. Young. Thin. Desperate. And in over his head. He wore a Kobe Bryant Lakers jersey and shorts that didn't quite fit him.

"It's brand new, man. I need the money." Mr. Cornrows.

"Do I look like a fuckin' bank?" Reggie.

"Hey, kid," I yelled from the door. The kid turned toward me. Reggie rounded the corner and peered at me, too. Both looked pissed and ready for a fight.

Reggie had over a hundred pounds and almost two feet on the boy. He was the tallest man I had ever known, especially when I was a young, scrawny teen fencing stolen jewelry.

"What the hell do you want?" Reggie asked, obviously not recognizing me. He looked the same as he had when I saw him last. He hadn't aged a bit.

I pointed to Cornrows. "I'm talking to the kid. What's your name?"

The kid shrugged his shoulders, looked at Reggie.

"What are you selling?" I asked.

Reggie straightened and put one hand up, as if this would be enough to block me. "You a cop?"

I turned to him. "Do I look like a fucking cop, Shadow? Shut the fuck up."

He eyed me, but didn't say anything. I knew he scared easy, and I knew he never kept weapons in the house. Other than the stolen goods, Reggie was essentially a good person.

The young man turned back to me. "I got some jewelry. It's not stolen." He was a bad liar.

"How much did he offer you?" I asked.

"Twenty."

I waved my hand at him. "Let's see it."

He showed me a handful of cheap gold rings and a man's gold watch. I could tell at least one of the rings was fake gold, but the watch was a decent take.

I turned to Reggie. "That's worth at least forty. That piece alone could draw bidders."

Reggie looked over the items more closely, searching for the value I saw in them. I knew he didn't see it. He was an easy mark as well.

"I'll give you forty-five."

The kid smiled. "Yeah, sure."

I reached for my wallet, but Reggie stopped my hand. "Fifty." He looked at the kid. "You stay with me, you get fair prices."

The kid looked confused. I thought about running the price up again, but decided I just didn't care enough about either of them to continue the charade.

"Fine," I relented. "Give him the money so I can get to why I'm here."

Reggie handed the kid the money and took the jewelry. "Get lost." He turned to me. "You just cost me fifty to keep a neighborhood junkie.

Who the fuck are you?"

I smiled. "A friend of a friend."

"I don't have friends."

"Neither do I."

He put his hands on his hips and studied me. "Do I know you?"

"You knew me once. When I was poor and desperate just like that kid."

"Little Luc. Holy shit!" He gave me a bear hug and stepped back. "Never thought you'd come back to the neighborhood. You beefed up some. Guess you're eating good now."

I wasn't here for the memories, although I felt a little bit of myself come back to life. I watched as Reggie stuffed the stolen goods in a bag and tossed it in the corner.

"When was the last time you saw my father?" I asked.

He huffed and turned his back on me. "Is he in trouble?"

I followed Reggie into the living room. He sat down in a chair two sizes too small for him. I remained standing. He had some new gang tattoos on his arm I didn't remember as a kid.

"He's dead," I said, glancing around the shabby apartment. It hadn't changed. He hadn't even painted or vacuumed. There were a few pieces of furniture and a huge saltwater fish tank. I stared at the fish swimming around in their glass prison.

"Yeah, I knew it was only a matter of time. Poor bastard."

"When was the last time you saw him?" I repeated. A large black eel stared back at me through the glass.

"Couple months ago. He dropped off some things. We watched a Lakers game. You know how big of a fan he was." I didn't, so I said nothing. Reggie continued without noticing my indifference. "He told me he was out."

"Out of what?" I asked.

He shook his head. "Done. Man, he was tired of living. His insides were eating him alive. Bad liver, stomach. Whatever's all in there. He was in pain. He stopped drinking, too."

I didn't believe it. "Did he come to you to fence anything?"

He smirked. "You know he was never good at stealing. Not without you. But he came around every now and then."

"You ever see him with a kid? Goes by the name of Chris Actar?"

"Chris? Yeah, once or twice. Nice kid. Took good care of the old man."

"Is he his—"

"Nah, I doubt it. Kid latched onto him last year. I think he's a runaway."

"My father didn't exactly like kids."

He shrugged. He lit a joint and leaned back. "Boy was trying to get into confidence like your old man. He couldn't lose the kid if he tried. The man was gettin' old. He needed someone looking out for him."

I couldn't picture my father old and dying. I couldn't picture him sober and clean, either.

"When he stopped by, do you remember what he dropped off?" I asked. It was a long shot, but it couldn't hurt to ask.

Reggie looked around, pointed to a stack of boxes in the corner. "Haven't seen him in over two months. It should be the top one there. Just the regular identity docs."

Reggie offered the joint to me. I shook my head.

I pulled the box off and opened it. It was full of papers. Birth certificates with names and official state seals. Social Security cards with various names. All of it looked legitimate, and I knew it was worth a lot. It was a great find, but I knew it wasn't what the cops were looking for. The timing wasn't right.

"What'd you give him for it?"

"Nothing. He said he didn't want anything. He was cleaning house. Just wanted to get rid of it."

That definitely didn't sound like my father.

"What about any electronics?" I asked. "Did he bring you a laptop?"

He shook his head. "Your father wasn't a thief."

I was glad someone was seeing things the way I remembered.

"How about someone by the name of Henry Dillon? That name sound familiar?"

Reggie shook his head. "Nah, don't know him. What's he look like?"

I shrugged. It would help if I knew a little more about the person I was trying to find. I considered taking the box with me, but decided I really didn't want to be caught lugging a box of illegal documents around.

"Do you know how my father got the birth certificates?" I asked.

"Your father knew someone who worked in a hospital. An administrator or nurse or something. She was working some hospital in Texas and used to mail him blank certificates every month. When you were born, she was working at Angels Hospital in LA."

I looked up at him. "Are you saying my certificate—"

A frightened look came over his face. "Oh shit, no. I don't think yours is fake. Tony never said anything like that to me."

I suddenly felt sick and couldn't wait to leave.

~~~

I still had my father in my thoughts when I arrived late to my second therapy appointment. There were only two cars in the parking lot, a black 2000 Jaguar XJR and a fairly new white Toyota Camry. I slid next to the Jaguar and peeked inside. It was clean, no papers or personal belongings in sight.

Dr. Holstein didn't appear upset with my lateness. She nodded when I walked in, pointed to the chair and opened her notebook.

"Tell me about your father," she said, as if reading my mind.

"He's dead."

"I got that from the last session. Let's discuss your relationship with him."

"I have no relationship with him. He's dead."

"You're repeating yourself."

"That's because you're not listening. I'm not here to go over the past in hopes you can find 'daddy issues' to blame my anger on. That's not what this is about. You're wasting your time." I considered getting
~~~

up and leaving, but I didn't. I liked the comfy couch and the way this lady looked at me.

"I don't think so, and let me explain why." She held up her hand to prevent me from interrupting. "Have you ever hit or attacked a police officer before Saturday?"

I thought about the question and couldn't remember a time when I had physically attacked a uniform. I had once broken into a cop's house and stolen his gun, among other things, but he had no idea I was responsible. I decided to keep the incident to myself.

"Not that I can recall."

"That's interesting, since you seem to live your life skirting the line between antagonizing and attacking. Also interesting because you mentioned the cops attacking you when you were a kid trying to survive on the streets."

I shifted in the seat, folded my arms over my chest.

"You are very conscious of the line. So I have to ask, when you crossed it on Saturday, did you unconsciously cross the line? Did you lose control of your emotions and react? Or did you assess the situation and consciously decide to throw coffee on the cop? Either way, you crossed the line, maybe for the first time. I need to know what made you do it. Right before you threw the coffee." She looked at her notes. "One of the officers told you your father was dead. Was that what triggered your action?"

I shook my head. "My father has nothing to do with this."

"Prove it to me, and I'll move on. Tell me about your father in the twenty-five minutes we have left."

"I haven't seen him in over fifteen years. I had no idea where he was. Nor did I care."

"You weren't close with him?"

"I don't know what that means."

"He raised you, right?"

"And I really don't know what that means. He was my guardian when I was a kid. When he wasn't drunk, he made sure the other bums left me alone. At least, until I learned to protect myself."

"Where was your mother?"

"Probably dead. I don't remember her. Don't try to make this about her."

"So your father was responsible for feeding and clothing you?"

I laughed. "No, I was responsible for that. My father was a con man, not a thief like so many people seem to think. He couldn't steal candy from a baby without getting caught. It's the only reason he kept me around. I had fast hands. The food we ate and the clothes we wore came from my hard work. Not his."

"How did you get off the streets?"

"That was my father's doing. I wasn't focused on getting a roof over my head, just on feeding myself, but my father needed money for booze. By eight or nine, I refused to steal alcohol, mostly because it was more dangerous and I no longer saw it worth the risk. He needed to run some cons and needed an address to do it. He conned Child and Family Services into getting us a place in Torrance and used the welfare money on drugs and alcohol. Then he set up a mail scam that drew in quite a bit of money. When I could, I stole it to pay for food and rent. The rest went to booze."

"He drank a lot?" she asked.

I didn't like where this was headed, so I steered her elsewhere. "I didn't notice so much, since I was going to school."

"You started going to school when you settled in Torrance?"

I thought of Mattie. "Yeah, my choice. My father wanted me to spend the day stealing, but I met Mattie and she needed me. I went to school to protect her. I did my stealing in the evenings to make Daddy proud."

"And you graduated?"

I nodded. "Barely. I was playing football by then, and a scout from UCLA spotted me. I got a full-ride scholarship."

"Impressive." She smiled. I could feel she was pleased with my responses, and I wondered where she was headed with the questions.

"Until I blew my knee out."

She looked at her notes. My cell phone rang. I let it go to voicemail.

"Did you have any friends other than Mattie?"

I looked at my hands and considered my options here. My interest in where she was going made me answer honestly. "I had a friend named Joey. He died when I was in high school."

"I'm sorry. How did that happen?"

I looked at her now. "When he wasn't stealing cars, Joey used to sell drugs for this Hispanic gang in the neighborhood. I explained how much easier it was just to steal money from them than to work the streets and put himself in danger with the cops. I stole from them, and they thought it was Joey. They shot him in front of me."

She made a note and moved on without a word of judgment on me. "Where did you live during college?"

The fact that she had moved on from Joey annoyed me. "The dorms, mostly, but I slept around. Anywhere I could find a bed."

"And after college?"

I wasn't sure why she was so interested in my sleeping arrangements. "I don't know. I moved around a lot."

"So, you've had no real home since the Torrance apartment?"

"I wasn't the settling down type. What are you getting at?"

"But you are now?" she asked.

I looked at my watch. I'd had enough of the questions. "I'm not that person anymore. I think our time is up."

Chapter 14

On the drive home, I checked my voicemail. It was Ward, wondering if I had located the stolen files yet and reminding me to call him as soon as I did. I wondered why he was so impatient to take down Ramirez. I considered calling him when I got to Mattie's, but I had another problem to deal with.

John was leaning against his car when I pulled into Mattie's driveway. He walked over to meet me as I got out of the car. His presence here was not a habit I wanted him to continue.

"I'm not going to bother talking to you anymore, Johnny." I walked past him and toward the front door.

"Luc, we need to talk."

I spun on him. "You lied to me. You said no secrets. You specifically said there was nothing going on here. A simple cancer death. A simple burglary charge. You lied to me."

"I didn't know about the kid until today."

The front door opened, and Mattie peered out at us. "What's going on?"

I lowered my voice. "Go back inside, Mattie."

"Luc, we're still looking into who this kid is," John said.

"What kid?" Mattie asked.

I didn't want to answer that. I knew where Mattie's thoughts would eventually land. "Mattie, please. Give me a minute."

Unfortunately, Mattie knows me better than I realize sometimes. She stepped out on the porch, gave me a look, and turned to John. "What kid are you talking about?"

"When Tony Actar passed at Guardian Home, there was a boy with him. He claims he's Tony's son."

Mattie looked at me. I held my hands up. "I just found out."

She turned back to John, and I knew he would receive the brunt of her anger. "Why are we just learning about this now? Where is he? Where has he been since Tony's death?"

"Apparently Child and Family Services took him Thursday night when they found Tony. They will take care of him and find a home for him."

"Bullshit," Mattie said. I smiled, even though I knew this wasn't going in my favor. "What's his name?"

"His birth certificate says Chris Actar," said John.

Now I cringed. "He has a birth certificate on him? Does it say Tony is his father?"

"Of course."

I turned to Mattie and pulled her inside. "Mattie, don't jump to conclusions," I said before she could say anything.

"He's your brother—"

"There you go jumping before thinking. We have no proof of that. A birth certificate doesn't mean anything. They can be forged."

"We're not letting that boy go into the foster system."

"He sure as hell ain't coming here," I said.

Mattie pushed past me back to John. "How old is he?"

"He's fourteen," John said. "But I don't know what I can do at this point. Child Services is not my domain."

"Make it your domain, John. Otherwise, I'll have my father take this to a judge. If you have a birth certificate, then Luc is the boy's next of kin. He needs to be with family, not in a strange place with strangers."

I closed my eyes and rubbed them. It was a long day, and I knew it was about to get longer.

"I'll see what I can do, but I can't promise anything," John said.

I looked at him, hoping he wouldn't be able to do anything. I didn't mind the boy going anywhere but near Mattie.

"Luc, I'm sorry about this. I really had no idea about the boy."

"Are you going to tell me why you're really involved in this? Why are you my point person, if none of this is Sheriff's jurisdiction?"

"Your father was suspected in the break-in at Ernesto Ramirez's office. LAPD is running with the case, but he's a big supporter of the LASD. The sheriff asked me to keep an eye on the LAPD's case."

I didn't mention that I already knew about the Ramirez connection. It was good that he didn't know I already knew. So far, Ward had kept his word.

"You think you have power to make people listen to you?" John continued. "This guy plays golf with the governor. He has a weekly meeting with the mayor. He wants his files back. LAPD is going to dig through your father's life until they find what he stole."

"Do they know what was taken? Why Ramirez wants it back so badly?"

John shrugged. "Just files. Probably financial, the way he's acting."

"What about a laptop?"

John's brow wrinkled. "There was no laptop stolen. Just files. Paperwork. Who told you there was a laptop?"

I considered calling out the lie, but decided I needed to keep Ward's confidence. I also had to be sure Ward hadn't been the one lying to me. "I told you before, my father's not a thief. Paper doesn't mean anything to him."

"LAPD has a strong case against him. They don't have any reason to doubt your father took the files."

I shook my head. "They're wasting their time."

Mattie was still steaming about the kid and made John promise to update her as soon as possible.

I spent the entire evening online searching for everything I could on Ernesto Ramirez and the Torrance Treatment Center.

Chapter 15

The following morning, I got a call as I was walking out the door. Spencer's request had been accepted, and Eugenia from the Torrance Medical Clinic called to tell me I could pick up my father's medical records. I agreed to meet her out front.

I arrived early and waited between the front doors and the parking lot. A young blond woman leaned against the wall, smoking and eyeing me. I wondered if she was a patient, before I realized she was wearing a badge from the Torrance Medical Clinic. She was small and thin, anorexic by my standards, and I wondered if the cigarettes were keeping her food cravings away.

Smelling the smoke, I considered asking her for a cigarette, but when she caught me looking at her, she turned her head and stared down the alley. Instinctively, I followed her gaze and saw I had a great vantage point of the back entrance of Guardian Home.

A group of homeless men were talking in the alley. They were too far away to hear, but I could tell from their animated gestures that someone wasn't happy. A bag lady in a long black trench coat sat against the wall nearby, muttering to herself and rocking back and forth.

She had a sign next to her asking for prayers. I had none to give, so I leaned over and handed her a few dollars. She looked up at me, nodded, and stuffed the money in her jacket pocket. She resumed her muttering and rocking.

"Please don't encourage them," the smoker said. She stepped closer to me. Her name badge said *Emily*.

"Don't encourage them to survive?" I asked. "It's only a few dollars to get her through the week."

"Handing out money only tells them it's okay to hang out on the street and beg. It tells them they'll be rewarded for being bums."

"No sympathy for the downtrodden?" I asked.

"Those people are either mentally disabled or drug addicts. They shouldn't be living on the street. They need to be in a hospital. They need someone to look out for them. You giving them money doesn't get them the help they need."

"Not everyone is sick. They're just trying to survive. They don't need a hospital. They need some caring and understanding."

"Living here isn't the answer. They come here bringing shopping carts, mattresses, and trash bags full of garbage—"

"Those are their belongings. They're homeless, and now you want to take their only possessions, too?"

"With their stuff comes the rats, and diseases, and crime," she continued. "It's become a breeding ground for vermin. They're stealing from each other, they're fighting each other. Regular people are scared to walk these streets. They worry about their safety. The stores down the street worry about their shopping carts. They have to hire extra security to protect their shoppers from the garbage and the panhandling."

"These people have rights, too. Just because they're homeless doesn't mean you can sweep them under the rug, or worse, ignore them."

"I'm not asking you to ignore them. I'm just telling you to spend your money helping the shelters keep these people off our streets."

"Not everyone wants to live in a shelter," I said.

"If they're living on the sidewalks, then it shouldn't be their choice." The woman dropped her cigarette and returned inside. I returned to watching the alley.

A few minutes later, Eugenia came out and handed me two thick folders.

"This is everything on Tony Actar," she said. "I hope it helps you understand the man you didn't know."

I opened the first folder and read a bunch of medical jargon. The ER had treated him twice for dehydration and pain. They gave him morphine and IV fluids. I wondered if it had been a scam to get the morphine.

The final pages showed Tony was found unconscious at Guardian Home and brought to Torrance Medical Clinic, where he was pronounced dead Thursday night at the age of sixty-six. Due to the patient's history of cancer, no autopsy was conducted. I wasn't surprised.

I closed the file. I didn't care enough to read through it. I would hand it over to Ward and see if he could find anything of use.

I wasn't ready to go into Guardian Home alone, but knew I couldn't put it off any longer so I called Orin and asked him to meet me. I needed coffee, and since the closest Starbucks was on Crenshaw Boulevard, I told him to find me there.

~~~

Guardian Home was a small homeless shelter in the heart of Torrance, just down the street from Torrance Medical Clinic. Anyone who stayed there knew the old nun who opened its doors, Miss Jessie. She was loving and caring, but she was also stern and expected everyone to play by the same rules. She didn't allow drugs or alcohol through the doors, and she refused to be scared of anyone.

When I was a kid, they would put a coffee cart on the sidewalk for anyone needing a coffee boost. I had found the place one day after searching for food. As a child, I didn't like the taste of the coffee, but found it would curb the hunger pangs for hours. I never walked through the doors of Guardian when I was a kid, but I had stolen my share of coffee.

Orin arrived as I was ordering at Starbucks. The woman looked at me strangely when I asked for a lemon slice, but said nothing. Orin ordered an iced coffee, and then we walked the two blocks to Guardian
~~~

Home together. Orin pecked away on his cell phone, oblivious to my discomfort as we inched closer to the homeless shelter. The breakfast line had disappeared, and only a few of the hungry souls still remained.

"Did you want to hear what I found out about the doctor?" Orin asked.

"What doctor?"

He sighed without looking up from his cell phone. I wondered why I was getting attitude from him.

"Doctor Stedman. The one you asked me to look up."

I had forgotten I had asked Orin. "Sure, but I think it's a dead end."

"Could be, but it's still interesting. Dr. Stedman works at Torrance Treatment Center. I've tried to reach him, but keep getting his voicemail. The receptionist won't give me any information." He handed me a piece of paper with the phone number.

Torrance Treatment Center. I wasn't surprised the file in my father's apartment linked back to Ramirez's Center, but I still couldn't see why my father would think a patient's file was worth stealing from the CEO.

Interested, I dialed as we walked. A woman's voice answered and told me I'd reached the Torrance Treatment Center. I asked for Dr. Stedman and was sent to his voicemail. I waited for his voice to finish, only to be told his voicemail box was full. I pressed *0* and waited for the woman to return to the line.

I looked over at Orin. "What about Henry Dillon?"

"I haven't found anything on Mr. Dillon. Zilch."

The woman's voice returned. I explained I was looking for Dr. Stedman. When she tried to transfer me again, I stopped her and told her the mailbox was full.

"Is he in today?" I asked.

This seemed to confuse her for a minute. "I can take a message and give it to him when I see him."

I thanked her, but didn't leave a message. I hung up, and Orin shook his head.

"Dead end?" he asked.

"Probably. I'll stop by later and see what I can find out. You stay on Henry Dillon. Since he was a patient of Dr. Stedman's, I have a feeling he might be harder to find than the doctor."

"Luc, we have a bigger problem."

"I know. I need to get a story here somewhere. Callahan's going to kill me if I can't produce something today."

"There's always the body in PV. They're having a hard time identifying it. I think the story's got potential."

"No dental records on file?" I asked. Since the body had been found in the water, I assumed fingerprints weren't going to be easy to lift. Most floaters had to be identified by dental records.

Orin shook his head. "Whoever they found, they either weren't reported missing or never went to a dentist."

It was intriguing, but I still wasn't interested. As we entered Guardian Home, I saw a group of men milling about the coffee stand. It was no longer on the sidewalk outside, and I wondered if that was because of the stolen cups of coffee.

"It's time to start thinking of the future," Orin said, eyeing his cell phone. "We need to stay on track and get a story to Callahan before he fires us both."

"Are you talking to me or updating your Facebook status?" I asked.

Orin looked up, but not at me. "I'll see if they know anything about your father," he said, walking off toward the group of men by the coffee stand.

Others, obviously volunteers based on their matching red vests, were clearing tables from the breakfast service. I watched as a young woman handed out cups of nuts to the few remaining people who had missed breakfast. She eyed me as I grabbed one of the cups.

"Who's in charge here?" I asked her when she had emptied her tray.

"Miss Jessie."

I tossed the nuts in my mouth and smiled at her. Not wanting a confrontation, she walked away.

I found Miss Jessie in a small office, talking to a tall bald man with torn jeans and bright red shoes. She didn't look any older than she had thirty years earlier when I had first seen her here. Her hair was gray and thin, and her eyes were sunken.

She looked up at me and pointed to the chair opposite her, as if she had been expecting me. "Sit down. Give him some coffee," she told the bald man.

I waved him off. "I'm okay."

Without looking at me, he dropped a mug in front of me, filled it halfway, and left.

I ignored the coffee and turned back to Miss Jessie. She was staring at the coffee mug. I wondered if she wanted me to drink. I didn't.

"I'm sorry to bother you, Miss Jessie. Do you remember a man dying here Thursday night?"

She looked up at me. "Of course I remember that, young man," she snapped. "I'm old, not senile. A woman doesn't forget something like that. I may not remember what I wore to school in fourth grade, but I remember a man dying last week."

Her anger made me smile. She looked back at the mug.

"Andy," she called out. There was no response. "I'll be right back." She got up slowly, grabbing different parts of the desk as she rose, and walked out the door.

I rubbed my eyes and wondered if I should just drink the coffee and leave. *Do I really care about my father's death this much?* Before I could decide, Miss Jessie returned silently and dropped a small paper cup next to my mug. In it was a slice of lemon.

I looked at her as she sat down. "You remember me?" I recalled her anger and quickly corrected myself. "After all these years, you remember how I like my coffee?"

She smiled. "You're the reason I put the coffee inside instead of leaving it on the sidewalk."

"I was told it was free. I wasn't stealing."

She shook her head. "You could have come inside. There was sugar and milk you could have added instead of stealing lemons from the neighbors."

I shrugged. "I didn't want to come inside and face you. You would have asked where my father was. I wouldn't have had an answer for you."

She looked sad now. "I wish I could have done more for you. That man wasn't a good father to you. You needed help. I tried calling Child Services, but without a name, they couldn't help me."

I offered my hand. "My name is Luc Actar."

Her cold hand shook mine lightly. "Your father was a drunk, and he abused you. You would have done better with Child Services."

I thought of Mattie and shook my head. "I guarantee I would have done worse. How did my father die?"

"I believe they told me he was battling cancer. I don't know why he wasn't in a hospital somewhere. He looked small and sickly, but so do so many of the people who walk through here."

"Did he leave anything here? Any belongings?"

She shook her head. "I think there were a few things, but Child Services took the box with the kid who was staying with Tony."

"Did the Child Services people leave a card or any way of contacting them?"

She opened her drawer, pushed some things aside. "I don't think so, but one of the officers left his card." She handed it to me. Detective Marquez.

"Did you know my father had a home in Lakewood?"

She shrugged. "He may have mentioned it."

"Do you know why he was staying here?"

"He wasn't staying here." She pointed to the coffee. "Are you going to drink that?"

I drank obediently. "Do you know a Dr. Stedman?"

She sneered. "Yeah, I know him. Dr. Jack Stedman comes by here every so often to kidnap my men. Says they're sick in the head."

"Kidnap?"

"He says he's helping them, but I think he's just trying to find new patients. He claims they're fifty-one-fifty and takes them away."

I was somewhat familiar with California Code 5150. It gives law enforcement and trained professionals the ability to institutionalize someone if they are a danger to themselves or others. They tended to be suicidal mental cases. I'd seen my share of fifty-one-fifties living on the streets. But I never liked the code. Something about giving up one's freedom always bothered me.

"What about Henry Dillon? Did you know him?"

"Sure, he was a regular, one of your father's friends. He's been gone for a while, though. I heard he was being treated by Dr. Stedman. Your father was asking about him, too."

"Is anyone else here friends with my father?

"Garrison Parks. He's still here." She pointed out the door. I didn't look. "He's the one talking to your friend."

I thanked Jessie and turned to leave, but she stopped me.

"We have Mass on Sunday, if you'd like to pray with us."

"Thanks, but I'm beyond saving."

"If you never ask for forgiveness for your mistakes, you're doomed to repeat them. Do you believe people can change?"

Thinking of my father, I said, "No."

I found Orin standing on the curb, still talking to Garrison. Despite the warm weather, Garrison Parks wore a thick brown jacket, and the pockets of his filthy black pants were pulled out. He smelled of rotten potatoes, and his hair was caked in mud, as if he'd been sleeping in a ditch. His shoes were held together with old duct tape that was starting to fail. He was also wearing a worn bike helmet, though I saw no bike in sight.

I didn't interrupt, since the man seemed to have a hard time spitting out his words. He was missing several teeth, and the remaining ones were tarred or cracked. His speech was slurred, but not from alcohol.

"I on' spoke to him a few time. I no . . . I not from roun' he'." He looked around as if he really had just walked into town.

Orin looked at me and held his hands up.

I translated: "He spoke to him a few times. He's not from around here."

Orin nodded. "That's what I got from the others. A few of them remember your father, but only saw him here a couple times in the past year."

"How long have you been here?" I asked Garrison.

Garrison looked confused. He scratched his nose, and I noticed a piece of paper in his fist. I grabbed his arm to look at it. It was a hospital bracelet from Torrance Treatment Center.

"Can I take this?" I asked.

Orin looked at me.

"May be nothing." I looked back at Garrison. His mind had already wandered to something else, so I took the bracelet. "Do you know Henry Dillon?"

"Sure, yeah. Ev'yone know Henny."

"Have you seen him lately?"

"No." He shook his head violently in case I didn't understand the one syllable.

"Do you know Dr. Stedman?" I asked.

He nodded and looked out at the street. I had a feeling I was losing his interest.

"Did Dr. Stedman pick you up here and bring you to the mental health facility?"

He nodded again, but continued to stare at the street. He pointed down the street at a woman smoking on the sidewalk. It was the same small woman I had seen smoking there earlier. She stared back at us, and Garrison dropped his hand.

I tried again. "What's wrong with you?"

His eyes narrowed on me. "Nada. I fine. You cop?"

My stomach turned. "Help me out here, Garrison. Did he give you any paperwork, or did he just take you?"

Garrison looked at his feet and didn't answer.

Orin saw I was getting annoyed with Garrison, so he pulled me aside. "Luc, where are you going with this?"

"Miss Jessie says Dr. Stedman is picking up patients from the streets here."

"I've heard of patient dumping, but picking patients up at homeless shelters is new to me. Why do we care that they're giving special treatment to the homeless?"

"He's kidnapping homeless people and using fifty-one-fifty to hold these people against their will for the seventy-two hours."

Orin shook his head. "Kidnapping? That's going to be hard to prove. Besides, I've seen some of these people. They could use a psychiatrist."

"They're homeless, Orin, not insane," I snapped. "They've been neglected and mistreated. They don't deserve to have their rights taken away as well."

Orin shrugged. "I'm just saying that worse things could happen to these people than receiving some attention for seventy-two hours."

"First, being homeless isn't a crime. Second, you've never been homeless, so you don't have the right to say what these people need."

"I'm still not seeing the story here, Luc."

I smiled. "The treatment center gets money from the state for every bed that's filled. They're padding their numbers with homeless people. They're stealing from the state. They're stealing from the taxpayers."

Orin smiled back. "Great theory, but look at your witness. He's not exactly reliable."

He was right. "Okay, we need to find Henry Dillon," I said. "He's got to be a more reliable witness. He may be at the treatment center, or he may be wandering the streets."

"If he's homeless and sick, we might not find him. Do you know how many people go missing every day? I think we need to focus our attention on the files your father stole. Maybe there's a smoking gun in there."

"The problem is we don't know where the files are or what they could possibly tell us. I think we have to go directly to Dr. Stedman and find out what he's doing."

Orin didn't look pleased as we separated.

Chapter 16

The Torrance Treatment Center was located near the Harbor Freeway. It was a large modern building with darkened floor-to-ceiling windows. I counted seven floors and a helicopter perched on top. There was also a security-controlled parking lot and cameras everywhere.

After I parked my Porsche in the large parking lot, I Googled the name and learned that the Torrance Treatment Center provided high-quality, affordable treatment services to adults and youth with alcohol and drug abuse and behavioral health problems. It was licensed and certified by the State of California and Los Angeles County. Their website stated they were open twenty-four hours a day, seven days a week. They dealt with inpatient care as well as outpatient services.

Despite the large building and the numerous cars in the parking lot, the waiting room was small and empty when I entered. A woman sat behind a plexiglass partition with a phone to her ear. Her jet-black hair fell nearly to her waist but was pulled back behind her ears, which glinted with rows of stud earrings. She also had a small nose ring.

She was deep in a conversation I couldn't hear. A ceramic clown figurine sat on the counter next to a sign-in sheet attached to a clipboard.

A large metal bookcase rose to the ceiling behind her, stacked full of files, color-coded and organized. Her desk was clean, spotless, except for a laptop, a phone, and a line of crazy-haired dolls with freaky eyes staring back at me.

I waited for a few minutes, but she continued her conversation behind the partition without a single glance my way, so I moved to the edge of the couch. *Judge Judy* was playing on the television mounted in the far corner, but the volume was down so low I couldn't make out the complaint. After waiting ten more minutes, I walked back to the screen, but the woman was still on the phone. I considered knocking just as a man in his early twenties walked in.

Without a glance at me, he reached over and wrote his name on the clipboard under *Patient*. Jeffrey Donovan. He listed his appointment with Dr. Brown at 12:30. He wore a dirty bandage on his right thumb and had a small tattoo of a spider on the back of his hand. He smelled of tobacco, and his teeth were yellow. The smell reminded me of my father.

After returning the pen and clipboard to the counter, he sat on the couch and stared at the television. I banged on the plexiglass divider. The woman looked up in surprise.

"She doesn't like that," Jeffrey said behind me. I stared at him until he looked away.

The woman slid the divider open and pointed to the clipboard. "Sign in."

"I'm not a patient," I said.

Her eyes shot open like the eyes of her dolls. I wondered if she was scared or just uncertain how to proceed with non-patients.

"I'm here to see Dr. Jack Stedman," I added.

"Do you have an appointment?"

"Let's say I do."

"What's your name?"

"Luc Actar," I answered, knowing she probably had access to his appointment schedule and I would be turned away before I could explain what I wanted. If I could just get Dr. Stedman to come out, I knew I had a chance.

She slid the divider closed again and picked up the phone. She glanced at me, then reached over to open the screen. "Jeffrey, go sit down. Dr. Brown will be out shortly to get you."

I glanced over my shoulder to find that Jeffrey had moved up close to me. He was so close, I reached back to confirm I still had my wallet. He smiled at me. He had blue eyes and deep dimples.

"I'm Jeffrey," he said, his lip bulging slightly with a wad of chewing tobacco.

I turned back to the receptionist and caught the divider before she could close it again. I pointed to the phone in her hand and asked, "Is that Dr. Stedman?"

She put the phone down. "Dr. Stedman isn't in today. I can schedule an appointment for you if you tell me what this is about." She had a bit of a lisp, and I suspected she also had her tongue pierced.

I lowered my voice. "I need to get a copy of my father's patient records."

She looked confused. "I'm sorry?"

"My father. Tony Actar."

She shook her head. "Our patient files are confidential."

"I understand that, but he passed away last week and my lawyers need a copy of his records." It was risky, but I felt mentioning lawyers might throw her off guard.

"Do you have a death certificate?" she asked.

"Not yet. It's apparently a long process."

She turned back to her computer. I knew I was losing her.

"When you receive the death certificate," she said, "you can make a request through our corporate management team."

"Look, I don't want to have to involve the lawyers and the judges. It can get ugly and definitely won't look good on the Torrance Treatment Center that they were unable to assist a patient's family in their time of grief."

She kept clicking away at her computer.

I pulled out my phone. "I can have my lawyers here with whatever paperwork you need," I bluffed.

"That won't be necessary."

"Really?" I asked, surprised it had worked.

"It's not necessary, because your father wasn't a patient here." She looked at me.

"Can you check an address for me? Maybe he was listed under a different name."

She looked at me strangely. Then she looked to my left. "Mr. Donovan, please stop eavesdropping. That's not polite. Dr. Brown will be with you in a minute."

I realized Jeffrey was still standing beside me. I decided to push in hopes she wanted us both to go away.

"Just a quick look," I begged. I gave her the Lakewood address.

She sighed, clicked, and shook her head. "I'm sorry. Nothing under that address, either."

I pushed again. "Can you check the name Henry Dillon?"

She dropped her hands in her lap. "Why don't you go ahead and call your lawyers?"

I thanked her for her help, and she closed the divider. I turned to find Jeffrey watching me.

"Too bad about your dad," Jeffrey said.

I shrugged and decided to change the subject. "Do you know Dr. Stedman?"

He backed up from me. "I'm not sick. I just need my paperwork signed to get out of here."

"But you are a patient?"

His head bobbed. "They gave me the choice between this and jail. I chose the shrink."

I knew the decision was a tough one for him, as it had been for me. I offered my hand. "I'm Luc Actar. I'm writing a story on the center."

His hand was moist as it shook mine.

"I'd love to interview you and get your impressions of the doctors and the care provided."

He pulled his hand back and stuffed it in his pocket. "I just want my paperwork. I'm not crazy. I need the paperwork so I can get back to my life."

He returned to the couch, stuffed a finger in his mouth, and stared at the television. The other hand lay on his lap. His fingernails had been bitten to the quick, leaving red scabs. He bit at the skin on his other hand.

I sat down next to him despite the smell.

"I didn't do anything," he said. He looked frightened of me.

"How long have you been coming here?" I asked.

"A few weeks. I just want to go home. They won't let me go home."

"You stay here?" I asked, confused.

He shook his head. "No. I'm an outpatient, but there's a restraining order out on me so I can't go home."

I nodded as if I understood. I really didn't care about his history. I wanted to ask about Dr. Stedman, but it appeared the name seemed to bother him.

"Do you like Dr. Brown?" I asked.

He nodded. "He's nice, so far. I only met with him once. I just need my papers so I can go home."

I wondered what papers he was talking about. "Where are you staying now?"

"I was at the Long Beach Mission last night. Not sure where I'm staying tonight. Hoping for somewhere safe."

I nodded, remembering the feeling when I was homeless. "Did the doctors here take you from the street? Did they force you to seek help?"

He shook his head. "The jail doctor forced me here. He said I was sick and wouldn't have to stay in jail. I didn't want to stay there. I just wanted to go home." He turned back to the television, and I was afraid I was losing him.

"Do you like *Judge Judy*?" I asked.

He grunted. He raised his left hand and stuck a finger in his mouth. I noticed another tattoo on this hand—a web.

"I don't like cops, and I don't like the courts," he said. "It's all bullshit." He turned to me. "They think because they have a college education, they can tell everyone what to do. Man, I had to stop smoking because no one allows it anywhere. You used to be able to smoke when you had a drink. Now it's illegal to light up in a bar. Isn't that crazy? I had to switch to chew just to get my tobacco fix. It's stupid. This country is stupid, telling everyone what they can and can't do." He shook his head. "They locked me up, but I'm a grown-ass adult. I should be able to do whatever I want. They sent me here, but I'm not sick. I don't need a hospital. So they let me out. I just need my papers so I can go home again. That's all I want, just to go home."

I was starting to feel sorry for the guy. He didn't seem crazy to me now, and I was wondering what the hell he was doing here. I was about to ask what he'd done to land in jail, when the back door opened and a doctor in a white coat called out to Jeffrey. The doctor was a round man with a full white beard that matched the hair on his head. If it hadn't been cut close to his face, I would have thought he was Santa Claus.

"Are you Dr. Brown?" I asked.

He nodded.

"I'm looking for Dr. Stedman. Do you know how I can reach him? It's vitally important."

"And you are?" he asked.

I introduced myself and explained I was with the *Crime Reporter*. He seemed a bit nervous and wouldn't look directly at me. He asked Jeffrey to take a seat for a few minutes and then stepped closer to me. I noticed that the beard was full of food crumbs.

"Off the record, Dr. Stedman doesn't work here anymore. I'm sure you can get confirmation from someone else, but I'll tell you what I've heard as long as my name doesn't appear in any articles."

I wouldn't normally make that arrangement, but without more information I wouldn't have a story anyway, so I agreed.

"From what I understand," Brown said, "Dr. Stedman stopped coming into work two weeks ago. Last week we were told to divide his patients among the remaining doctors."

"Did he have any reason to quit?" I asked.

"There are rumors, but I can't confirm any of them."

I decided to be direct and stop wasting my time and his. "I've heard he was kidnapping homeless people off the streets and calling them patients."

Dr. Brown looked shocked, his eyes round as marbles. "I don't know anything about that."

I gave him my card. "I'd really like to hear Dr. Stedman's side. If you talk to him, can you have him call me immediately?"

He took the card, but wouldn't promise anything. "If you want to know more about Dr. Stedman, you should talk to Ernesto Ramirez. He runs the management of the entire facility. He gave us the directive. Talk to him."

I thanked him and said goodbye to Jeffrey, who waited patiently on the couch. He was pretending to watch *Judge Judy*, but I knew he had heard every word I said.

~~~

"You're early," Dr. Holstein said when she opened her door.

I shrugged. "Trying to beat traffic."

She offered me a seat, and I took one. She offered tea, but I declined.

"Was there anything you wanted to talk about today?" she asked as she poured herself some tea.

"No. You're the shrink. It's your program."

She nodded and opened her notebook. "Okay. Tell me about Mattie."

"No."

She put the tea cup down. "Are we going to go back and forth like yesterday?"

"Look, I talked about my father despite not wanting to. It wasn't useful, but I understood your reasoning. We're not talking about Mattie. Period."
~~~

"You don't see the logic of talking about Mattie? The incident took place in her home, in front of her. You mentioned you were concerned about her with the police. I think it's valid to question her role in this."

I shook my head. "This has nothing to do with Mattie."

She looked back at her notes. "You didn't throw the coffee at the officer who told you your father was dead. You threw it at the officer who mentioned that Mattie had let them in the house."

I stood. "I said I wasn't going to talk about Mattie. If you're going to continue on this path, I can leave now."

"Sit down, Luc. You came early because you wanted to talk. I know how to read people. I know my job, so let me do it. You might find I can be of help to you."

I sat. She smiled, and I realized I didn't like her hold over me.

"Your reaction is exactly why I want to discuss her." She held her hand up to stop my protests. "We won't talk about your relationship. You obviously care enough about her to keep her out of this. It's interesting, but I won't push."

"Thank you. We can talk about anything else."

"Even your father?" she asked.

"Sure, whatever."

She wrote a note in her book. "What's going on with your investigation into his death?"

"Medical records show he died of cancer. Not much more to go on there."

"Does it make you sad to think he died alone?" she asked.

"Apparently he wasn't alone. Some kid claiming to be his son was with him. He's fourteen. Probably a con artist just like him."

"Well, that's interesting, isn't it? Have you met the boy?"

"No. Don't plan to, either. He's not my brother."

"But he just may well be. You don't have any family. Don't you want to meet him?"

"I have Mattie. She's my family. I don't need or want anyone else."

"But she's not your family, Luc. She is your future, your dreams. She reminds you of what you can be. Family keeps you grounded. You don't have anyone to remind you of where you came from."

"I have the scars to help keep me grounded. I don't need a reminder of my childhood. Where I came from isn't pretty, remember? Why would I want to remember that?"

"Because it's who you are. Those experiences, whether good or bad, made you who you are. This boy may have some of the same experiences. You'd probably be amazed at how similar you are and how much you two can help each other. Forgetting your past isn't the way to deal with it."

"If I go back, I'll lose everything I've gained so far. I've moved past all of that. I don't need to deal with it. I just need to keep moving."

"Tell me about the last time you saw your father."

"I don't remember."

I was glad she didn't push, but she made a note in her notebook. It made me consider how I could steal it from her. "Do you resent the fact that your father didn't take care of you?"

"No, I don't resent him at all. He was a drunk. He did what every other drunk does."

"You're allowed to be angry with him. You don't have to make excuses for him."

"I thought I was here to rid myself of my anger."

"I'm concerned you could misdirect your anger. With all that anger built up over the years, you could snap and take it out on another person. An innocent person."

I said nothing.

She asked, "Do you drink, Luc?"

"No. Not like him."

"What does that mean?"

"My father drank to escape. I drank to keep the cold away. He couldn't put the bottle down. I put it away when I met Mattie."

She made another note, and it annoyed me.

"You were constantly fighting over alcohol with him," she said. "Did this escalate physically?"

"It always comes down to that, right? People think he hit me, so I turned out bad, but he's the one dead, not me. I survived."

"He abused you?" she asked.

"No more than I abused him. We fought. I won more than I lost. It's not that hard beating up on an old drunk. There is no way my attacking a cop had anything to do with my father. I've grown up and moved on to a much better life. I'm not a child anymore, and I have no feelings for my father either way. Not anger, not sadness, not regret or anything. I just don't care that he's dead." I wondered if that was completely true. If it was, then why was I researching his death? "Look, I need to get to Mattie's house before she starts to worry. Are we done?"

"See you tomorrow," she said, standing up. She offered her hand. "Despite what you feel now, I am sorry for the loss of your father. It does mark the end of a part of you. You need to deal with that."

I headed for the door. "Only the bad part ended."

Chapter 17

As I drove north, my mind kept returning to my father. I couldn't help noticing a blue Chevy pickup truck following close behind me. I changed lanes a few times, and the truck changed as well. I decided it was best not to go to Mattie's house until I learned who was following me. I couldn't imagine the police being so ill-trained as to be that obvious in their pursuit. Even though I would have hated a cop following me around, I was more concerned with the alternative. Whoever was in the blue truck could know about the folder and what I had done to Carl Palfy.

I exited the freeway and slammed on my brakes, and the truck almost slid right into me. He honked his horn and sped past me. I watched him make a right-hand turn on the next street and wondered if I was just paranoid. I had been unable to see the driver and too distracted to write down the license plate. I was getting sloppy and knew it could only end badly.

I kept driving, and somehow ended up driving straight to the Torrance apartment building I had shared with my father. I parked across the street and looked up at the desolate apartment building and wondered what I should be feeling. The little grass patch had died and turned to dirt and weeds. The paint was faded, and the entire place reeked of piss.

I walked toward the first apartment door. Number 101, where Joey had lived. He was there when I first moved in. He wasn't there when I moved out. I pulled a cigarette from my pocket and took my time lighting it. Breathing deep, I pushed the door open.

The room was bare. Even the carpet had been taken. If something can be sold, there's a thief out there willing to work to steal it.

I walked into the tiny kitchen, glanced around, and walked out to the attached garage.

Only the bottom four apartments had garages. Joey had turned his garage into a gym, full of stolen weights and punching bags. His father had been a boxer. At least, that's what he had been told by his mother. He had never met the man. Lucky for me, Joey hadn't taken after his father. I had spent hours in that garage, but now it was bare, no bags to punch.

Joey had dropped out of school when he was only thirteen. He had been caught stealing twice and decided it was easier to sell drugs. He was two years older than I was, but back then I thought of him as my younger brother.

I walked out to inspect the other apartments. An old Chinese man had lived in apartment 102 next to Joey and his mom. We called him "Mr. Bird." I never knew his real name. He was scared of us and rarely came outside. I may have seen him only a few times during the six years I lived upstairs. He was scared of criminals.

We wouldn't have hurt him. He never did anything to either Joey or me, and he never called the cops on us. So that made him straight in our books. He probably had no idea that the only reason his house was never broken into was because two criminals like us protected it.

I wondered if Mr. Bird was still alive and where he might be living now.

Apartment 103 was an open turnstile. Every few months a new person moved in. We rarely saw anyone move out and had to assume they left in the middle of the night. That happened a lot in run-down apartments like this. The landlord was just as crooked as the tenants. No one complained on either side.

I couldn't remember anyone ever living in apartment 201, although I doubt it was empty.

As I had done a million times as a kid, I walked up the stairs and looked out toward the street. It was quiet for a Monday afternoon. Soon there would be children walking home from school and cars speeding home for dinner.

A homeless man watched me from across the street. His shopping cart was overturned, and an old burgundy blanket covered his belongings. He looked permanently planted on the corner, and he was shaking his head at me.

I tossed my spent cigarette over the balcony like I had done so many times before. Habits come back at strange times. I looked back at apartment 204 but didn't move toward the door.

Too much had happened since I had left this place. I wasn't that scrawny kid anymore. At least, not from the outside. People didn't see a scared, hungry kid. I wasn't sure what they saw, but they didn't see that.

Mrs. Mason in apartment 203 had said I was nothing but a common criminal. I didn't know what that meant. What was common? But she liked me anyway. She used to leave bread outside our door for me. I knew she didn't leave it for my father. It was only there after my father left for the night to get drunk.

She had heard most of our fights. Her living room shared a wall with my bedroom, and it was that bedroom where most of the fights would start. She called the cops a few times during that first year. She even got him arrested once, but they never came to take me away.

I wouldn't have gone, anyway. Within a few months of moving in here, I was going to school with Mattie. There was nothing that could have driven me away then. I belonged here.

I pulled another cigarette out and wished I had something stronger. Maybe a bottle of Jack Daniel's.

I picked the lock and opened the door. The floors that had once been covered by a dirty shag carpet were now bare, and the walls were covered with graffiti.

I remembered the first time I had walked into this apartment. I was just a young kid, and it seemed so grand. It was so much more than I had ever expected. We had gone from living on the dangerous, filthy streets to a two-bedroom apartment with a kitchen.

It had all seemed unreal, like a dream, but it quickly turned into a nightmare. My father's drinking became heavier, his demands more intense, and his anger fiercer. The fights became more frequent, and I was unable to run from the beatings.

Shortly after we had moved in, I met Mattie. As I grew closer to her, my hatred for my father intensified. The pull to go to school, to be near Mattie, outgrew my desire to steal for my father. I tried to pull away from him, but my old life always came rushing back. The kitchen would be empty, so I'd have to steal groceries. The rent would be due, so I'd have to steal a car.

When I moved out at eighteen, I had hoped to never see this place again. I had buried Joey and turned my back on my father. The former had been difficult, the latter way too easy.

I wanted success. I wanted happiness. I wanted a life. And I wanted to never be hungry again. Pain was my past. Hope was my future. Mattie gave me that hope.

I was twenty-two when I returned. The place was already abandoned except for a few squatters. I scared them away when I returned, drunk and bloody, after my altercation with Carl in the alley.

I had thrown away that hope. Or at least, I thought I had. I had come here to die or to be dragged away in handcuffs. That was my fate, but it wasn't the police who came for me. Spencer had come and picked me up and taken me back to our dorm room. He hadn't asked any questions. I wondered if things would have been different if he had.

I looked at the corner where I had spent two weeks straight. The blood and vomit were no longer visible. The rats had probably taken care of the cleanup.

I walked into the small kitchen. The ugly yellow linoleum had been pulled up, revealing a scarred and sticky floor. Spent joints and trash littered the counters. The cupboards had been removed from the walls. Even the sink was missing.

The kitchen had once held dishes, not that there was any food. No, the only reason we had dishes in the sink was in case the social workers stopped by unannounced.

My father soon got rid of the knives, though. I had quickly learned to defend myself with any type of weapon found in the house.

My room had been off the kitchen. It was supposed to be a dining room, but we didn't need one of those. Now the door was missing, but I couldn't find the strength to cross the threshold into my old room. Instead, I sat in the corner of the kitchen and wondered why I had come back here.

I closed my eyes in the cold room and remembered a time before the apartment, when my father and I would be lucky to find an abandoned building to sleep in. We'd sit around a makeshift fire to stay warm, hoping the police wouldn't roust us for the night.

~~~

A ringing woke me. Surprised I had fallen asleep, I scanned the room for danger. The ringing continued. I answered my cell phone and heard an angry Orin on the other end.

"Glad to hear you're still alive, Luc. Planning on coming back into the office today?"

"I'm taking the rest of the day off." I rubbed my eyes and heard static on the line.

"You're cutting out, Luc. What—"

"Oh, sorry." I walked out the front door and was blinded by the sun.

"—like you're in some sort of tunnel. Callahan isn't happy."

I watched a patrol car cruise slowly down the street. I wondered for a second if it was there to watch me. The homeless guy on the corner paid it no attention. His eyes were still turned in my direction.
~~~

"I'll call you back when I get somewhere with better reception," I said. I closed the phone and headed toward the stairs.

I crossed the street, but walked away from my car. The homeless guy still stared at me. He had to be close to eighty years old. Unshaven and wrinkled, he was missing most of his teeth. I stayed just far enough away to avoid inhaling his scent of dog shit.

I pulled out my wallet and handed him a twenty. He squinted at me, and I wondered if he was blind.

"How's it going?" I asked.

"I don't want your money," he rasped. "It's only guilt that makes men want to help someone like me. I'd rather you carry that guilt around with you. It'll make you a better person than giving me money and going on with your life without that guilt."

"Trust me, old man. I have enough guilt to carry around for all of us. Take this as down payment for what I owe the world."

This, he seemed to understand. He nodded at the money before it disappeared in the layers of clothes.

"You here a lot?" I asked.

"Never leave. It's home, ya know?" The old man scratched his thick gray beard.

I knew. "You ever see anyone over there?" I pointed to the apartments.

He shook his head. "Nah."

I could smell alcohol and almost asked him to share, before realizing I was starting to lose my footing on the thin line I was now walking. I knew I needed to get back to Mattie.

"That place is haunted," the man said.

I laughed. "Yeah?"

He didn't laugh. He looked at me. It was hot out, but a chill ran through me. I lit another cigarette.

He finally asked, "Did you see the ghosts? When you were up there, did you see them?"

I took a pull on my cigarette and looked back at the building. Another patrol car cruised past. The driver took an extra long look at me. I smiled at him, but he kept driving.

"Yeah, I saw them."

The bum snorted. I closed my eyes and enjoyed the sun on my face and the nicotine running through my blood.

~~~

I cut past Santa Monica Boulevard and headed up the hills. I ran into the liquor store for a fresh pack of smokes and then walked to Spencer's new apartment. His bachelor pad, he called it.

I walked up the stairs to number three and knocked on the door. Since there was no answer, I picked the lock. I plugged Mattie's birth date into the alarm panel, and the system turned off.

I grabbed two glasses from the kitchen cabinet and an open bottle of scotch from above the refrigerator and made myself at home. With a cigarette between my lips, I settled into the black leather couch. I poured the scotch in one glass and used the other for my ashes.

I dialed Ward's number, but got his voicemail. I left him a message letting him know I had received my father's medical records and for him to call me about the stolen files.

Half a bottle of scotch later, Spencer walked through his door. He glanced at me before dropping his briefcase. "You really need to stop doing that," he said.

I wasn't sure if he meant breaking into his house or drinking, so I didn't respond. Instead I got up and retrieved a glass for him. When I returned to the living room, he had removed his jacket and tie. He looked tired, his eyes distant.

"Long day?" I asked, handing him the glass of scotch.

He nodded and sat down next to me. "What are you doing here?"

I lifted the bottle. "Needed a drink."

"I know it's been a while, but there's a place called a bar that serves alcohol to crazy men like you."

I shrugged. "Didn't want to pay for it."
~~~

"We both know you have more money than I do. You should be doing the buying."

"I'll think about it next time." I lit my last cigarette.

"You gotta stop smoking. It'll kill you."

"No, smoking doesn't kill. Cancer kills. If those damn doctors could just find a cure, we could enjoy smoking in the way it was intended."

I drank more, and neither of us looked at each other.

"Why aren't you home?" he finally asked.

"Don't start, Spencer."

Silence interrupted the argument neither of us wanted. I drank and let the silence take over.

"Did you get your father's files from Torrance?"

I nodded. "Thanks for that."

"Anything interesting?"

"Probably not, but I'll pass it on to Ward and see what he can get from them."

"Why bother? Your father's dead. Move on. You used to tell me the past is the past. You never wanted to look back, afraid of what would come back to haunt you. Whatever you're doing, stop. Don't put Mattie through this."

I got up. I wanted to hit something, so I thought it best to get away from him. I glanced at him and noticed that he still wore his wedding ring.

"Why are you here, Luc?"

"How come you're still wearing that thing?" I asked.

He looked confused as he stared at his hand. He began to fiddle with the ring, but didn't take it off. He looked more than tired; he looked physically beat. Being the new partner at his law firm definitely wasn't agreeing with him.

"Would that make you feel better?" he asked.

"Hell yeah."

"Tough shit. You know, things aren't always about you. You need to stop being so damn selfish."

I could tell something was bothering him, and I knew I was about to step where I shouldn't, but it didn't stop me. I sat back down and filled both our glasses. "You're still holding on."

"I loved her, Luc. I still do." He rubbed his tired eyes and took a drink. "It's not something I can just shut off. Especially to please you."

"If she changed her mind, would you take her back?"

He looked at me, the honesty showing through the pain. "In a heartbeat."

I didn't like the answer, but I couldn't blame him for it. I understood. I took another deep pull on the cigarette and considered how different our lives would be if I hadn't returned to Los Angeles.

Spencer's phone rang, and he grabbed the cordless off the table. His face straightened when he heard the voice. Figuring it was work, I got up to pace and give him his privacy.

I saw pain in his eyes, and my worry for him moved me closer to eavesdrop. He was still my best friend.

"Yeah, he's here." He turned his back to me, and I knew it was Mattie. I sat back down on the couch and waited for him to hang up. When he finally did, he grabbed the bottle of scotch from the table. I felt bad for him, even more so because his pain was caused by me.

"You were right yesterday," I said. "I shouldn't have started digging into my father's life. I should have walked away, but now I can't. I don't want Mattie near this, but I can't walk away."

"Luc, I can't help you." There was a strange sound in his voice.

I looked at him. "What are you talking about?"

"This isn't working. I love her too much to watch you screw this up with her. I can't watch her be hurt, and I can't help you do it to her. You should go. Go be with her, and stay the hell away from me."

I stood. "Spencer, you're my best friend."

"No, I'm not. I'm the guy who's been helping you out of jams your entire adult life. I can't do it anymore. I don't have the patience or the time in my life to follow you around and pick up the pieces."

"Is that what you've been doing? Following me around and picking up the pieces? I thought you were following Mattie around like a fucking lost puppy dog."

He rolled his eyes, and a smirk appeared on his face. I wanted to smack it off.

"Of course you knew," he said. "Why would I think differently? Yes, Mattie and I have been having lunch together the past few weeks. It's not what you think."

Weeks? I felt my stomach drop.

"She knows you're hiding something from her. She's been rather upset by it."

"And you were just itching to be there to help her through it, right? How come you didn't mention it to me? I thought we were friends."

He laughed. "She's my wife."

"Ex-wife. She never loved you." It was a low blow, but I didn't care.

"Get out."

I finished my scotch and resisted the urge to throw the glass against the wall. Dr. Holstein would be so proud. As I walked down the stairs, I wondered what more could be thrown my way.

Chapter 18

"Forgive me, Father, for I have sinned," I muttered to myself as I watched the lone old woman slide out of her Pontiac Grand Am and walk toward the church. Instead of going to Mattie's, like I should have, I decided it was time to see what was in the file my father kept in his mattress.

The service or sermon or whatever had let out at least an hour ago, so I knew the woman was going into the church for confession. She was in her seventies, at least, with gray hair and drooping eyes, her shoulders hunched from either age or regret. She clutched a small green handbag. The matching dress hung to her ankles. She walked slowly, then disappeared inside the building.

I wondered what evil things one does at that age.

I leaned against the building and stared at the doors. I had no intention of going inside. I didn't need to be saved. I'd been taking care of myself my entire life. I peered down the street to my father's apartment complex before returning my eyes to the street in front of me and the church.

Twenty minutes later, the old woman emerged from the church and returned to her car. She looked lighter than when she arrived.

I laughed as I thought how quickly her sins had been forgiven and forgotten. I would need five hours. Or five days.

The sun had disappeared below the horizon. The red sky had turned brown, then gray, and finally descended to black. Darkness had left everything quiet. Only three cars had passed since the woman had left. The priest walked out and spoke to a small crowd of bystanders outside the church. I watched them as night descended onto the street. By all appearances, it had gone well. They smiled and shook hands, not knowing I lurked only a few feet away.

No one had looked my way while they wandered back to their cars. Oblivious or naïve—or maybe it was still easy to ignore me as people went on with their own lives.

The air was warm with enough humidity to make it uncomfortable as I sat and watched the activities at the church. I wondered why priests always wore black. *Thieves and priests,* I thought, looking at my own black clothing. I wondered what the connection was.

I stretched my legs and checked my watch. I had missed dinner. I thought about calling Mattie, but I had left my cell phone in the car. I heard a helicopter above and remembered why I stayed out of Lakewood. Sky Knight, the world's first 24-hour helicopter law enforcement program, was centered here. I cursed the helicopter as it flew away in the night sky, looking for criminals like me.

I glanced back at my father's apartment building. The front apartment, the one rented by the large Hispanic man who favored boxers, still had a light on. After three hours, I held out hope he would go to bed early. The hooker in the back apartment hadn't made it home yet. I didn't expect her to make it an early evening. It was a good evening for making money. Hot and desperate.

I wished for a cigarette, but had lit the last one over an hour ago. Something moved to the side of the church, drawing my attention. I identified it as a raccoon and returned to my inspection of the street.

I wondered what I would say to the priest. "Forgive me for my life?"

As the church grew dark, I fought the weariness overcoming me. I tried to remember the commandments, but couldn't. I couldn't count my sins, either.

Thou shalt not steal?

Was I supposed to ask forgiveness for everything? I had done much of it just to survive, to keep fighting the systems that tried to keep me down. To live. I didn't regret any of it.

Thou shalt not kill?

I had killed.

I checked my watch again, rubbed my eyes. I couldn't remember when I had last eaten, yet I craved only caffeine and nicotine.

Thank goodness I wasn't Catholic, like Mattie. I never understood how they carried around all that guilt. I didn't need faith, I just needed luck. I guess there are only two types of people in this world—those who believe in good and those who do evil.

I glanced back at the apartment. The light was finally out. No movement in the front apartment. I stared at the darkness in the window.

Mattie would be going to bed soon, too. She would be upset if she knew where I was or what I was about to do, but she wouldn't find out. The less she knew, the happier she would be.

I watched for a few more minutes before turning back to the church. It was dormant now. Faith had gone home to bed. Time for the wicked to take over.

My eyes roamed the street once more. Satisfied, I pushed off from the wall and stretched my sore muscles. I strolled back to my car, conveniently parked across the street from the window, now dark. I looked at my watch before opening the passenger seat and retrieving my gloves. The weather was unusually warm, and the gloves could have drawn unwanted attention. If someone even noticed me.

I slipped them on, listening. I thought I heard an owl or hawk screech.

I crossed the street and picked up my pace as I walked past the window I had watched all evening. I wondered if he was a light sleeper. The walls looked thin, and I was pretty damn sure that if he heard me breaking into his neighbor's apartment, I wouldn't have to worry about him calling the cops, but rather about the weapon he'd choose to confront me with.

My father's apartment was dark, as I expected it to be. There was no outside light to warn anyone I was there. I glanced once more at the front apartment and thought I heard him snoring. If I had been a religious man, I might have prayed he stayed asleep.

I didn't bother picking the weak lock on the door this time around. One swift kick at the knob, and the door swung open. I slipped in, closing the door behind me.

I listened for any activity next door. Nothing. Maybe he was a deep sleeper.

Darkness swallowed me. I didn't bother with the lights. I didn't need to see; instead I listened and then moved.

I walked to the bedroom, stepping on trash along the way. I reached into the mattress and grabbed the file. Marquez and Carter hadn't been very thorough. I left the bedroom and followed the same path I had taken, glass crunching under my feet.

I was so preoccupied listening for sounds from the front apartment that I didn't realize I wasn't alone. I focused my eyes on the front door when I heard the unmistakable sound.

The hammer made the slightest of clicks when it was pulled back. I froze and knew I was in trouble. I carried nothing. No weapon.

"Don't shoot," I whispered. I hoped whoever held the gun to my back was calm enough to keep their finger off the trigger. I pushed my arms away from my body so I couldn't be a threat.

I strained to see the front door, but knew I was too far. The darkness could help, though. Shooting a moving suspect was difficult, even for an experienced shooter. Shooting someone in darkness was a tougher feat. I had a good chance of surviving the first shot, but I had been shot before. I knew the pain.

Very slowly, I twisted my head and looked into the darkness. I strained to find the slightest beam of light that could help illuminate my surroundings. As my eyes adjusted, I tried to identify the revolver pointed at me. *Smith & Wesson?* I couldn't be sure. I hoped the safety was on.

Then I focused on the eyes behind the weapon.

"Jesus Christ," I muttered.

I almost didn't recognize the face as my eyes adjusted to the low light. One eye was obscured by dried blood, now black, that had sprouted from a nasty gash just above the eye. The blue eyes had turned red and were surrounded by bruises.

"What happened, Georgia?"

She blinked at the sound of her name, but didn't respond as she struggled to hold herself in a sitting position on the couch.

"Who did this to you?" I stepped forward. Her hand jerked, and I stopped. "Can you lower the gun, honey? I'm not going to hurt you."

I took another cautious step, but the gun didn't move. I was close enough to take it from her, but I didn't want to risk scaring her and making it go off accidentally.

I scanned her bruises. She had been beaten badly. She needed stitches, probably in more than one place.

"You need a doctor."

"No," she whispered, her voice cracking. I barely heard the word.

"Honey, you don't have a choice. I'm not leaving you here to bleed to death."

Her hand lowered. I wasn't sure if it was from weakness or confidence in me.

"You can keep the gun for now, if it'll make you feel better, but you're coming with me."

I reached out slowly and cupped one hand gently behind her back. She flinched but didn't pull away. Her back felt wet, and I hoped it was only sweat. I could smell her flowery perfume. She didn't fight me when I pulled her to her feet. I don't think she had the energy to walk.

I steered her toward the front door and was surprised when she moved along with me. She took small steps, her knees barely lifting.

When we emerged from the dark apartment, my eyes left the gun and scanned the street. Thank God it was still empty.

She didn't say anything as I drove, but her eyes were focused on me. Because I knew someone who could help, I drove out of my way to UCLA Medical Clinic. When I pulled into the parking lot, her eyes finally turned from me.

"You won't be able to take that in with you," I said, referring to the pistol in her lap.

She shook her head, and I saw tears spring out. They were bright red. She pulled the gun closer to her, but kept it aimed at me.

"Honey, you can't bring it in there. You can leave it in the glove compartment and have it back when we're done."

She thought about that as I turned the car off. I got out, giving her the time and space she needed to finally let go of the only protection she had left.

I walked to the other side and opened the passenger door. Her hands were empty. I supported her back as I led her into the emergency room. I didn't sign her in. Instead I requested Dr. Ralphe, and the woman confirmed he was there and paged him. Dr. Ralphe had been my doctor after I was shot protecting Mattie from a killer who had taken us hostage in her house. Dr. Ralphe had been nice to me despite my constant complaints. Probably because it was his job.

He looked annoyed when he spotted me. Then he saw Georgia. He waved a nurse over to take her. She gave me a pained look before following the nurse to a room.

Ralphe sighed, obviously upset with me. "Stay here." He also disappeared behind the curtain.

I paced. I thought of calling Mattie, but it was already late and I didn't want to tell her I was sitting in the emergency room waiting for a beat-up hooker.

Instead I called Ward. When I got his voice mail, I left an unpleasant message for him to call me. If I didn't hear from him soon, I would track him down and beat the shit out of him.

My feet ached as I watched the emergency room slowly empty. Dr. Ralphe came out first. He didn't look happy. He ran a large hand through his thinning black hair, sighed, and looked around for me.

"Is she a prostitute?" Dr. Ralphe asked me.

"What the fuck does that matter? I'm paying you."

He shook his head. "If I discriminated in this emergency room, I'd never have treated you." He pulled me into the corner and waited for a group of people to pass. "How much do you know about her?"

"Not much," I admitted.

"How old is she?"

"I don't know. She's been on her own for a while, though."

"What about her name?"

"She goes by Georgia."

He nodded. "Well, she's got a pretty big gash above her eye. She needed a dozen or more stitches. She's also got several cuts on her hands and arms. I need to get X-rays and a CT scan." He sighed. "Whoever attacked her didn't realize she would fight back." I could tell he didn't want to continue, but he did. "She's got rope burns on her wrists, so she was restrained for a little while."

"Was she raped?" I whispered.

"I can't be sure. She won't talk to anyone. She refused a rape kit."

"Ah, shit." I wanted to hit someone.

"Luc, I'm going to have to notify the police."

"No."

"Whoever did this to her deserves to go to jail," the doctor said.

"Whoever did this deserves a bullet to the head."

"She needs to be admitted. We need to keep her overnight. There are papers to fill out."

I shook my head. I knew what he was asking.

"I could lose my license. I have an obligation. At the very least, I need to contact Child Services."

"Why?"

"She's only a kid, Luc."

"No paperwork. I don't want anyone knowing she's here." I thought about the five grand in cash I still had in my car. "You'll receive a donation. Leave it at that. Keep a close eye on her, Ralphe."

I pulled one of my business cards from my wallet and wrote on the back. "Tell her when she's ready to leave to see my friend, Genie. She'll take care of her." I handed him the card.

Chapter 19

"You missed dinner," Mattie said as I opened the door.

Surprised she was still awake, I looked on the wall to see that the alarm hadn't been set.

"I wasn't hungry. Why isn't the alarm set?"

She was dressed in simple blue jeans and a white T-shirt, but diamonds sparkled on her ears. I knew the earrings had been a gift from Spencer and wondered why she was still wearing them.

She leaned in to kiss me, but stopped short. "You're smoking again?"

I reset the alarm. "You really don't want me to give you a list of my crimes tonight." I avoided looking at her and made my way to the stairs.

"Wait. We have company."

I stopped and looked at her. Her smile had changed to concern. I heard the television from the other room.

"We need to talk first."

I didn't want to talk. I marched to the living room and found a gangly teenager sitting on the couch, watching the big-screen television. A punk in torn jeans and a Red Hot Chili Peppers T-shirt. His feet were up on the coffee table, his shoes worn with holes. He had wild hair that was begging for a haircut. Charlie sat at the boy's feet and barely looked at me when I came in.

Mattie's old guitar leaned against the chair. I realized I hadn't seen it in years. For some reason that made me even angrier.

"Chris," Mattie said, "this is Luc." She turned to me. "Luc, this is Chris Actar."

Big eyes turned to me. Defiant, yet intrigued. The eyes staring at me weren't of a child, but someone with confidence and control. A kid with a plan.

"Hey," Chris said. I saw the slight hesitation before his eyes turned back to the television. I recognized it. A con just realizing he had picked the wrong mark. He was thin, but not from awkward youth or growth spurts. I knew the signs of malnutrition.

"Mattie, can you leave us alone for a minute?"

"Luc—"

"Mattie." I looked at her, then whispered, "Give me a minute."

"Be gentle with him. He's just a kid." I knew she didn't like the look in my eyes, but she sighed and went into the kitchen anyway. I waited until I heard her putting away dishes.

"Get up."

Charlie's ears perked up at my tone, and he slowly got up and moved to my side. I put my hand on his head to let him know I wasn't mad at him.

The kid ignored me, so I repeated myself. The dog let out a small whimper. I knew he didn't like when I got angry. I clenched my fists, counted to ten, and then relaxed my hands. I wouldn't fight in Mattie's house.

The kid finally got up, stretched, turned the television off, and turned to me.

I moved faster than he expected and had him up against the wall. One arm pinned his chest, while the other held his thin wrists above his head. I stared into his green eyes.

"You picked the wrong mark, boy."

"I'm not a con," he said as he squirmed to get out of my grip.

I realized how thin he really was. I held him tighter so he couldn't move. If he was able to get free, I'd have to hit him to keep him still, and I really didn't want to do that here.

"You smell like pot," I said.

"And you smell like nicotine. At least my vice isn't addictive."

I expected a smirk, but got a stone glare instead. I wondered if I had looked like that at his age.

"So you're a smartass kid," I said.

Something flickered in his eyes, and I saw the control falter. "I'm not a kid."

Ah. His Achilles' heel.

"What are you? Fourteen?"

"Do you remember yourself at fourteen?" he snapped back. He attempted to push my arm away, but I held it tight.

At his age, I was stealing money from rich people and stripping cars for parts. And always looking for a way out.

"Don't compare yourself to me, boy. Who are you?" I stared into his eyes, hoping I could read him, but he turned his head away.

"My name's Chris Actar. Guess we're brothers."

"I don't think so."

"Brotherly love is dead in LA. Thankfully, Mrs. Hardwin has a heart for family."

"You're not staying here."

"Mrs. Hardwin says I am. It's that or I hit the streets. Maybe you can give me some pointers to keep the pedophiles away. Mattie would want to make sure I'm safe and all."

I cursed. "You can stay tonight, but tomorrow you can find a new mark."

"Yeah, I guess this one's already taken."

I released him and hit the wall next to his head. Charlie barked once, then lay down.

"Don't make me hurt you," I said.

He rubbed his wrists. "I'm not scared of you. You hit a kid these days and your face is plastered on the evening news."

"You told me yourself, you ain't a kid."

"Luc!"

I turned toward Mattie's voice. I saw her concern and cringed. "Sweetheart, let me finish this."

Her expression changed to anger. "In the kitchen. Now."

I gave the kid a quick glance. He had a smirk on his face that told me he now knew my weakness. I stormed into the kitchen. Mattie followed me.

"Luc, that boy is not your personal punching bag."

"He's not my brother, either," I said.

"You don't know that."

"What I do know is that kid's a liar. Probably a con."

"He said Tony's his father. Even if it's not true, he was living with your father when he died. Can you imagine what he's been through?"

"That doesn't mean I have to save him."

"So it's okay to let another child suffer like you did?"

"I can't be responsible for him. He's fourteen. He can leave."

"You didn't," Mattie said.

I looked at her. "I had my reasons for staying. You know that."

"Your father's dead. This child is alone. He has no one. Do you remember what that felt like?"

Because I did, I didn't respond. As she walked back to Chris, I realized my restless nights were about to return. I grabbed my cell phone and made a call to Jim to give him an update on Mattie's new houseguest.

Chapter 20

I was jolted awake early the following morning by the shrill sound of my cell phone. I was in the middle of a dream, but the only thing I could remember was the look on my father's face the last time I saw him.

I rubbed my eyes and looked at my watch. I hadn't meant to fall asleep. The couch had been so uncomfortable, but it was the only spot in the house where I could keep an eye on everything. The sound of my cell phone tore through the quiet house before I could open it.

"You got yourself a runner." At least Jim was still awake.

I held the cell phone to my ear with my shoulder and grabbed my keys. I noticed Charlie sitting at alert at the front door. I ordered him upstairs.

"Where is he?" I asked Jim. I wasn't surprised that Chris had fled. In fact, I was hoping he would. I would learn more about him if he was on the move.

"He just left the house and is walking down toward the corner."

I looked at the alarm panel and wondered how he had disarmed it. I re-armed it and walked out the door.

"You want me to follow him?" Jim asked.

"No, I got it." I unlocked the Porsche. "Keep an eye on Mattie for me."

"Malibu's a safe neighborhood."

"So I'm told."

I reached the corner and spotted a lone kid walking in the shadows. I kept my lights off and watched from a distance as Chris walked down the dark, deserted road toward Pacific Coast Highway. At the corner, he crossed the street to the restaurant that was now closed and dark. He made a call at the pay phone, watching the street with the phone to his ear.

He waited. I waited. I hoped he wasn't observant enough to spot my car in the distance. Unfortunately, he spotted the cop car before I did. As it turned into the parking lot of the restaurant, Chris dropped the phone and took off running. He jumped a short wall as I put the car in gear. The officers took off on foot after him.

I knew the neighborhood better than he did, and I knew all the exits. I pulled the Porsche onto the street and cruised past the empty patrol car just as the officers jumped the wall in pursuit.

I turned left, then right, and searched the street. I put the car in neutral and stepped out.

Chris emerged from the back of a house and came running straight at me. He was so focused on the cops behind him that he never saw me. I grabbed him as he tried to run past.

"Get in the car, you idiot. You'll never outrun them."

He didn't have the strength or the breath to fight me. I pushed him down in the seat and sped off toward PCH.

"Where are we going?" he asked, lifting his head. I pushed his head back down to his knees.

"Taking a cruise in case they spotted my car. Why are the cops looking for you?" I eyed the old blue backpack he was clutching as he tried to catch his breath.

The kid didn't reply. He stared out his window as I cruised past a stop sign. No sign of the cop car or the pursuing officers. I pulled the car over and stared out toward the ocean. The sun would be rising soon.

"How did you get a car like this?" Chris asked.

I looked at him and realized he was impressed. "Get out." I pushed him out of the car, but held onto the backpack.

He got out and stared back at me. I pulled out a bag of weed from the backpack and stuffed it in the glove compartment. I rifled through the rest of the bag and found a birth certificate. Chris Actar, born in Texas to a woman named Virginia Actar. My father was listed as well. It looked legit, just like the others I had seen at Rev's apartment. I stared at it for a minute. Chris said nothing.

After a few minutes, I got out of the car and armed it. "Let's take a walk."

He didn't move. I pulled out my wallet.

"One hundred dollars. You talk, you get the money. I need answers, and I don't want to beat them from you."

"I didn't steal anything." He stuffed his hands in his pockets, hiding as much as he could from me. "How'd you get so rich?"

"What does it matter?" I asked.

"Being rich is kinda cool."

"Being rich doesn't make you cool. Just look at Donald Trump."

My phone rang. It was Jim.

"You got two pigs at your front door. Suits, not uniforms. Mattie just opened the door."

"Shit. She better not let them in the house again."

"She's just talking to them right now. LAPD."

"Probably Marquez and Carter."

"Cops sure like you these days. They're leaving."

"Thanks, Jim. Keep an eye on the house. Make sure they don't do anything stupid."

I called Mattie next. The kid kept his eyes on me.

"Luc, the two detectives were just here asking about Chris. The same two detectives that were here on Saturday."

"You didn't let them in the house, did you?"

"No. They said they were just checking to make sure Chris was okay."

I rubbed my eyes. "What exactly did you say?"

"I said he was asleep, and it was none of their business."

"You lied to the cops?" I couldn't help but laugh.

"They lied to me first. Where's Chris?"

"He's with me. We have some things to discuss. You don't need to worry. We'll get things worked out."

I hung up with Mattie and watched the waves crash on the rocks as the horizon transitioned to a fiery orange. A lone seagull stood on the rocks, looking out to the tumultuous ocean. I thought it should stay on dry land, but after a few minutes it took off over the ocean.

Chris walked over to the sand and sat down next to me.

"Why'd you sneak out?" I asked.

"You obviously don't want me there."

I didn't deny it, but I knew he hadn't left because I had hurt his feelings. "Why are the cops after you?"

"The two detectives, they won't leave me alone."

"Marquez and Carter?" I asked. "The ones investigating the burglary?"

He nodded. "I don't know anything about the burglary."

He was a bad liar, and I knew right then I didn't want him talking to the cops, either.

"Did they question you when Tony died?" I asked.

He shook his head. "Child Services wouldn't let them. I told them I was too traumatized." He smirked, and I knew he was hiding something.

"Who'd you call back there?"

"A neighbor. We look out for each other when Tony's not around."

"Georgia?" I asked.

"How'd you know about her?"

"She's a nice girl." I decided against telling him about my late-night break-in and our visit to the hospital. "You were living with Tony at the Lakewood apartment?"

"Look, those cops won't leave me alone. I don't want to talk to them."

I realized Chris was running because he knew something. I needed to know what that was. It would take more than a conversation at the beach. I considered my options.

"Fine," I said. "I can prevent them from talking to you."

"You can?" He looked up at me.

I nodded. "I'm officially next of kin. You stay with me, I call the shots. You go running loose, then the State calls the shots. At some point Child Services will make you talk to the detectives."

He seemed interested in my option.

"Here are the ground rules," I said. "You do what I say. Nothing more, nothing less. If you're on my side, I protect you. You step out of bounds, I feed you to the cops myself."

"Sounds fair. Do I still get the money?"

I put the money back in my wallet. "When I'm convinced you're not pulling a con, you can have it," I lied.

"Can you really keep the cops from me?"

I smiled and stared at my growing shadow. "If my father told you anything at all about me, he should have told you I can do that. I can also keep secrets. Tell me about the burglary."

"I didn't have anything to do with it," he repeated, looking back toward the waves.

I knew from his lie that he was clearly responsible. Now I just needed to find out what had happened to the loot. I figured I'd give him some time to open up at his pace. "Okay. Any idea where Tony would hide something he stole?"

"Tony wasn't a thief."

He was right, and the fact that he knew that would mean he knew my father pretty well. Eventually he'd tell me everything.

Chapter 21

After dropping Chris back at the house with Mattie, I headed into the office early. Orin was already there, looking more discouraged than normal. He told me he'd found a home address for Dr. Stedman, but neighbors hadn't seen him recently. Orin was working a contact to see if he could find the man's phone records.

He still hadn't found any information on Henry Dillon. I gave him the file from my father's apartment and told him about my night, leaving out the hooker and the hospital.

He opened the file and skimmed the information. "April fifteenth, checked in under fifty-one-fifty by Dr. Stedman. Claimed he was suicidal. He met with Dr. Stedman three times in the seventy-two-hour period. Diagnosed as paranoid schizophrenic. He apparently was well liked among the staff and the other patients. On his last day he was told he should stay for more therapy and apparently agreed." Orin turned the page. "A copy of the form with his signature."

I shrugged. "Doesn't prove anything."

He looked up at me. "Apparently Henry Dillon was really sick. Dr. Stedman did the right thing here, Luc."

"Keep reading. Three days after agreeing to voluntary commitment, Henry refuses to leave his room, claiming someone is trying to kill him.

Dr. Stedman meets with him in his room, but he's unable to convince him to stay. Henry checks himself out that evening. Three days later, he's at Torrance Medical Clinic bunking in the same room as my dad. After he's released, both he and Dr. Stedman disappear."

"Which may be completely coincidental. He's a sick homeless man, after all." Orin closed the folder and dropped it on the desk. "I'm sorry, Luc. None of this sounds sinister."

"We need to find them to be sure. My father broke into Ramirez's office for a reason. We need to know why."

"I thought you didn't believe your father stole anything?"

I still didn't, but after meeting Chris, I realized the kid was definitely capable of the job, and my father would have no problem using the kid to his advantage. But I needed to find out what the advantage was. I told Orin about Chris and my early-morning discussion with him.

"Do you want me to dig and find out who this kid really is?" Orin asked.

I shook my head. "I need a story for Saturday, and I think our best efforts will be spent on locating Henry Dillon. He may have the files we're looking for. I'm going to make another visit to Torrance Treatment Center and find out where the hell Dr. Stedman is hiding out."

"What about Detective Ward? Maybe he can help track down both of these guys for us."

"I've been trying to reach him on his cell, but he's not answering my calls." I glanced at my watch. "Maybe I'll see if I can get an official statement from Ramirez, too."

"You're actually going to confront Ramirez with only rumors? We haven't even talked to Dr. Stedman."

"We're running out of time. I think the best approach is the frontal assault. I'm going to force a face-to-face meeting with the guy. I'll ask about the burglary and then segue into his doctors kidnapping the homeless to bump up his patient numbers."

"Luc, this is a bad idea. This guy knows some people high up. He can squash you before you even walk in the door. I'm sure he's got better security than he had before the burglary."

I knew Orin was right, but I also knew Ramirez was overly interested in my father's investigation. I hoped it would be enough to get him to agree to talk to me.

We were just finishing our game plan when Callahan appeared in the doorway. He always looked like a ball of nerves to me. He was losing his jet-black hair quickly, and his eyes were red because he rarely slept. His hands bunched into fists as he talked, and he could never stand still. I felt nervous just looking at him and often avoided him for that reason alone.

I stood, hoping he'd get the impression I was leaving. I definitely didn't want him to pin me in my office.

"Luc, I need a story. What are you working on?"

"Can't talk now, Callahan. I'm on my way out for a few quotes."

He blocked the doorway. "No more bullshit, Luc. Let's hear what you're working on."

Resigned, I sat back down and tried not to look at him. "We're looking into Ernesto Ramirez. We've heard that a doctor on his staff is kidnapping homeless people for the hospital." I decided not to tell him we had no actual proof of this yet.

Callahan's face turned bright red. "No. We're not running a story on Ramirez." He shook his head. "No way."

"Why not?" I asked, shocked. "This is a great story!"

"Ernesto is one of our few remaining advertisers. He helped push this paper off the ground, and he happens to be a personal friend of mine. No story on him." Callahan continued to shake his head, as if it were a nervous tick.

"Lucky for me, I don't give a shit about money bribes or friendship," I said. "This story will rock LA."

"This isn't up for discussion, Luc," he shouted. He always hoped raising his voice would shut me up, but it never worked.

"No need to be a dick, Callahan. You may be my boss, but you can't stop me from writing the story."

"No, but I don't have to print it. You forget, I still call the shots here. You better have another story for me by tomorrow—one I can print, or you can pack up whatever shit you have in this office and get the hell out." He turned to Orin. "I want you on the Palos Verdes John Doe murder."

Orin stood abruptly, as if he would say something, then lowered his head. He muttered, "Yes, sir," and walked from the room.

"You're a fuck-up, Luc. I should never have hired you back. No matter how high you think you've climbed, you'll always drag yourself back down. Well, you're not dragging this paper down with you."

Callahan stormed out of the office. I was too pissed to fight back, and deep down I knew he was right. I slammed my laptop closed and pulled open the drawer with the tequila bottle. Taking a shot, I searched for my cigarettes. They weren't there.

I unlocked the other drawer and found the pack of cigarettes lying on top of the folder that had been mailed to me. I got up and slammed my door closed. Returning to my seat, I tossed down another shot of tequila before opening the folder once again.

That day came rushing back at me. I remembered the anger and pain I had felt when I learned Carl had hit Mattie. I remembered the guilt hitting me like a steamroller. I hadn't stopped the relationship, even though I knew it would end badly. I knew he wasn't right for her, and I knew he would mistreat her. I knew she would be in pain, yet I didn't stop it.

I wasn't sure at the time why I hadn't stopped it. Maybe I felt it wasn't my place, but I knew it was. I was responsible for making sure Mattie was okay. I was ultimately responsible for her well-being, and I had walked away from that responsibility.

She had told me it didn't matter where someone came from. It didn't matter the difference in wealth or the type of family. I wanted to believe her. I wanted to believe there could be a positive future for someone like me.

Carl and I weren't that different. We had both grown up on the streets in Torrance. He sold drugs for a small local gang. I stole money and drugs from those same gang members. We both hoped to make something better for ourselves, and we both resorted to violence when things didn't go our way.

I hadn't gone to the alley to kill him that night. I had never thought I could take a life so easily. But it was easy. So easy, I knew I could do it again, if Mattie was ever threatened.

I flipped the page and stared at the autopsy report. The damage described had all been done by my hands. I turned the page again and read the detectives' notes on the scene. I stopped when I saw Mattie's name. The detectives had questioned her. She had never told me. I wondered if she had known all that time that I was responsible for this. I closed the folder and wondered again why it had been mailed to me.

I considered dropping the Ramirez story. I still had no evidence, other than some offhand comments from Miss Jessie and a forgetful homeless man. I needed to find someone who would talk to me. Before I could find the answers I knew Ramirez could provide, I needed to learn more about my father and why he would get involved with Henry Dillon and Dr. Stedman.

What would my father have to gain by stealing from Ernesto Ramirez? Did his chance encounter with Henry Dillon at the hospital spark the entire plan? If so, what would Henry want from Ramirez? Was there something he was trying to get, or was he so delusional that he really thought someone at the treatment center was trying to kill him? I needed to know what was stolen, but Orin was right. It was too soon to approach Ramirez with only rumors. I knew Henry Dillon was the man who linked everyone, but it was easy for a sick homeless man to disappear. It would be much harder for a prominent doctor to vanish. I decided to find Dr. Stedman on my own.

I locked the file back in my drawer and headed out to the Torrance Treatment Center.

Chapter 22

I found Dr. Brown much more willing to talk to me this time around. He met me in the hallway and directed me to the cafeteria on the second floor. I followed as he waddled down the hallway. His heavy breath increased with every step. I hoped he could make it down the hallway without having a heart attack, and was thankful when we reached the cafeteria so he could catch his breath.

Elevator music played softly, and I could hear the kitchen staff in the back getting breakfast ready. We walked across the spotless, shiny white floor and stood in front of another man in a white coat behind the counter. He had a kind, soft smile.

Brown ordered a coffee and offered to buy me one, but I declined. After pouring in about a cup of sugar, he pointed to an empty booth. The place was just starting to wake up. Two other guys in white coats wandered in. They waved at Dr. Brown but went to order their breakfast.

I spotted his receptionist in a far booth with several folders spread out before her, an iPod on the table, and ear buds in her ears. She looked smaller when she wasn't hiding behind a partition. Her big eyes stared holes in me from across the room as she sipped from a mug. Dr. Brown didn't seem to notice her.

"I was interested in your claim yesterday about Dr. Stedman," he said. "I did some checking, and I'm very concerned about him."

"Would you be willing to go on record?" I asked, turning my attention back to the man sitting across from me.

"You're a reporter, right?"

I nodded. "For the *Crime Reporter*."

He nodded, stared into his coffee. I wondered if he was still catching his breath or regretting the fact that he hadn't gotten something to eat.

"I don't want you to name me by name, but you can quote me as an anonymous source. Dr. Stedman's files were all sent to Mr. Ramirez under orders directly from him. The files were sent a few weeks ago. I can't seem to get a copy of any of the files no matter how many times I ask. I've taken on the bulk of Dr. Stedman's patients, but have little background on any of them. Dr. Stedman disappeared the following day."

"What do you mean he disappeared?"

He shrugged. "No one has seen him in almost three weeks. Most of us thought he quit. There's been a lot of tension between Dr. Stedman and Mr. Ramirez, and we figured Dr. Stedman had had enough. But several of us have tried to reach him with no luck. After you stopped by, I got concerned. I contacted his sister, and she went by his house. It appears he hasn't been home in some time. I'm afraid he may have taken off or he's in some sort of trouble."

I asked Dr. Brown for any contact information he had for Dr. Stedman and his sister. I made a note to follow up with her. I found it interesting that Dr. Brown seemed concerned for his coworker enough to contact his family, but still referred to him as *Dr. Stedman*. I wondered if it was a doctor thing, to show respect or something. I found it too formal.

"Were any of his patients institutionalized on fifty-one-fifty?"

"I can't tell you for sure, since I don't have the files, but I believe a few of them were. Even so, those patients have to be processed and evaluated within seventy-two hours according to the law."

"What happens after the seventy-two hours is up?"

"Usually the patient is released to a family member, but that's not always possible. Some patients need more counseling or drug therapy and decide to stay here."

"They agree to stay?"

"Yes. Many of these people are very sick. They need constant medical care and medication. If they stay here, it's the patient's choice."

"If you don't have the patient's files, how do you know it's their choice to stay? How do you know these patients aren't being coerced into signing away their freedom?"

He sighed. "Most of the patients here have voluntarily given up their freedom or are seen on an outpatient basis. If they agree to stay here, they understand they can leave at any time. There is only a small population that has been committed involuntarily. We follow the law here. I don't believe Dr. Stedman would commit someone unless they were a danger to themselves or someone else."

Dr. Brown pulled up his thick arm to check his watch and made a comment about having to get to his office. I noticed that the receptionist was still watching us from her booth.

"Can you give me the patients' names?" I asked before Dr. Brown could get up.

He shook his head. "I can't do that."

"Can you contact them and see if they'll talk to me?"

He thought about this and finally nodded. "I can try, but I can't promise any of them will call you." He glanced at his watch again. "I should get back. What else do you need?"

"If a directive was given at this hospital to pick up homeless people, how high up would it go? Would Ernesto Ramirez know?"

"I've never heard of such a directive. Why would Mr. Ramirez want to do that?"

"The hospital takes money from the state. The more patients he has going through the hospital doors, the more money he sees."

"I don't believe everyone is blinded by money." He sighed again. "But there's very little that goes on in this facility that he doesn't know about."

It was enough for me. I thanked the doctor and told him to call me as soon as he got in touch with any of the patients. I didn't watch him leave, but instead focused on the receptionist. She seemed quite interested in my conversation with Dr. Brown, and it was time to find out why. I stayed in my seat and motioned her to come to me. She glanced around and waited until Dr. Brown had disappeared down the hallway. The other men who had arrived for breakfast had also left.

She tucked her iPod away and made her way to me. I motioned to the seat Dr. Brown had vacated, but she remained standing.

"Whatever he said to you was a lie," she said.

"I can't imagine you could hear anything from where you were sitting, and even though you were watching us closely, I don't think you can read lips that well."

"He's a liar. I know he's telling you all kinds of lies about Dr. Stedman, but he's a good doctor."

"Why would Dr. Brown lie about Dr. Stedman? Is there bad blood between them?"

"Not from Dr. Stedman. Jack likes everyone. He's always trying to help everyone. Dr. Brown is just jealous of him. He had more patients and was making more money. Dr. Brown just wanted him out of the way. He loves that Dr. Stedman quit. He loves the attention he's getting from Mr. Ramirez."

"Sit down and talk to me. Tell me what you know about Stedman leaving. Why did he quit?"

She didn't sit. Instead, she fidgeted with the rings on her fingers. "I don't know. I wish I knew. He tells me everything, but he didn't tell me he was leaving. One day he was here, and the next, Mr. Ramirez is pulling his files. It's not fair. He was a great doctor, and he helped a lot of people."

"Do you know if most of his patients were homeless?"

She looked at me and finally sat down. "He has a soft spot for homeless patients."

"Where did he find these patients?" I asked.

"His sister. They're really close. They talk all the time. She was trying to help these people, and Jack agreed. These people need help. They wouldn't be homeless if they were on the right medication and under doctor supervision."

"Not all homeless people are sick," I said, standing up.

She looked confused. "I've been working here a long time. You'd be surprised how sick some of these people really are."

~~~

As I left the cafeteria, my cell phone rang. Ward was finally calling me back.

"Where the hell have you been?" I asked him.

"I have a deceased six-year-old and a foster mother who can't remember when she last fed him. I've been on-scene for two days."

I said nothing and let the silence hang there, hoping he understood I wasn't going to take the brunt of his anger for that one. I could hear Ward take a deep breath.

Finally, he asked, "Have you found the stolen files or laptop yet?"

"No. I wanted to let you know I got my father's medical records, though. Do you have someone that can dig through the medical jargon?"

"Sure. Drop them off, and I'll review them." I heard a woman screaming in the background.

"I can head over to the station now," I said.

"Leave them in my desk. I'm going to be here a little bit longer, and I don't want anyone seeing them. Do you have any idea where your father stashed the files?"

"No, but I know what Ramirez is trying to hide. His hospital is apparently kidnapping homeless people and using fifty-one-fifty to cover his ass."

Ward was quiet on the other end.

"Ward, you still there?" I asked.
~~~

"Yeah. Luc, you promised this wasn't going to end up on the front of the *Crime Reporter*."

"Guess I broke my promise," I said. "This is too good to let go. I can bury Ramirez, and you won't have to lift a finger."

I walked out to my car and noticed Detectives Carter and Marquez leaning against my Porsche. I wondered how they had found me here.

"You can't go after Ramirez," Ward said, his voice rising. "You need to stay away from him. We had a deal, Luc. This is just for the missing files."

"You can thank me later." I closed the phone.

Detective Carter straightened when he spotted me. Marquez remained leaning against the car, his arms folded.

"I thought the deal was I go to anger management and you boys leave me alone," I said. I looked at Marquez. "Get away from my car."

Marquez didn't move.

Carter stepped between us. "What are you doing here, Mr. Actar?"

"Free country, Carter. I don't have to answer that."

He nodded. "Okay, I'll give you that. Mr. Actar, we need to talk to Chris."

I smiled. "Good luck."

Carter took a deep breath as if the words were hard to speak. "We need your permission to talk to him."

"Look, he had nothing to do with the burglary you think my father was responsible for. He won't help you."

"Chris mailed something when he was with Child and Family Services. They mailed it without looking at the address or asking what it was. We need to know what was mailed and where."

"You think he had the files Ramirez is looking for?" I could tell that Martinez was very uncomfortable talking about his case to me. I wondered if it was because I knew more than he did now.

"We've been unable to find them anywhere else your father went."

I unlocked the Porsche and said, "I bet Ramirez is going to be real upset to learn your case rests on the shoulders of a fourteen-year-old boy who refuses to talk to you."

"Luc, we just need five minutes with him."

"As his legal guardian, I'm going to politely decline your offer." I got in the car and drove away, proud that I hadn't attacked either one of them.

Chapter 23

The square brick building that housed the headquarters of the Torrance Treatment Center had large columns and sharp corners. The top corners were decorated with gargoyles that stared menacingly at the surrounding parking lot. Their mouths were open to allow water to flow out.

I wondered why anyone would have put the gargoyles on the building. It didn't rain hard enough in Southern California to worry about water damaging the building's exterior, and they definitely didn't portray an inviting presence in the neighborhood.

At the ground level, a large winged lion sculpture looked posed to attack anyone entering with bad intentions. It's eyes stared blankly, feathered wings arching upward. The lion's mouth was open as if caught by surprise. I gazed at it for several minutes, trying to determine the purpose of putting such a strange creature outside an office building.

It was quiet in the parking lot as I sat in my car, but I could see several layers of security that would have kept me from attempting a burglary here. I had to respect the kid for not only succeeding, but having the balls to even try.

I located Ernesto Ramirez's car, a shiny red BMW 6 Series coupe parked in a spot marked for the chief executive officer. There were a few other cars but very little foot traffic, despite the approaching lunch hour. The only other person I saw was a large Hispanic man leaning against a wall near the front door, looking bored. He didn't notice me across the street as he kept an eye on the entrance; his surveillance consisted of the parking lot and the door. He was armed, but not in uniform. A bodyguard, as opposed to security.

With the bodyguard in place, I knew I wouldn't have a chance to talk to Ramirez alone. Since Orin couldn't find a home address, my only hope was to follow Ramirez if he went out.

I had just nodded off when I heard a car engine start. I looked around and saw the bodyguard drive out of the parking lot in a silver Toyota truck, a phone to his ear. I wondered if it was his lunch break or if he would be right back. Ramirez's car was still in its spot.

I didn't know how much time I had, so I jumped from the car. I kept my head down, even though I knew the cameras would catch me anyway.

Inside the building, I smiled at the receptionist on the phone, but continued walking. She tried to stop me, but I mouthed the word *bathroom*. She looked confused but continued to talk into the receiver.

The office had dark hardwood floors that echoed with every step I made. I continued down the hallway, hoping to find the right door. I opened a set of double doors, only to find an empty boardroom. The receptionist continued talking, but I hurried anyway. I spotted the surveillance cameras, but there was nothing I could do about it.

At the end of the hallway was a back emergency exit. It didn't appear to be alarmed. As I turned to go back down the hall, I saw the glass door. Etched in the shaded glass in large letters, TORRANCE TREATMENT CENTERS. Under that, CHIEF EXECUTIVE OFFICER ERNESTO RAMIREZ. Under the name was a gray pitchfork-looking logo with a red snake wrapped around the center.

I opened the door and found Ernesto Ramirez sitting behind a large dark mahogany desk, his shoes off and his feet propped up on it. He wore a black tie, a starched white shirt, and an expensive black jacket. He seemed dwarfed behind the desk. He couldn't have been more than

140 pounds and looked more like a high school nerd to be picked on than a high-powered CEO who made cops shudder.

He didn't look surprised to see me. He didn't bother to remove his feet from the desk. "What do you want, Mr. Actar?"

"Aw, I'm flattered you know who I am," I said, closing the door behind me.

Leather-bound books filled the shelves, and fancy artwork decorated the expertly textured walls. It was meant to give a warm feeling, but the room was cold. There were no personal effects, no wedding photo, no mementos. I wondered how someone could actually work in a room so void of emotion. Then I remembered my own office at the *Crime Reporter*.

I thought about making myself comfortable in the chair that faced him, but I had a feeling that if I sat in his chair, he would think he had the advantage over me.

"Unless you're here to return the documents your father stole from me," said Ramirez, "you have no reason to be here."

"I don't have anything, but I'm dying to find out why you're so upset that they're missing."

"I run a business here, Mr. Actar. I have a board of directors to report to. I need to prove that our financial and executive information is safe and secure. You have an editor to report to as well, right?"

I smiled. "Did Callahan call you?"

"Get out. I don't have time for you today. If you want to talk to me, bring me the files your father stole."

"I'm not ready to leave. I have the entire front page of the *Crime Reporter* to fill, so I'm going to need some quotes. Tell me about Henry Dillon."

I thought I saw a flash of recognition, but he said nothing, so I continued.

"He was a patient at Torrance Treatment Center. Dr. Stedman kidnapped him from outside the Guardian Home."

"I don't know what you're talking about," Ramirez said. The look on his face almost had me believing him. His eyes squinted and he looked like a snake peering at his prey, but he made no attempt to fight back.

"Here's what I'm talking about. I have a witness who states Henry Dillon was picked up on a fifty-one-fifty last month. Now he's missing. I hold you responsible for him. What do you think the public will think of this? And prepare a good answer. I'm going to quote you."

He ignored my questions and opened a drawer in his desk. I waited to see if he would pull a gun on me or call his bodyguard. I knew I was running out of time.

"Even if you don't answer, the story will still make the top headline on the *Crime Reporter*," I said.

He flipped through several folders, finally selecting one and throwing it across the desk at me. "I got a better headline for you. How about 'Journalist likes to beat up his whores.'"

I opened the folder and looked at the picture on top. It was a photo of me helping Georgia into my Porsche. I didn't bother to flip through the rest.

"You really think this would bother me?" I said, throwing the pictures back at him. "I don't live by the media. I won't die by it. Go ahead and release the pictures. See if I give a shit."

"You might not, but I'm sure Mattie would," he said.

I straightened. Mattie would be upset, but I could deal with it. The fact that he even mentioned her pissed me off. He was looking smaller to me now.

"You're right," he said. "I shouldn't have bothered with the pictures, but they were just so easy. Since you want to play hard, I'll play hard." He looked through the folder. "Oh yeah, you provided a bribe to a school official to ensure Mattie got the job at the private school, didn't you? And she's working with a lawyer to get guardianship of that child."

I wondered just how long he'd been keeping tabs on me. I remained quiet so I could hear the entire threat before deciding how I could rip his head off.

"What a shame. With just one phone call, I can have Mattie arrested for child abuse. She'll not only lose her job, but there won't be another school in the country that will touch her. And the child? I'll make sure Child and Family Services takes the kid and buries him so deep in the foster system, you'll never find him again."

"You bastard." I shot forward, hurtling myself over his desk.

He tried to duck from a blow he was sure was coming. Instead, I reached out and wrapped both my hands around his throat and squeezed. I pushed him against the wall. His eyes bulged and the smirk fell from his face as I raised his puny body off the floor. His feet flailed wildly, kicking my shins. I squeezed harder and watched him gasp for air.

"Was that a threat?" I asked.

His face reddened. I knew I could take his life, but I wasn't past control, and I wasn't crazy. I knew this wasn't the time or place for him to die. I released him, and he crumpled to the floor.

I heard a woman scream and knew I had overstayed my welcome. I walked to the door and smiled at the scared receptionist who had walked in on our discussion.

"I'll just use the bathroom at home," I told her.

From behind the desk, I heard coughing. The fact that he was still breathing disappointed me a bit.

"I'm not scared of you, Ramirez," I said over my shoulder. "You just met your match. Game on."

I walked toward the back exit in hopes of not running into the mammoth bodyguard. I swung the door open.

"Mr. Actar?"

I looked up to see Jeffrey Donovan, the patient I had met in the waiting room of Torrance Treatment Center, standing in the alley. He looked pale, his hair even thinner. He had scratches on his arms and neck. I wondered if he was physically sick as well as mentally.

"Jeffrey. What are you doing here?"

He stuffed a finger in his mouth and began chewing. In between bites, he said. "I have a meeting with Mr. Ramirez to get my papers.

What are you doing here?"

"Just having a friendly discussion with Ramirez," I said. "You know Dr. Stedman, correct? Do you have a minute?"

He shook his head and spit on the ground. The smell of his chew was intense, and I stepped back.

"No, sir. I just came to get my papers for court. If I keep my mouth shut, I can have my papers and stay out of jail. I can't talk to you."

"Is that what they promised you? Keep quiet and stay free?"

"I won't go back to jail. I did the therapy. I did what the doctors told me to do, but they lied. I want to be free from all of this. I want to go home." His head jerked back to the alley, his eyes darting here and there. I wondered what drugs they had put the poor guy on.

"I'll do what I can to keep your name out of this, Jeffrey, but I need you to talk to me. Tell me what you know about the doctors at Torrance Treatment Center."

I moved out of the way as he reached for the door, shaking his head again. "No. I need to go. I have an appointment. It'd be best if you left me out of whatever you're doing, and I won't bother you with what I'm doing." He walked through the door.

I noticed the receptionist watching me from inside with a cell phone to her ear. I heard a siren in the distance and knew it was time for me to leave.

Chapter 24

I skipped lunch. The thought of eating when Mattie was probably having lunch with Spencer made me sick. I drove to Irvine and arrived early at Dr. Holstein's office. The Jaguar was missing from the lot this time. The Camry was in the same spot it had been all week. When I got to the lobby, I learned that Dr. Holstein was still at lunch, but her receptionist called her and she arrived ten minutes after I sat down in the lobby to wait.

Dr. Holstein said nothing of my early arrival. She followed her routine and offered me tea. I declined and watched her pour herself some and settle in her chair with her notebook on her lap.

"Let's talk about your friends today," she said.

I thought of Spencer. "I don't have any friends."

"You have no one that you can talk to other than Mattie? Who do you talk to when you can't talk to Mattie?"

"I used to talk to Spencer, but he's having a hard time with his divorce. He blames me, and now we can't be friends."

She nodded. "That must be hard."

"I don't need him."

"Did you talk to him about your childhood?"

"No. He wouldn't understand."

"What about Mattie?"

"I'm not talking about Mattie."

"Is there anyone you talk to about your childhood?"

"Why are you making this all about my childhood? I'm an adult. I have adult problems now."

She jotted something in her notebook. "What type of problems?"

"I'm about to lose my job. I had a huge fight with Spencer, and my father's new son is living in Mattie's house."

"The boy moved in with you?" she asked.

"That's what you focused on? What about the fact I have no story for this week and my editor is having a fucking cow?"

"Okay, we'll take one problem at a time. Why don't you have a story?"

"I have a story, but he won't print it. Money and power override the truth in this city."

"So write a different story. I'm sure there's a lot of crime going on here you can write about."

"I don't want to write about just anything. I want to write this story."

"Why did you become a journalist, Luc?" she asked.

"Because I like attacking people who lord their power over others. It's the only thing I'm good at."

"Luc, your boss is telling you to write something else. If you want to keep your job, do it. It's not your paper. This is about listening to authority."

"No, this is about the truth. He's trying to cover it up like everyone else. I don't care enough about this job to sit by and ignore this."

"Okay, then losing your job is not a problem. Let's move on to your other problem. What was the fight with Spencer about?"

"Because I'm sleeping with his ex-wife and he's still in love with her."

She crossed her hands on her lap. "Do you love Mattie?"

"I'm not talking about her."

"Sometimes in this life we have to choose. I think you've made your choice. Spencer knows this. He's going to need more time to deal with the new situation. You have to give him the time and space he needs."

"And what if he decides we can't be friends?"

"You have to be okay with his decision. You don't regret yours. Tell me about the boy. What's his name?"

"Chris. Mattie let him move in last night. I'm trying to get him out."

She smiled. "What's he like?"

"A punk kid. He's a thief and a con."

She laughed. "He reminds you of yourself at his age, right?"

"No. I was nothing like him."

She apparently ignored me as she continued, "And you don't want Mattie seeing that. She might remember what you were like."

I realized Dr. Holstein was focusing on Mattie again. Standing, I said, "I'm done here."

As she was making another note in her notebook, I walked out. The doctor didn't bother to stop me.

After leaving the office, I took a few minutes to watch the street before pulling a slim jim from the trunk of my car. I had the Jaguar's passenger door open in seconds. I sat in the passenger seat so I wouldn't draw attention to myself as I searched the glove box. I found a Mercury Insurance card with Mary Holstein's name and address. I copied the address and continued looking around. I found an LAPD robbery homicide business card with Carter's name on it. John had been right. Holstein was probably related to Detective Carter. Returning the card, I locked the car.

I was suddenly finding it very hard to walk away from such a sweet ride.

~~~

I arrived at Mattie's house to the sound of laughter and music and the strong smell of marijuana. I heard Charlie barking from the back yard. I found Chris on the living room couch with his feet up on the table, strumming Mattie's old guitar. Two girls were sharing a joint and giggling next to him.
~~~

I wished I had a gun to scare the girls straight, but instead I cleared my throat. Chris stopped playing. The girls looked over, but didn't seem bothered at my presence.

"You two girls, get out," I said, pointing at them. The blonde frowned at me, as if at any minute she would burst into tears. She pulled on a sweatshirt to cover the tiny tank top she was wearing.

The other girl cocked her head at me, ready for a fight. "Why?"

"Because that boy right there is about to get his ass kicked, and I'm sure he doesn't want an audience."

Chris took the joint from the girls and put down the guitar. "Scram," he said. His mood had changed from lighthearted to serious. If I wasn't mistaken, I even saw concern.

The girls walked out. I heard one mutter, "Asshole," but I wasn't sure if she was referring to me or to Chris.

I followed the two girls out and left the front door wide open as I watched them walk hand in hand down the street. I sat on the porch and wondered what my options were. I wanted to kick his ass for real. I wanted to smack some sense into him and tell him how stupid and dangerous his little game with me was. But I still needed him to talk to me. I had a feeling I wasn't going to get my way, and I didn't like the thought of losing this battle.

Chris joined me on the porch a minute later. The joint and the guitar were gone. I said nothing and let him think about how much trouble he could be in. He leaned against the closed door just out of my reach, but I could see the slight look of fear in his eyes. He refused to look at me.

Twenty minutes passed in silence, and I knew he wanted me to talk first. Finally he pulled out a cigarette and lit it.

I took one step, reached for the cigarette, and watched the fear jump up again. "What is this?"

"Just a cigarette. It's not illegal."

"It is if you're fourteen." I dropped it on the ground and stomped it. Then I remembered that Mattie would see it. I picked it up and threw it in the grass.

"No victim, no crime," he said.

I laughed. "Did he teach you that?"

"Maybe." He looked away.

"I don't know how I ever learned anything from that man," I said.

This kid had no idea what the real world was like. I wondered how long he had actually been on his own or if he had run away and straight into Tony's Lakewood apartment. He had a lot to learn about crime, life, and how to survive. He apparently hadn't been living with Tony very long; otherwise he'd be a lot sharper.

Chris looked at me. "How do you define a crime?"

"It's a crime if you get caught. Otherwise it's just living."

"Did he teach you that?"

I leaned back. "The streets taught me that. Tony never taught me anything worthwhile." I looked at Chris. "I know you did the burglary job. You stole the files for Tony."

"I didn't do anything."

"I sure as hell know he didn't do it. And not many people can do a job like that. I think you have that ability."

He looked at me now. He didn't admit it, but I could tell he was proud of that fact. Maybe proud that I knew it.

He finally shrugged, but his eyes were studying me. "I don't understand why everyone is getting so upset."

"I already know you stole the files. Did you look at them?"

He nodded. "I glanced at them. They were just medical records."

"How many?"

He shrugged again. "Three boxes full."

"What happened to them?"

He put his hands in his lap, then rubbed his legs as if he was cold. "I gave them to Tony."

"What happened to them after that?"

"Don't know. He gave them to some guy that wanted them."

It still didn't make sense. "Who was this guy?"

"I don't know. Tony didn't want me to know him, and he didn't want the guy to know about me. He said it was to protect everyone."

He paused. "Are you really going to kick my ass?"

"Still debating," I said.

"The pot wasn't mine. I didn't know she had it." I was surprised he was even bothering with a defense. It's what a normal kid from a normal family did. A kid on the street wouldn't bother with a defense unless speaking to a cop.

"You can't break the rules and then blame someone else. It's still your ass on the line."

"I'm not good at fighting," he admitted.

I looked at him and realized he was worried. He wasn't looking like a street kid anymore. Something was wrong.

"Why not? You lived on the street, didn't you?"

"No one ever taught me."

I noticed he hadn't answered the question about living on the street. His timid response also told me Tony hadn't touched the kid. If Tony had raised his hand to Chris, he would have had to fight back to survive, like I had. I had to wonder why. Was Tony too sick to fight? Or did he find this punk kid too intimidating in his old age?

"I'm done debating. It's time you learn how to fight and how to defend yourself." I pointed to my car.

"Where are we going?"

"Can't fight here. This is Mattie's house."

Chapter 25

"You're late," Mattie said as I locked the Porsche. I was preparing myself to be yelled at when I saw her eyes jump open. She pushed me out of the way and reached for Chris.

"What happened?" she asked, pulling him inside.

"It's just a black eye," I said. "Nothing broken. It'll heal in a day or two."

She threw me an angry look. "Go get him some ice," she ordered.

I rolled my eyes and headed for the kitchen.

"What happened?" Mattie repeated as she followed me, still clutching Chris as if he were a baby.

"Let him go, Mattie," I said. "He's fine. Next time he'll learn to duck my right hand."

She did let go of him and turned on me. "*You* did this?" I knew the tone and knew I wasn't going to win this fight. I looked over at Chris, and he was smirking.

I grabbed an ice pack and threw it at him.

"Ow," he said when Mattie looked at him. The smile was gone, and a look of pain had replaced the glint in his eyes. He was a better con man than I realized.

"It's not what you think," I said. "We were having fun at the gym, that's all. I promise. We just went a few rounds in the ring, but he forgot to keep his hands up."

"I can't believe you, Luc. He's only fourteen years old. He's just a boy."

I smirked at Chris now and saw how annoyed he was at being referred to as a boy.

"Well, he handled himself like a man. That is, until he walked in here and started pouting for sympathy."

"Jerk," he said.

"Luc, Child Services hasn't finalized any of the paperwork. If they think you're an unfit guardian, they'll take Chris away."

Before I could tell her it was fine with me if they took him, Chris spoke up. "I'm fine, Mrs. Hardwin. We were just having fun, and I dropped my hand. It won't happen again."

She turned to Chris and cupped his face with her hand. I remembered her doing that to me after a fight with my father.

"This isn't your fault, Chris. Luc needs to grow up and be responsible for once. I'm glad you had fun, but now I have to explain to my mother why you have a black eye."

"Your mother's coming here?" I asked.

"Mom and Dad are both on their way here now. I'm making dinner. Go clean up. We'll talk about this later."

"Why don't I order something, Mat? You've had a long day at work, and I'm sure you don't want to cook."

"Don't worry, I've taken care of everything," Mattie said, "We're having Cajun chicken."

I groaned as she walked away. I looked at the boy. "Whatever you do, don't complain about the food."

"Why?" he asked.

"Cajun just means she either burned the chicken or over-seasoned it."

"My head hurts," Chris muttered. "Maybe I should skip dinner."

"Take a Tylenol and walk it off."

Mattie is the spitting image of her mother, Virginia. Sweet, caring eyes, debutant posture, and a beautiful smile that drives all the men crazy. The two women are the epitome of elegance and grace. As they sat in the living room listening to Chris play Mattie's old guitar, her father, Bill Connor, and I watched from the kitchen with drinks in our hands.

"How much do you know about the boy?" Bill asked. Bill was the head of a large law firm dealing mostly with criminal defense. I knew he was just as suspicious of the boy as I was.

"Not much, unfortunately."

"He reminds me of you at that age."

I didn't want to compare myself to the boy and found it weird that everyone else did. "Tony never hit him. He doesn't know how to fight, doesn't know how to protect himself."

"That's good."

I said nothing.

"She's attached already," he said. "She won't let him go now."

"She's going to have to. He's not staying."

Bill laughed. "Virginia told me the same thing about you. Look how you stuck around."

At dinner, I watched the boy as he picked at the burnt piece of meat on his plate. It took him several minutes to pry off a small chunk that appeared edible. He didn't look optimistic as he took the first bite. After just one chew, he spit it out.

"Shit," he said. "I can find better food at the bottom of the dumpster at Guardian."

I kicked him in the shin under the table.

"Fuck!" he shouted.

I looked at Mattie and her mother, but neither said anything. It was Bill who spoke.

"Young man, we don't use that language at the table."

I cringed. "Sorry, Dad."

Bill shook his head as if it wasn't my fault, but I knew it was. And I knew Mattie would blame me.

The boy looked at me. "Why the hell do you call that old man Dad? Tony was your dad."

"It's a sign of respect. Tony was never a father. Bill treated me like a son, so he gets the respect." I pointed to his full plate. "Eat. You don't know where your next meal will come from."

"Tony raised you. You're the person you are because of him, and you don't even know anything about him!"

"That asshole did nothing to help me become who I am," I said, raising my voice. "But you're wrong. I know more than I need to know about Tony, more than you'll ever know. I know he chain-smoked unfiltered Marlboros. I know he loved Jack Daniel's whiskey. I know that when he'd had too much, his left fist became stronger and I had to guard my kidneys. I know that when he got busted on a con or had to walk away from a big score, I needed to sleep with a knife in my hand."

"Luc, stop!" Mattie said.

I looked at her, angry and embarrassed at the same time. I couldn't believe she had just snapped at me in front of her parents and the boy. I threw my napkin on the table.

"I'm no longer hungry," I said, standing.

"It's probably the chicken," the boy muttered as I walked out of the room.

~~~

I could hear Chris strumming on the guitar as I hid in the office. I unlocked the drawer and pulled out a small box, but didn't open it. Inside was the ring that held my future, yet I couldn't look at it.

I turned up the scanner and heard an officer call for a 187 by Los Alamitos Bay Harbor. I copied down the information I was able to ascertain. The LA Sheriff's was reporting to a call about a floater in the water near Portuguese Point. The body had been found by a couple near Smuggler's Cove, an area that used to be frequented by nude sunbathers but was now a hot spot for lovers.
~~~

The officer requested backup for crowd control. Ignoring the music from the other room, I considered making a trip to the scene. It was late, and a crowd gathering at a crime scene was slightly interesting. Then I overheard an officer in the background. It sounded like he said "same guy."

I grabbed my cell phone and texted a deputy I knew in the Lomita division of the LA Sheriff's, the area responsible for Palos Verdes. He confirmed, under promise of anonymity, that the police believed the victim was probably killed by the same person responsible for the death of the floater found just north of the peninsula.

Two dead bodies in one week, possibly the same killer. I wondered if Orin was already on the scene. He'd probably have the top story in Saturday's paper. It annoyed me that I was now interested in a story he had brought me and I had so quickly dismissed.

I heard the door squeak and looked behind me to find Chris standing in the doorway, his hands jammed in his pockets. I looked at the doorknob that had been locked. I hadn't heard a sound, and the smirk on his face told me he was proud of that fact.

"How'd you do that?" I asked.

He pulled one hand out and revealed a pick.

"Impressive," I said. "Close the door."

The smile faded, and the hurt-boy look returned.

"Come in and close the door," I said, starting to see a way to get this kid to open up.

He closed the door and dropped himself into a chair. "I heard you were good with a pick," he said.

"Not at fourteen. I didn't master the pick until I was eighteen." I took the pick from him and examined it. Then I dropped it in the desk drawer. "I stopped using it about that time, too."

"Why?" he asked.

"Cops search you and find that, they'll try to pin every unsolved burglary on you. It's safer to just use what you can find and discard it when you're done."

"Tony teach you that?" he asked.

"Like I told you before, Tony didn't teach me anything. What song were you singing out there?"

"'After the Thrill Is Gone,'" he answered.

I grunted. "Don't you know any new shit?"

"I know some Chili Peppers, but that doesn't get the women to open their wallets. Old women like the Eagles."

"Mattie's not old."

He shrugged. "When are you going to ask her?" He pointed to the ring box in my hand.

I ignored him and put the box back in the drawer and locked it.

"It is for her, right?"

Again I said nothing. I didn't want to talk to him about Mattie, but I didn't want to tell him to shut up, in case it ruined the trust I was starting to build with him.

"You don't seem like the religious type."

"I'm not," I said.

"So you're just trying to do what's right for her. I get it. Problem is she's already married."

"Divorced," I corrected.

"In the eyes of the law, maybe, but in God's eyes, she'll always be married. Catholics don't recognize divorce."

I waited for him to continue. I could tell by his cocky stare that he had more on his mind. He continued to stare at me like he pitied me.

"What?" I asked. "You think sleeping with a married woman bothers me?" I laughed. "Not my first time. Never bothered me before."

"Well, you never know. She may still say yes. Maybe she doesn't want you to burn in hell all by yourself."

"You believe in heaven and hell?"

"You lived on the street. Now you live here. How can you tell me heaven and hell don't exist if you've lived in both?"

"What did you mail from Child Services? The cops are starting to hound me, and I need to know so I can direct them elsewhere."

He looked at the floor, and I knew he was closing up again. "I told you I handed over the boxes of files to Tony. That's all they care about."

"I can't protect you from the cops if you don't tell me everything." Still no response, so I made a leap. "It was the laptop, right? What was on it? Where did you send it?"

He stared at me and finally said, "I gave the laptop to Tony with the files. I don't know what he did with it."

I figured he was lying, but wasn't sure why. I already knew he had mailed something from Child Services. I needed to know where he had mailed it. I had an idea, but before I could question him further, there was a knock on the door and Mattie appeared. The way she stared at me, I wondered if she had heard us talking.

"My parents are leaving," she said.

I pushed the kid up from the chair. "Go say goodbye and thank them for coming."

The boy grunted but got up and left. I could tell it hadn't been that long since he'd been part of a family somewhere. It made me wonder why he'd run away.

"I don't want him here by himself tomorrow," I said. "Can you take him to school with you?"

She nodded. "I'm sorry about earlier."

"No big deal." I glanced at the locked desk. "When you grow up hungry on the street, pride is the first thing you lose."

Chapter 26

Dr. Brown called at a quarter to nine that night. He told me he'd only been able to reach one of Dr. Stedman's patients who was willing to talk to me. He gave me the phone number of a Benny Pon. I was running out of time for my story, so I called Benny right away and asked if I could come over. He sounded more than willing to talk and gave me his address in Hawaiian Gardens.

I drove fast down the 605 and got off at Carson Boulevard. Turning left onto Carson, I drove past one of the older casinos still standing in Southern California. Palm trees lined the street. A woman begged on the corner with a cardboard sign. If Hawaiian Gardens looked anything like the state of Hawaii, I couldn't figure out the draw.

I turned down Benny's street and knew immediately I didn't want to leave my Porsche parked outside. He lived in the last house at the end of a cul-du-sac. A group of Hispanic teenagers hovered at the house next door. Their pants were low on their waists, and I was pretty sure one had a pistol in his pocket. One of the boys pointed at my car. I whipped a U-turn and drove back to a laundromat at the corner. A cop car was parked in front of the Mexican restaurant next door. I parked next to the cop. I armed the car and hoped it would be there when I came back.

As I walked down the street toward Benny's house, I watched the group of teenagers. Up close, they looked like junkies. They watched me as I knocked on Benny's door.

Benny Pon was an ugly, fat man with the eyes of a hyena. He was younger than I had expected, probably only in his twenties, but he had a limp in his right leg and the wrinkled, ruddy face of a longtime smoker. He wore a dirty white T-shirt, and his pants hung low on his wide waistline. The ensemble was topped off with white socks and Adidas slip-on sandals. I didn't ask about the limp, mostly because I didn't care, but also because I had a feeling he wouldn't tell me. He didn't seem like a friendly fellow when he opened the door, but he invited me in anyway once I told him who I was and why I was there.

He said that he lived with his brother and his wife, which explained why the house was better taken care of than I had expected. The interior was tidy and sparsely decorated with IKEA furniture, but there were little reminders of the neighborhood: bars on the windows, an alarm panel, and motion detectors. His brother was either paranoid or had been introduced to the world of crime as a victim.

Benny didn't offer me anything to drink, but I didn't mind. He agreed to have the conversation recorded, and muted the hockey game he was watching. I told him I'd be quick and wouldn't take up much of his evening, but he waved his hand at me as if I were a child and turned back to the game.

"You're a reporter, you'll stay until you have what you need. Go ahead and get on with it."

I had spent the drive out there formulating the questions in my head. Now, observing his attitude, I decided I had a much more important question.

"Why did you agree to see me, Benny?"

He looked at me now, leaned back in the chair, and smirked. "You're Tony's son."

"You knew my father?" I asked, surprised.

"The doctor said it was you, and I figured you wanted to know about your father."

I sank further in the chair. "Not really. I'm actually more interested in Dr. Stedman. Can you tell me how you became a patient?"

He laughed. "I was high. This was two months ago. I'm clean now." I didn't believe him, but knew he said it only to go on record. I nodded, and he continued. "Dr. Stedman found me wandering outside the Guardian Home like he finds most of his patients. He asked me a few questions, then handed me a piece of paper and told me I wasn't able to properly take care of myself. He said I was a danger to myself. I don't remember what I said to him, but he offered me a place to stay and a warm meal, so I got in his van. When the drugs wore off the next morning, I realized they wouldn't let me leave."

"Did you do the full seventy-two hours?"

He shook his head. "Once I found out I couldn't leave, I called my brother. They allow you one call a day, I think. He works at a law firm. They couldn't hold me. I couldn't wait to get out of there."

"Your brother's a lawyer?"

"No, no. He works as a maintenance guy in the building. He's been there several years, and the top floor is a law firm. I told him what happened, and he asked one of the lawyers to help. My brother came down and picked me up with some legal paperwork. I have to stay here with him now, and the lawyer told me to stay away from Guardian Home for a while."

"How long were you at the facility?"

"I called my brother as soon as I woke up. I think it was around noon. He was there that evening to pick me up." He turned toward the television and watched the action on the screen, apparently bored with my questions. The game was almost over, and I hoped he would turn his attention back to me.

"Did you meet with Dr. Stedman?"

"Yeah, I had one session with him. I mostly yelled at him for taking me. I don't think he had the right, no matter what I said to him while I was high. I think it's kidnapping. I told him so."

"What did he do?"

"He just listened and wrote some bullshit on his notepad." Benny pointed to my own notebook, which I had yet to write in. "Then he said I needed help and he would try to help me if I agreed to stay on."

"Did you see any other doctors there?"

He shook his head. "Nope, just Dr. Stedman." The smirk returned. "The receptionist checked me out when I was leaving. She's a hot one, young and single, but she's only interested in Dr. Stedman. She told me she doesn't date patients. Whatever."

"Any idea why Dr. Stedman picked you up? Did you threaten to kill yourself or threaten anyone else?"

"No way, man. I don't do violence. I'm all about feeling good." He turned back to me. "I *was* all about feeling good. Now I'm working on getting a job and stuff."

I nodded. "Could you have done anything that would have drawn Dr. Stedman's attention and make him think you were mentally unwell?"

He laughed. "No. I think some woman at Torrance Medical Clinic called to complain about me walking along outside. I was on my way to Guardian, and I guess she didn't like the look of me."

"What woman?"

"Small blonde. And I mean real small. She's tiny. She works at the clinic, and I see her from time to time outside smoking in the alley. I heard she complained to Jessie about the people she helps there."

I wondered if the mystery woman was the same woman I had spoken to outside. How many small blond smokers could work there?

"Did you know Henry Dillon?" I asked.

"Sure, I met him at Guardian a few years back. Why?" Benny asked, turning back to the game. I watched the last few seconds tick away on the game clock.

"Is he under Dr. Stedman's care?"

"He was picked up under fifty-one-fifty a couple of weeks ago. He stayed for almost a week, then bailed."

"Do you know where I can find him?"

He studied me. "Why are you looking for him?"

"I'm just trying to write my story on the treatment center and how they're mistreating the homeless. I just want to talk to him."

"He's been missing for a few weeks now. Nobody's heard from him. Just fell off the face of the earth."

"No one disappears, Benny. Someone knows something. Tell me who to talk to."

"There's no one left to talk to. Everyone I know involved has disappeared or died. Maybe it's good to be away from there for a while, you know what I mean?"

"Involved in what, exactly?"

"The burglary," Benny said. "Isn't that what you're really doing here? You want to know about the job your father pulled."

I suddenly felt I was talking to the right person. "What does the burglary have to do with Henry Dillon's disappearance?"

Benny straightened in his chair, now ignoring the television. I finally had his full attention. "After Henry got released, he came to see me. He was always the nervous type, super paranoid. He thought everyone was out to get him. That's how Dr. Stedman picked him. He asked him if he'd ever wanted to kill himself, and Henry told him the world was a scary place to live. Dr. Stedman figured he was a danger to himself and committed him for three days. Henry came out even more paranoid, though. He kept telling everyone that someone was watching him. He said someone was going to kill him. But, you know, like I said he was just super paranoid."

"Why did he come see you?"

"He wanted me to steal patient files. I told him he was crazy. There was no way to break into that facility, and I wasn't about to commit myself voluntarily just to steal some useless files."

"Did he say why he wanted the files?"

"He said someone asked him to break in and steal them. He was apparently pretty scared of this guy. He didn't want to tell me at first, but he had to if he was going to get me to help. He freaked out when I said no. I used to be a thief, but not anymore. I'm clean now."

"Yeah, you said that. Was that the last time you saw him?"

He nodded. "Yeah, but I heard things."

"What things?"

"I heard Henry was hanging out at Guardian Home again, but I haven't been back since I got out of the treatment center on the advice of my lawyer friend. A friend of mine who helps out down there said Henry tried to commit suicide and ended up in the hospital, Torrance Memorial. That's where he found your father. I guess he was in the bed next to him. What are the chances, huh? They hadn't seen each other in years, but Tony jumped at the chance to help Henry."

"Why?"

He smirked. "The only reason Tony does anything is for himself. I'll get to that part. My friend told me that Dr. Stedman had left Torrance Treatment Center and the files had been moved to some offsite office."

"So my father supposedly stole the files for Henry. Did he deliver them?"

He nodded. "That's what I heard. He stole all the files, and he delivered them to Tony as promised."

"What about the laptop?"

He grinned. "That was Tony's insurance policy. That was the only reason he agreed to help Henry. It had a backup of all the files. Tony's a smart guy. Did I tell you I worked with him on a con once? He found some doctor's prescription pad and used to send me off to pick up drugs all over town. We made a lot of money."

I was still on the laptop as Benny continued to rattle on about my father. "He was going to blackmail someone with the information, wasn't he?" I asked, interrupting Benny. "Was it Ernesto Ramirez or Dr. Stedman?"

"Possibly. He may have also planned on going after whoever was holding Henry Dillon by the short hairs. He didn't like his friends being messed with."

"What happened to Henry after Tony delivered the files?"

Benny shrugged. "No idea. No one has seen him since."

When I returned to the laundromat, the patrol car was gone. The alarm on my Porsche was also blaring. Three kids watched me from inside the laundromat. I thought about going inside, but I was too tired to fight. I turned off the alarm and got in the car.

The ignition was popped off and dangled broken. Amateurs. I couldn't start the car with my key. I cursed and looked back at the laundromat. The kids were gone.

I pulled the wires, hotwired my own car, and drove back to Malibu, thankful to be out of Hawaiian Gardens.

Chapter 27

I was in a horrible mood when I arrived at the office the next morning. I had woken up to find Orin's story about the Palos Verdes murder victim on the front page of the *Reporter*.

The LA Sheriff's detectives had confirmed that the second victim in Los Alamitos was cut up and mutilated in a similar fashion to the victim found near the PV Peninsula over the weekend. They had yet to identify either victim, but were getting close. Orin had even included a sketch of the first victim. Both were male, with the first victim listed as between the ages of thirty and forty-five. The second victim was much older. The detectives confirmed that one killer was suspected for both murders.

Orin had caught a good story, and I was extremely pissed about it. But I had no idea my morning was about to spiral out of control.

When I walked into the small reception area, Natalie immediately picked up the phone. She avoided looking at me. Maybe she saw my nasty mood, or maybe she didn't want to deal with my attitude this morning. Ignoring her and my desire for a cup of hot coffee, I headed toward my office. When I got there, I tossed the paper in the trash and booted up my computer. I had a story of my own to write, and my story would make the top of Saturday's paper. Everyone would soon forget about the murder victims washing ashore.

I tried to contact Genie first, hoping and praying I was right in thinking that Chris had mailed the laptop to Georgia and she had found her way to Genie after leaving the hospital. The phone continued to ring at the Paradise Club. I hung up as Orin walked in with a grin on his face. I took a deep breath and waited for the bragging to begin.

"Did you read the front page this morning?" he asked.

It was a stupid question. I read the paper every day. "Must have missed it today. Did you get anywhere on the search for Henry Dillon or Dr. Stedman?" I asked, changing the subject.

His smile faded as his gaze moved to my trash can. "You're an asshole, Luc. I just want you to know that. Not everything has to be about you."

"So you didn't find anything? Well, lucky for me someone on this team actually worked last night. I found a patient willing to talk, and I'll need your help writing up the story for Callahan. We're going to fry Ramirez on the front page tomorrow."

"Team?" he said. "This has never been a team. Good luck convincing Callahan to print anything you write on Ramirez."

Callahan walked in and interrupted my coming attack on Orin. Orin's smirk returned.

"Orin, I want you down at Lomita Station," said Callahan. "They've finally identified the first victim. I want a write-up for the front page."

Ready to defend my story, I stood. "Callahan, I have credible witnesses stating that Dr. Stedman and the Torrance Treatment Center have been kidnapping homeless people to fill beds. It's a clear violation of their civil rights."

"Luc, don't bother. You're fired."

"What? Just because I have something against a friend of yours? Do you realize what kind of shit storm you'd create by firing me?"

"Yeah, but it will probably just sell papers, and that's been my intent all along. You've done nothing to help this paper. We're about to go under, and you refuse to care about anything but the Saturday byline. I can't afford to hold onto you in hopes you'll find the next big story. Clear out your desk by this afternoon."

They both turned and left me alone. I sat wondering if there was anything in this office I needed to pack up this time around. I searched the drawers, but my cigarettes were gone, and the bottle of Tequila was empty. I unlocked the bottom drawer and pulled out the file, revealing the framed picture of Mattie and me underneath. I dropped the file back in the drawer and slammed it shut, leaving both the picture and the file in the darkness of the drawer. There was nothing left for me to take.

As I headed down the stairs, I tried the Paradise Club again, and Genie answered on the second ring.

"Luc, you need to stop calling here and go underground."

I heard an argument in the background. "What's going on?"

"The cops were here this morning and searched the place. They mentioned your name and some guy named Chris. They didn't search long, and they left in a hurry."

Before I could ask where Jim was, my call waiting beeped. Seeing it was Jim, I promised Genie I'd make it all up to her.

"Luc, Mattie left the school," Jim said when I switched over. "She headed home, and I followed her. She was met by several cop cars."

Panic gripped me as I reached my car. "What the hell is going on, Jim?"

"I don't know, but I'm outnumbered, and it's only a matter of time before they spot me. It's too hot for me here—plus I need to check on the bar. Genie just called and told me the police were there, too."

"Go, Jim. I'll take care of it."

I called the house, and Mattie answered. She sounded as frantic as I felt. "Luc, the cops are looking for Chris."

"Don't tell them where he is."

"I already did. I didn't have a choice. They have a warrant for his arrest. They're going to the school right now."

I dropped the phone in the passenger seat and drove as fast as I could to Mattie's school, keeping an eye on my rear view. If the cops were looking for Chris, I knew they would be watching for me. Since they hadn't met me at the office, I guessed I was already too late.

My fear turned to anger as soon as I parked my car at the school and spotted the sedan parked across the street with two men sitting inside. Cops. They straightened when they saw my car. I got out and ignored them, but I heard the door open.

"Mr. Actar, can we have a word?"

I glanced back and saw two men in suits. Obviously detectives. I didn't recognize them, so I increased my pace. "I'm busy. Make an appointment."

I turned to walk toward the front gate of the school, but one of the officers put his hand on my shoulder.

Dropping my shoulder, I turned back to him. "Don't touch me."

"Mr. Actar, we'd like you to come with us."

I laughed. "This is about Ernesto Ramirez, isn't it?"

The two officers exchanged a quick glance and stepped closer to me.

I backed up again. "Tell Ramirez he can screw himself. I don't scare easy."

Following the officers' gaze, I turned to see Carter and Marquez walking from the school office. Shuffling his feet between the two large men was Chris. He was already wearing handcuffs.

The two detectives next to me were smiling now. "Your choice. Our way or yours?"

The detective closest to me had his own handcuffs out now. The fear returned. I couldn't explain it, but it paralyzed me. I watched the cuffs coming closer and then felt the other officer grab my arm.

So I swung.

I hit one of them before the other could grab me. Then I felt someone kick me from behind. In a matter of seconds, there were four of them tackling me to the ground. I felt a kick in my back, and I stopped fighting.

I felt steel tighten around my wrist for the second time in a week. I didn't fight the cuffs, knowing the detectives could make them too tight for me to feel my fingers.

"Do you have any idea who I am?" I yelled.

The detective I had hit wiped his nose. "Yeah, we do. That's why we're enjoying this so much."

"Get the kid," someone yelled.

I turned my head and saw Carter walking back to where they had left Chris. He hadn't run. He only stared at me. He looked sick.

And I felt guilty.

The larger detective grabbed my keys. "Check the car."

"I see a stripped ignition," the other detective said.

"That's probable cause," Marquez said, smiling at me as he pushed his knee into my back. I turned back to watch the detective open the passenger door.

"Don't you dare put a scratch on my car."

"We got drugs and a bag of cash," the detective announced.

"Shit," I muttered. "There's five grand in there, so it better all be there when I get my car back," I yelled.

"Bingo," the officer yelled. "We got us a pistol. Looks like a twenty-two." He fumbled with it. "Loaded, too."

"Read him his rights," Carter said.

I laid my head on the pavement and closed my eyes.

Chapter 28

The two officers drove me to the Malibu substation and left me alone in a small interview room. I was hungry and tired, but I knew better than to sleep with cameras watching every move I made in there.

I knew they could lock me in the slammer for forty-eight hours before presenting a case to the district attorney. Most smart people knew to stay quiet and hope the cops couldn't find the evidence to hang you in that time frame, but I didn't want to spend the next two nights in jail. My only hope was to talk my way out of this mess and convince the cops not to go to the DA.

An hour passed with nothing from the outside world. I waited without moving. No pacing, no show of anger. I just waited. Finally a deputy came in and re-read my rights to me. I signed the paperwork, waiving my right to silence. He asked if I wanted to contact anyone. I considered this, but there was no one I wanted to witness this. I waved him off and he left me alone again.

Another half hour passed before the two detectives who had arrested me returned to interview me. The larger one introduced himself as Detective Peters and asked all the questions. The other detective remained silent. I tried to speed things along, since I knew Mattie would be worried.

They asked about the gun in the car, and I explained that it wasn't mine and I had found it Wednesday night. I could tell Peters didn't believe me. I explained the money was from a business deal and the stripped ignition was from prankster kids. No, I did not report the break-in.

Peters focused on the gun, and I knew it was the only thing they could hold me on. I was starting to feel better about my situation when there was a knock on the door. Both detectives disappeared.

When the door reopened five minutes later, it wasn't the officers. It was Bill Connor.

"What the hell are you doing here?" I asked. I remained sitting, but I could feel my anger jump up. I didn't want him here.

"Don't say another word," Bill snapped at me. "A scared boy called me. He was worried about you and remembered you once told him he could always count on me to help."

I lowered my head into my hands. "I'm sorry about that," I said, thinking of Chris. "But I'm not a young boy, and I definitely don't need your help."

I heard him drop his briefcase on the table. The sound echoed in the tiny room. "Well, well. I had no idea you had passed the bar exam. Congratulations, Luc."

I looked up. "I can handle this myself."

"Yeah, you're doing a great job so far. Tell me, are you playing the stupid criminal or are you really that stubborn?"

I pushed up from the table. I wasn't in the mood to be nice anymore. I wanted to beat the shit out of someone. Bill just happened to be the closest thing to me.

"Don't play the rich, pretentious lawyer thing with me, Bill. I ain't that poor, broken child that needed your help to stay in school. I can handle my own problems now. And I think I can safely say I have more money than you. So don't you dare throw that in my face."

He didn't flinch from my anger, as I had hoped. Instead, his eyes narrowed on me as he leaned in. "Sure, but mine's clean. I can walk out of this room whenever I want. You can't. Because of that, I'm free to talk. Sit down and listen."

"After all these years, I won't have you treat me like some scared kid. I refuse to let you look down on me anymore. I'd rather go to jail."

"I'm not here for you. Hell, if I had my way, I'd let them lock you up. It would be the only way to keep you from my daughter. But she loves you, which makes you family, despite your constant screw-ups. Now sit down, son, and let me explain something."

I glanced at my wrist, only to realize they had taken my watch from me. Frustrated, I relented and sat. I pretended it was my anger that prevented me from looking at him.

"I once walked into my kitchen and found a very young, very thin boy sitting at my table with my innocent daughter," he said. "I remember thinking how sickly you looked. And through the grime, I could see you were bruised. Bruises from life on the streets, as well as from abuse handed out by those who should protect and love.

"I wanted to throw you out. Not just because of the dirt you brought into my home, but the pain that came with it. I didn't want my daughter exposed to the abuse, neglect, and pain you were forced to live with. Her mother definitely didn't want you near Mattie, but I watched you as she talked to you and saw the hope in your eyes. I offered you something to eat. Remember that?"

I smiled despite my anger. "An apple. I gave it to Mattie."

Bill laughed. "Yeah. You were starving, but refused to take a handout."

"I'd rather steal it."

Bill contemplated that before he continued. "I watched you leave that day and walk back to your home, to the father who beat and neglected you. You never complained. Maybe it's your stubbornness that prevented you from asking for help, but I couldn't stop thinking that a kid who could survive on the street could go anywhere. Could run anywhere. Yet you always went back to that little two-bedroom apartment and took the abuse. You could stand up to anyone and anything. There was nothing in this world that could break you.

"Luc, I never once looked down on you. I was too busy looking up to you."

I had no words. Nor could I look at him. I'd had no idea he felt that way.

Bill cleared his throat and unfolded the stack of papers he had dropped on the desk with his briefcase. I watched his hands move swiftly and confidently through the stack. "Now. We have some work to do if we're going to have you released on bail."

"The cop grabbed me first. I warned him to take his hands off me. He didn't." I paused. "I can explain the gun."

He nodded and kept reading. "I'm not worried about the gun, the drugs, or the money. I'll have that out on an illegal search of the vehicle. I'm more concerned with the arrest warrant LAPD is trying to get signed as we speak." He looked at me. "I have a few friends who like to give me a heads-up on arrest warrants for murder."

"Murder?" I shouted.

His eyes studied me over the rim of his glasses. "Didn't know about that, did you? Yeah, well, my guess is the sheriff's detectives are only holding you here until the warrant gets signed and LAPD can take custody of you. Right now they're having a hard time getting a judge to sign, but if they can get more evidence on you, it won't take long. Have you seen a copy of the complaint?"

It made sense, since no one had yet to book me for anything. I got up to pace. "The gun isn't mine," I said. "It belongs to this girl. If someone died by that gun, it had to happen before I got it. I've only had it a few days. They can't connect me."

"You're not seeing this the right way. You're already connected to the victim. They still have to match the murder weapon."

I looked at him, and my stomach dropped. I thought about the bloody Torrance alley. I thought about the picture of Carl Palfy. "Who the hell do they think I killed?"

"Mr. Ernesto Ramirez." I winced, and he shook his head. "I think it's probably too much to ask that you've never heard of him and thus would have no reason to want him dead."

I remained quiet, thinking about the one and only time I had ever seen Ernesto Ramirez. I was pretty positive I had left him alive.

Bill continued to read his notes. "The judge's secretary who called me said the warrant request mentioned that you threatened to kill him yesterday?"

"I can't say I didn't want him dead." I thought of Mattie.

"Well, lucky for you, no judge has been willing to put his name on a warrant and become your next target in the papers. They've requested more information. Which means, you don't talk to anyone."

There was a knock on the door, and the two detectives reentered.

"Can we wrap this up so we can move Mr. Actar to lockup?"

"He's done talking to you," Bill said. "You can book him now, and we'll have the charges dropped by morning."

I looked at Bill. "I need to get to Mattie."

He shook his head. "No way, Luc. Anything you say now can be used against you. I think we need to go over the facts first."

"I don't care. I didn't do this. I need to clear this up now."

"The judge has already gone home," Bill said. "You aren't getting a bail hearing tonight."

"I need to get home to Mattie, Dad. Get me out of here."

Bill saw the desperation on my face and turned to the cop. "You're charging him for the weapon and drugs?"

The detective nodded.

"Bring in the prosecutor," Bill said. "Let the DA know we'll help with the Ramirez case to get these charges dropped."

~~~

The marathon interrogation began slowly. I was introduced to a female prosecutor by the name of Carol Crunnion. She was a hard woman with sharp facial features and a stern attitude. She was annoyed to be there, and she showed her extreme displeasure that the infamous Bill Connor was also there. I explained that my lawyer insisted on being present during the interview, but I would tell them whatever they wanted to know. Although she didn't like the arrangement, she agreed
~~~

to hear me out and the charges would be dropped if the answers were helpful and honest, with one caveat: if she felt I was guilty, she'd watch me rot in prison. I was pretty sure she was telling the truth, but since I knew I was innocent, I was willing to take the chance.

Also in the room was Detective Peters from the LA Sheriff's, who had arrested me, and another tall, dark-haired man with shaky eyes, who smelled like a cop as well. He wore a suit and only introduced himself on the record as Rick Nelson. No title or affiliation. He stood in the corner, his arms crossed over his chest, and kept his eyes on me the entire time. Everyone else ignored him, but I noticed that Detective Peters looked at him with disgust before turning his back on him.

"Let's start with Mr. Ernesto Ramirez," Carol said. "Did you go to his office yesterday?"

"I didn't threaten to kill him," I said, hoping to move the conversation along. They wouldn't let me pace, so I found myself tapping the table.

"Luc, let's confer before you blurt out stupid answers." Bill put his hand on my arm. I could tell he was uneasy.

I shook my head. "We don't have time for games. Let's get to it. I didn't kill him. We had an argument, and I didn't appreciate being threatened, so I attacked him."

I saw Bill wince.

"He threatened you?" the prosecutor asked. She seemed genuinely interested in my answer. Maybe she didn't like Ramirez, either. Maybe he had threatened her, too. It wasn't impossible with his track record. Or maybe it was just a trick to make me confess.

"He threatened my—" I looked for the right word. "He threatened my family."

I felt Bill studying me. He said nothing as I waited for the next question.

"You attacked him?" she asked.

"I was angry. I wanted to hurt him, but I didn't. His secretary can confirm he was alive when I left."

She looked at her notes, jotted something down, and asked me to describe the encounter exactly as it happened. I told her how I had waited in the parking lot, how I walked past the secretary, and how I asked him for a quote. I explained that he refused to offer a quote for my story and then threatened to take Chris away. I decided not to mention the specifics of the article I was writing or the folder he had threatened me with.

"Did you go back?"

"No," I said, frustrated.

"How did you get the gun the officers found on you?"

I couldn't hide my embarrassment as I tried to determine the best answer. I couldn't exactly tell Bill the prostitute left it in my car when I took her to the hospital.

"I was working on a story. I stopped by this house on Wednesday evening to see if I could talk to some neighbors. A neighbor was willing to talk to me, but she looked like she'd been in a fight. She was holding the gun, probably worried that whoever had started the fight would be back to finish it. I thought she needed a hospital, so I drove her to the ER. I told her to leave the gun in the glove compartment. I forgot all about it."

"Interesting story. I'm sure we can corroborate with the doctors. Her name?"

I rubbed my temples with the heel of my hand. "She wasn't officially admitted."

I thought I heard her laugh, but when I looked up, she was concentrating on her notes, the same angry look on her face.

"How old was this girl?" she continued.

"I don't know." I wondered if they knew she was a hooker. They probably had the pictures Ramirez had taken. I wondered for a second if they would hang me with Ramirez's evidence.

"And where is she now?" Carol asked.

"I left her at the hospital."

"What about the five grand in cash the detectives found in your car?"

"It's my money. I loaned a friend some money to open a club. She was paying it back."

"Do you have papers to prove this?"

"Sure," I said, knowing I could write something up in a matter of minutes and Spencer would sign off on it. At least, I hoped he would still help me out.

We went through it all three more times, before Carol finally looked up from her notebook. Everyone in the room looked exhausted.

"Okay, let's go back. Why did you visit Mr. Ramirez in the first place?"

"Shit," I muttered. "I was writing a story. I wanted his side."

"About him?"

"Yeah, I told you already. Look, if you get Detective Ward, he can help corroborate some of this, and I won't have to keep repeating myself."

I heard the cop who was standing in the corner finally move.

"Detective Ward?" he asked, pulling out a notebook. For the first time, he looked interested in what I was saying. "What does Detective Ward have to do with Mr. Ramirez?"

I didn't answer. I looked around the room at everyone. Carol Crunnion was looking down at her notes and wouldn't look at me. Detective Peters coughed and leaned back in his chair. Bill was rubbing his head.

The room had suddenly gone very quiet.

Chapter 29

I turned to look at the tall stranger. "Nelson, right? Why don't you introduce yourself before I answer any of your questions?"

The man ignored my question and returned one of his own. "Did Detective Ward ask you to look into Mr. Ramirez?"

I didn't answer.

"Mr. Actar, did Detective Ward ask you to approach Mr. Ramirez for any reason?"

"No."

He leaned closer to me. "Did Detective Ward tell you about the burglary?"

I didn't like how he kept repeating Ward's name. I looked back at Detective Peters and saw him shaking his head, but he wouldn't look up from the floor.

"When did you and Detective Ward discuss Mr. Ramirez?" the man asked.

"You're Internal Affairs, aren't you?" I asked him.

He ignored me. "Did Detective Ward give you the five grand to kill Mr. Ramirez?"

I turned to Bill and shook my head. I was done answering questions. Bill stood.

"This conversation is over. It's time you made a decision. Charge him and send him to lockup or let him go." He looked at Carol Crunnion. "You know you don't have enough to prosecute. Do you really want to risk letting him sit in a jail cell tonight in hopes you'll get some smoking gun?"

"Mr. Connor, I appreciate your opinion on the matter, but your client didn't convince me he's not part of some conspiracy in the murder of a highly important figure in Los Angeles. We're going to have media crawling all over everyone to get this story, and we need to have our facts straight before I make any decisions. Mr. Actar was one of the last people to see Mr. Ramirez alive. He threatened him hours before he turned up dead. I can't ignore the facts."

"I didn't kill him," I yelled. "I was at home eating dinner with my lawyer and his family, damn it!"

Crunnion and Connor continued to argue, each trying to out-shout the other. Detective Peters said something under his breath and shoved the chair back, but even the screeching sound didn't stop the yelling. Nelson stepped closer to me to ask me a question, and then stopped.

Suddenly all conversation ceased. I turned to see that John Carliss had stepped into the room during the commotion.

He turned to the others in the room and said, "Leave us." Everyone but Bill scurried out of the room.

"You too," I said, pointing to Bill.

Bill shook his head. "That's not a good idea, Luc."

"Get out, Bill."

"I step out of here, and you're completely on your own," Bill said.

"I've always been on my own."

Bill continued to argue, but soon realized I wasn't relenting. "Mattie won't be happy," he said. I knew it was his last-ditch effort. I noticed John smirk as he waited for my answer.

"Tell her I'm sorry. It's better this way."

John sat down across from me and waited for Bill to leave. The room was suddenly very empty and quiet. I had spent the last half hour staring into the angry face of Carol Crunnion. I was hoping Johnny would be easier to deal with.

I was wrong.

John searched my face. "You're in deep shit, Luc."

"I know. Can Maclay help me?"

"Sheriff Maclay doesn't want to dirty his hands with you. You're radioactive right now, and you dragged Detective Ward down with you. He doesn't see how we get out of this without looking bad. Damn it, Luc. I should have let the LAPD lock your ass up last weekend and saved everyone the trouble. I put my career on the line by going out on a limb for you, and this is how you repay me?"

I tried to interrupt.

"Shut up, Actar. Why didn't you come to me? I've always done everything I could to help you. I've never lied to you. If you had questions, you should have asked me. All I wanted was for you to talk to me and leave my detectives alone. Leave Ward out of whatever story you were trying to dig up here. Now you've ruined his career, probably his life. Detective Ward is a great detective. You've screwed him. You've screwed everyone that can help you. I'm surprised Bill is even here to stick up for you. I have to wonder how long it will take before you drag him down, too."

"Johnny, I know I screwed everything up. You're right. I shouldn't have doubted you, but I didn't know who to trust. Ward came to me. You're right about him. He's a great detective. I thought he could help me, and I wanted to help him. That's it. Do you know what they have on me?"

He nodded. "It sure as hell looks like Detective Ward paid you to take Ernesto Ramirez out of the picture."

"Come on, Johnny. You know that's bullshit. I may be capable of murder, but you know Ward."

"And right now that's the only thing keeping you from sleeping behind bars tonight. They want you to roll on him. It's not going to be enough to admit to murdering Ramirez. They want a confession that implicates Detective Ward, too."

I put my head in my hands. "I didn't do it. The gun isn't even mine, John, but it was in my possession yesterday. Ward didn't even know I was going to see Ramirez."

"Ramirez was stabbed, not shot."

I looked at him and saw he was serious. "Thank God for that. I know I didn't have a knife in my car. I didn't kill him. You have to believe me."

He nodded. "Okay. Let's start with your story and your encounter with Ernesto Ramirez. Tell me everything. Don't leave anything out, and I'll see what I can do."

~~~

It was past midnight when I was finally released and given my car back. They decided to hold onto the drugs, money, and pistol, but thankfully, could find no reason to hold onto my car. I didn't complain about the rest. I was tired of fighting, and I had no one left to back me up.

I had six calls on my voicemail. Four were from Mattie, asking where I was. One was from Spencer, asking me to call, and the last one was from Mac, informing me in a very calm voice that the police were at LB Motors serving a search warrant of my business. No other information was given. I deleted all the messages and drove the silent streets back to Mattie's house. The air was still not working, forcing me to sweat the entire drive.

When I pulled into the driveway, I was surprised to see Spencer come out on the porch. He shook his head when he saw me.

"It's not what you think," he said.

I wanted to laugh, but didn't have the energy. "You came running over here the second I was out of the picture. You can tell yourself it's because she needed someone and I wasn't there, but we both know why you're really here."

"She's not happy."

"It's been a long day, Spencer. I don't have time to deal with you, too." I walked past him and grabbed the door.

"They took Chris."
~~~

After a long, tiring day fighting cops, I had forgotten all about the boy. "I'll get him back. Don't worry about it."

"Yeah, I'm sure you can."

I watched Spencer walk to his car before I headed inside to face whatever Mattie would throw at me. I expected her to be upset, but when I found her in the office, I could see I was very wrong. If she had been sad, I would have been okay. If she had been angry, I would have faced it. But as she looked up at me, I realized she looked hopeless and defeated.

She waited for me to say something. I couldn't think of anything to say, so I let the silence drag on.

"I'm tired, Luc. I'm too tired to fight."

I realized I needed her anger. I needed her to feel something. I didn't want her to give up on us. "Don't look at me like I'm one of your students, Mattie. I'm not one of your charity cases. I'm not some lost child you can save."

"Then stop acting like one. For God's sake, Luc, you were arrested for murder!"

"And you're not asking for my side. Do you think I did it?"

She sighed. I felt my headache coming back.

"I know what you're capable of," she said. "I know what you can do when you're angry."

I opened my mouth to speak, but found I was having a problem with the words. I closed my mouth and turned away so I didn't have to look at her—to look at her disgust with me.

"That's what's wrong," I replied. "You look at me and see . . . that." The alley. The blood. Even I couldn't ignore it. "I should never have told you."

"That's the problem, Luc. You don't tell me anything. You keep things hidden and then tell yourself you're doing it to protect me, but that's bullshit. You refuse to open up to me, afraid I might see something I don't like."

"You're right, Mattie. Because I told you about Carl Palfy, you look at me and you can only see a killer."

"No, I look at you and see a man who doesn't regret killing. A man I know would do it again—"

"You're damn right I would do it again. That bastard hit you. He deserved to die. I'm not going to explain myself again."

"And Ernesto Ramirez? Did he deserve to die?"

"I didn't kill him. I was here at home with you and your parents when Ramirez was murdered, but I sure ain't crying for him now."

"What about the drugs? The gun? Oh yeah, and the five grand in cash."

"Spencer told you?"

"He didn't have to. The police were here. They had a search warrant."

I looked at the desk and back to her. "They were in the house? Did they take anything?"

Her face snapped so fast I almost didn't brace myself in time. Her anger had me stepping back from the blast. She struck out at me, slapping my arms and chest. Nails scratched at my neck.

"They took *him*, goddamn it! They took Chris."

I grabbed her arms, but she continued to struggle against me. Then the tears came. I pulled her into my arms and tried to calm her down.

"I'm sorry."

She pulled away, the anger showing through the tears. "No, you're not. You've never been sorry for anything your entire life. You couldn't wait to get that boy out of here and out of your way."

"Mattie, I'll get him back."

"No." She wiped her eyes, but the anger and tears still spilled out. "No, you won't. I don't want you anywhere near him. The boy has been through enough. Let Spencer take care of it."

"Like Spencer takes care of everything?"

"I won't have you stealing him back. At some point you're going to have to learn you can't steal everything. You can't kill those you disagree with."

"You want me to stand aside and do nothing?" I asked. "I can't figure you out. What the hell do you want from me?"

"I want you to talk to me. I want you to open up and not keep secrets from me."

"You mean like you've kept it from me that you've been dating your ex-husband?"

"Really?" She pulled away from me. She shook her head and her voice dropped to a whisper. "I know you have your demons to fight, but I'm not one of them."

"Then why do I always feel like I have to fight for this?"

"You don't have to anymore."

~~~

I had nowhere to go. I drove to the *Crime Reporter* office and broke in to retrieve the police file I had left in the desk. With the cops watching me closely, I knew a search warrant of my office wouldn't be out of their reach, and this was the last thing I wanted the police to be questioning me about. With the alarms blaring, I left with the file and the framed photo of Mattie and me.

I drove past Spencer's apartment and threw the photo at his door and sped off. I drove until I was out of gas and found myself back in Torrance. I called Detective Ward as I parked in front of the Torrance Liquor Store, but got no answer.

The liquor store looked the same as when I had stolen food there as a teenager. A Korean man stood behind the counter and looked seriously disturbed to see me. I took out my wallet and he seemed to relax a little. I bought a bottle of his cheapest tequila and a pack of unfiltered Marlboros, the type I had often stolen from my father. I paid for the reminders of my past, stole a lighter, and headed out. I walked behind the store to the alley. A black pickup truck was parked there, probably the Korean's.

I sat on the gravel lot with my back to the store, staring at the wall that had once been splattered with blood.

I drank.

I smoked.

I read the police file from front to back and drank some more.
~~~

I stared at the photos of what I had done.

The Korean man came out and asked me to leave.

I stared at the wall and smoked.

He threatened to call the cops.

I left, wondering why I was trying so hard to forget my past. I was exhausted and felt like shit. I considered sleeping, but the heat of the day was still sweltering in the darkness. I knew of only one place that always stayed cold.

Chapter 30

I woke up on the scarred, cold floors of my old room in the abandoned Torrance apartment building. I wanted to sleep and not wake up. I could hear ghosts talking through the walls and knew I had drunk too much. A sliver of light peeked in through the broken window.

As the sun continued its relentless path upward, I watched the patch of sunlight move slowly across the room toward my face. I blocked out the noise from outside and the noise from inside my head as I waited for the sun to continue its journey toward the end.

My cell phone had no service here, and I wondered how long I could stay before someone would find my lifeless body. I let the cold take over and wondered why the hell I had even come back to Los Angeles. I had escaped once before. Why hadn't I stayed away?

I had just vomited when Orin walked in. He looked at me, wrinkled his nose, and sat on the floor across from me. The sun was still lighting the room. I glanced at my watch and realized very little time had actually gone by.

"What do you want?" I asked. I grabbed my last cigarette and lit it, looking around for the bottle of tequila I had started the night before. Anything to get the taste of vomit out of my mouth.

"Arrested and homeless in the same day. Back to square one."

"You talked to Mattie?" I asked, drinking the last of the tequila.

"I called the house this morning. She sounds as bad as you look. At least they let you keep the car."

"It's my car. Why would they keep it?"

Orin folded his arms over his chest. "It's not stolen?"

"Why does everyone think I stole the Porsche?" I asked.

"Because you're a car thief."

"Retired car thief. I'm a journalist now."

"Actually, you're an unemployed journalist."

"What the fuck do you want, Orin?"

He shook his head at me. "One cigarette. That's all it took."

"It wasn't the cigarette." I slid the folder over to him. He caught it and opened it to the first page.

I looked away as he read.

"Who's Carl Palfy?" he asked.

"I was still in college. I was done playing football due to banging up my knee, and I was struggling with my classes. I hadn't spoken to Mattie in probably four months. She was seeing someone, so I tried to walk away. I thought it was best for her, but I had this weird feeling I needed to talk to her." I shifted positions so I could reach the bottle of tequila. "You know, she has this way of hitching her voice up a notch, just slightly noticeable. She does it when something's wrong. Even when she says she's fine, I can hear it. Isn't it funny, that I notice that?"

I looked up at him. He was no longer reading, just staring back at me.

"She told me she was fine, but I heard the voice. I pushed until she told me. She'd just broken up with her boyfriend." I pointed to the folder. "Carl. He hit her. He didn't like something she said, so the asshole backhanded her. Across the face. He hit Mattie in the face." I shook my head and tried to steady myself. I heard the page turn and knew Orin was looking at the picture of the alley.

"So you did this?"

"My father never hit me in the face. Never once. I always thought it was a respect thing. It was one thing to be hit by someone. It was a whole 'nother thing to let everyone else know about it, but . . . you know, I don't know if I believe that anymore.

"When I was doing that to Carl, I wasn't picturing him. I was picturing my father. I hit and I hit and I never let up. I couldn't let up. That man had beaten me too many times. I needed some sort of closure. I got it that day and I wanted it to be over. I was tired of fighting. I crawled out of that alley and came here. I was too chickenshit to swallow a bullet, so I tried to kill myself with the bottle."

"Sounds familiar."

"Turn the page."

He flipped the page and continued to read the report.

"They talked to Mattie," I said. "She had no idea what happened, so she didn't bother to make anything up. She's not the lying type, anyway. They tried to find me, but I was lying on this floor, hiding from everyone." I pointed to the folder. "Halfway down. They found my father. I didn't even know where he was."

Orin was still reading. "He gave you an alibi?"

"Yep." I nodded. "The damn bastard told them I was with him at an AA meeting. Had two witnesses, too. Told them I would probably deny it because of the scholarship. He had it all planned out. Cops believed it. They didn't even bother to follow up with me. He was always one hell of a con man."

Orin turned the page and continued reading. I put out my cigarette on the floor.

"He protected me," I said. "I had screwed up beyond saving, and he found a way to keep me out of prison. I had no idea. I've spent my entire life thinking he's a drunk asshole. Maybe I was wrong all along. I blamed him for all the horrible things in my life, but I survived."

Orin closed the folder and pushed it back toward me. "He was an asshole. Don't try to rewrite history because of one statement he gave to the police more than ten years ago. I don't know what his intention was, but I do know you just screwed up your life and Daddy's not here to fix it. You need to fix this with Mattie."

"She threw me out. She doesn't want anything to do with me."

"So you're just going to accept it? You're just going to wallow in self-pity and let the best thing that ever happened to you walk away?"

"What do you want me to do? Cry?"

"You don't regret anything?" he asked.

"No, Orin. Mattie knew what she was getting herself into. I'm done trying to be something I'm not. I survive better when I know who I am."

"What are you going to do about this?" He pointed to the folder. "Are you going to turn yourself in?"

I looked at him and realized I shouldn't have shown him the file. What the hell was I thinking? I grabbed my lighter and lit the entire folder on fire. Orin said nothing as it burned.

"It never happened. This conversation never happened. I'm not going to prison."

Orin shrugged. "You know, no matter how many times you've been shit on, it's still your option to sit and mope in it, or wash it off and move on." He sniffed me. "You need a shower, and we need to get going."

"Where?" I asked. "I'm unemployed and homeless. What's the point?"

"Because for once, I have the story, and you're going to ensure it's on the front page of the *Reporter*. Stop thinking of how this affects you and start thinking about everyone else. Today, try to help someone else for a change."

I looked at him. I wasn't convinced.

"Get up off your ass. I found Henry Dillon. His mutilated body washed ashore in PV this past weekend. I need you to find Detective Ward for me."

I straightened. "Are you serious? The floater is Dillon?"

"I was with the Sheriff's all night. They're still confirming the second body they found, but they whispered to me that it's looking like your missing doctor. His sister is on the way to the morgue to confirm now."

"Both guys are dead? How long have they been dead? How did they die?"

"Answers I hope to have by the end of the day. I need to head back there now. I'm meeting with Emily Stedman in an hour."

"Emily. That sounds familiar. Does she work at the Torrance Medical Clinic? Thin woman, smoker?"

"Yeah, she works at the clinic. Why?"

I shook my head. "I met her. She doesn't like homeless people around the clinic. She was calling her brother to get them off the street."

Orin nodded. "Great. If she's involved in this somehow, she can provide some great quotes."

"You're writing a story?"

"That's kinda what I do, Luc. Blame it on my OCD. But I need your help."

"Why?"

Orin sighed. "Do you know why the US uses the jury system?"

"What the hell are you talking about?" I asked.

"Do you know why we have a group of your peers instead of trusting a judge or a cop to decide on cases? It's a proven fact that a group of individuals, who bring their own life experiences and can discuss and deliberated are better at discovering the truth than a single person."

"What are you saying, Orin?"

"I'm saying you couldn't find the truth by yourself. Neither can I. We need to work together. We need Detective Ward's help too. We need to find out how Ramirez was murdered and how it's connected."

"Ward can't help. He won't have access to the case. Best-case scenario, they've put him on administrative leave. Worst case, he's behind bars."

Orin frowned. "What happened?"

"IA thinks he wanted Sergeant Ramirez so bad he offed her husband." I thought about Maria.

"Do you know anyone else who can get us inside information on the Ramirez murder?"

I stood up. "We need to find Ward."

"You just said he can't help."

"He won't know about the case, but he's the only one who can get Maria Ramirez to talk to me."

Chapter 31

I drove all over Southern California looking for Ward. I started at his precinct and was told he wasn't there, and they refused to give me any information. Even after explaining I was no longer working for the *Crime Reporter* and that I was asking as a friend, no one would help me. Next, I drove by his home in Hacienda Heights, but the place was empty. I had never been inside, and in fact was pretty sure Ward wouldn't want me there, but I picked the lock and spent a few minutes trying to figure out where Ward would be.

I had no idea where Ernesto and Maria Ramirez lived, so Orin was running down that lead, but my guess was that Ward would stay far from her. I checked several of the local restaurants, but no luck. Finally I decided to call in a favor to a guy I knew in Internal Affairs. He was a clean cop and often gave me a heads-up if a dirty cop was being investigated. I figured if Ward's name came up in my interrogation, he was definitely being watched by someone in IA.

My contact called me a half hour later and gave me an address. I pulled into the parking lot of the Long Beach bar where Ward and I had drinks less than a week earlier. I parked next to Ward's car and looked around to see if I could spot the IA officer watching him. I didn't.

I said hello to Chuck behind the bar, and he pointed me to the corner booth. Ward was slouched in the booth with a drink in his hand and his eyes staring at me. His suit looked worn and tired, just like him.

"What the fuck are you doing here?" he asked when I sat down. His eyes were red, but I wasn't sure if it was from anger or pain.

"You came here because of me, didn't you?"

"I came here because you told me the cops stay away from this place. I don't know why I didn't just listen to Carliss and stay the hell away from you. Did you see them out there waiting for me?"

I shook my head.

"They're out there, and you meeting me here is not going to help my defense. I just spent the last three hours with my attorney. I'm not speaking to anyone until I see a warrant. They can follow me as long as they want." He looked at me. "Did you kill Ramirez?"

"Wow, way to be blunt," I said. "No, I did not, and I have an alibi to prove it."

He nodded and pushed his beer toward me. "I can't drink alcohol this early."

"Did *you* kill him?" I asked in return.

He didn't answer.

"I can call Bill, and he can meet us."

"I don't need your lawyer. I can take care of myself."

"Tell me you have an alibi, Ward. Tell me they aren't going to chase both of us on this."

He laughed loudly now. Chuck turned to look at us.

"I have the best alibi ever," Ward said. "I was with her. It clears me of the murder, but only piles more suspicion on me. I've probably lost my shield, lost my life, but at least I still have my freedom, right?"

"You were still seeing her?"

"No, not really. I just went over to talk to her. I was actually hoping he'd be there, though. I wanted to confront him after all the shit he put me through. He tried to ruin my career."

"What happened when you got there?"

"He wasn't there. I assumed he was working late. I don't know." He rubbed his face. "I really screwed up this time. The last time, I don't know, I wasn't thinking. This time, I didn't care. We didn't talk about any of it when it ended. Maybe that was the mistake. Now I have no idea where we stand." He paused. "I guess it doesn't matter. Her husband's dead. Jesus Christ. You know, I'm not sorry about it."

"You know if you had asked me to kill him for you, I would have."

"Don't tell me that. I'll have to arrest you."

I couldn't resist. "You don't have a badge anymore."

"I'll always be an officer," he muttered. "The shield is just a symbol the city hands out. You do realize you reek of tequila, right?"

I smiled at him. "No water in my old apartment, and I was kind of in a rush to see you. I think whoever killed Ernesto Ramirez also killed Dr. Stedman and Henry Dillon."

"Who?"

"Dr. Stedman worked for Ramirez at the facility. Henry Dillon was a patient. Both were killed and apparently dumped this week."

He muffled a curse. "This is bigger than I thought."

"It has to be someone at the hospital. I need to know what happened before Dr. Stedman disappeared and why Ramirez was keeping it quiet. I need to speak to Maria."

Ward shook his head. "No. She's had enough already."

I knew Ward well enough not to press the issue. If I pushed him in a direction he didn't want to go, he'd not only push back, he'd push me out.

"Let's get outta here," I suggested.

He shook his head. He looked defeated and ready to give up. I knew the feeling. I thought about what Orin had said to me that morning.

"Life sucks, Ward. Get over it. Time to move on. Time to wash it off."

"What the hell did your father get himself into?" he asked. "What was in those files, and why the hell did he want them?"

"They were patient files. From what I can figure out, Henry Dillon asked my father to steal the patient files from Dr. Stedman. I have no idea why they weren't in Dr. Stedman's office at the treatment center. For some reason Ramirez had requested them. My father stole the files and delivered them to someone. Whatever was in the files was worth the deaths of three people."

"We need to know why the files were moved," he said.

"The only person who knew that is dead. I think we should focus on what the files could show. My guess is they prove Dr. Stedman was kidnapping homeless people, and Ernesto Ramirez knew all about it."

Ward made a sound that wasn't quite a word. "You're still trying to find an angle here for a story?" He shook his head. "It doesn't play for me. Ramirez was a dick, but he wasn't a criminal. Maria would've known."

"Ramirez used the police for his benefit. It's not that far of a stretch to jump to criminal. Why else would he hide the files in his office to begin with?"

"He wasn't hiding the files." He stood up. "Let's talk to Maria." He sat back down and cursed. "I can't leave here and go see her. I have IA following me."

"Have her come here. There's a back door that leads to the alley. It's dark and private back there. She can park there, and IA won't see her."

Chapter 32

The black Honda Accord crept down the alley and eased to a stop alongside Detective Ward. A woman I didn't know was driving. She put the car in park and started arguing with Maria in the passenger seat.

"Who's the driver?" I asked.

"Maria's sister," Ward said, staring at the car.

"Is she single?"

Ward didn't answer.

"I'm just asking. She's hot. You could have gone for her instead."

"Shut up, Luc."

Maria climbed out of the passenger seat. Her hair was slicked back in a pony tail, and her eyes and nose were red. Despite the heat, she wore a long black sweater, the sleeves long enough to cover her hands. Her arms were crossed over her chest, and she looked pissed to see me.

"Why am I here?" she asked Ward.

"Exactly like I told you on the phone, Maria. We need to talk about Ernie's death."

"Why is he here?"

She wouldn't look at me. To me, Maria Ramirez didn't look sad. It could have been that the anger at seeing me had replaced the sadness, but I actually believe the cop in her had taken over and she had shut out the human emotions. I didn't apologize or tell her I was sorry for her loss. I sensed she didn't want or need my sympathy.

"I want to find out who killed your husband," I said. "I need your help. You can help me, or you can shut yourself up in your house and wait for the cops to do it. But you know my track record, and I can tell you right now, I'm several steps ahead of the cops already. I've connected your husband's death to two other victims found this week."

She said nothing for a minute, and then dropped her arms. She looked down at her hands, and I noticed a tissue gripped tightly in her palm.

"What do you want to know?" she asked, looking up. She stared me down as she waited. She didn't look at Ward now.

"Exactly what was stolen from his office?" I asked.

"All of Dr. Stedman's patient files."

"Anything else?"

She shook her head.

"Why did your husband have the files?"

"Ernie had noticed the influx of patients from the homeless communities. Many of these patients were being kept longer than the seventy-two-hour hold allowed by the state. He confronted Dr. Stedman, but Dr. Stedman claimed all of his patients were in need of physiological evaluation. He claimed he was just doing his job."

"So Ramirez asked for his files?"

"No, not at that time. He started doing background searches on all of his doctors, and he noticed some financial irregularities in Dr. Stedman's accounts. Before he could confront him, Stedman disappeared."

"What kind of irregularities?" I knew the search of Dr. Stedman's financial records was probably done without his consent. I suspected the sergeant of breaking the law to help her husband, but the fact would have to be used against her at a later time. Now was not the time to make her mad at me.

"He was receiving payments of up to five hundred a month in cash deposited to his account. It could have been nothing, but my husband was concerned it was connected to the influx of patients."

"He thought someone was paying Dr. Stedman to pick up patients?"

"We had no idea what was going on. Ernie requested all of the files be brought to his office so he could review them. The boxes were stolen before he even started his review. He had the files in his office when the break-in happened."

"What about the laptop Ward mentioned?"

She looked at Ward now. He nodded, but wouldn't look at me.

"Two days after the doctor disappeared, my husband picked up his laptop and brought it home. The laptop had all the electronic files. We weren't too concerned about the break-in at first, until we realized the laptop had been stolen, too."

"So someone broke into his office *and* your home?"

"Not someone," she said. "Your father."

I ignored the nasty tone in her voice. I was more concerned with what wasn't being said. "Was the laptop in the report?" I was thinking about John and why he didn't know about the laptop.

She shook her head. "The LA Sheriff's detectives were working on the break-in at the office, and they weren't taking it too seriously. My husband requested LAPD to take over, but he didn't feel a need to have them in our home, so we didn't tell them about the laptop."

I knew she was keeping something from me, but couldn't figure out why. Ward wouldn't look at me.

"You told me about the laptop," I said to Ward. "How did you know?"

He took a deep breath, and I knew it wasn't good. I remembered what he had said earlier in the bar.

"Carliss told you to stay away from me," I pressed. "You didn't. You always follow orders. Why did you come to me and tell me about the laptop?"

"When you showed up at the bar, Maria thought you might be able to locate where your father would hide the documents and laptop. She told me everything and asked if I could find a way to make you help."

"You asshole," I said, jabbing a finger at Ward. "You lied to me from the beginning. You were never there to help me. You pretended to be my friend just so you could get into her pants?"

Ward jumped toward me and shoved me up against the wall. His speed was impressive, but his anger overwhelmed me.

"This isn't third grade, Luc. We're not friends! We've never been friends. Just because your daddy beat you and I was raised in foster care doesn't make us bonded." He put in finger in my face. "You're a car thief, masquerading as a journalist determined to take down law enforcement. You use everyone around you to try to improve your life without worrying about how it affects them, and then you turn around and call them your friends. I don't need friends like that."

I tried to push him off of me, but he shoved me harder against the wall. I felt something dig into my shoulder blade.

"You may not know what it's like to have a family, but I do. The cops you go after, that's my family. My brothers."

"Your brothers were looking to stab you in the back yesterday," I yelled back. "Your family is watching your every move, waiting for you to screw up. Sure looks like you're the fuckup of the family."

He smirked. "And I bet your father would be proud of the life you've conned everyone for. You use me for your stories. I used you for the job. That's the extent of this relationship. You got it?"

I pushed his finger out of my face. "I came here today to help you clear your name."

"Bullshit. You came here because you know Ramirez's death points to a larger story, and you want your name on the byline."

"I was fired yesterday."

He laughed. "Looks like everyone is starting to see Luc Actar as the scumbag criminal you really are." He released me, turned, and walked back into the bar.

"I was here to help you," I said to the closed door.

Chapter 33

Mary Holstein's home was situated in the Aliso Viejo hills. The tract home had no security that I could see. It was a two-story home with a freshly cut lawn, blooming flowers, and not a weed in sight. Her beautiful Jaguar XJR sat in the driveway.

I walked up the three steps and knocked on the door. She opened it with a smile on her face, but it disappeared when she recognized me.

"What are you doing here?" she asked.

"I missed my session yesterday on account of a false arrest. I need to make up the session."

"This is my home, Luc. I don't do sessions here. Why don't you make an appointment for Monday?"

"Monday's too late. I had until the end of the week to finish the therapy."

"How did you find me?" she asked.

I rolled my eyes. "You're wasting time. I know you don't want to work on a Saturday, but I only need one more session so I can close this up and get the cops off my back. Just one hour, please."

She relented and opened the door to me. She showed me into a formal living room with two couches facing each other. I could tell the room was barely used. Chinese art hung on the walls, expensive-looking vases decorated an end table. I wondered if she ever spent time in this stuffy space.

She excused herself, saying she would bring tea or coffee. I declined. Watching her go, I stood and looked around the room.

I could hear her talking in the kitchen, her voice low. I looked at my watch. I sat back down and waited patiently.

She returned a few minutes later with two glasses of lemonade. I had hoped she'd offer something to eat, since I was starving, but she didn't.

"Let's get started. Tell me about what happened yesterday."

"The cops thought I killed someone. I didn't. I lost my job, and Mattie kicked me out. I'm homeless again."

"Why did Mattie kick you out?"

"Because it's her house and she doesn't want a lying criminal in it. I don't blame her."

"You've been living there for several months now. Why do you still call it her house?"

I thought the question strange. Out of all the things she could be focusing on, she focused on my pronouns. "It's her house. She bought it. I no longer live there with her."

"A change in environment might be a good thing right now. Sometimes our surroundings give us cause for irritation and anger."

"Are you really going to focus on that instead of asking about the murder I was arrested for?"

"You said you didn't do it."

"And you believed me?"

"I have no reason not to believe you. You're not sitting in a jail cell right now. I think the reason you're sitting in my living room has more to do with Mattie than a false arrest."

I leaned forward. "Do you really think I threw coffee on that cop because of Mattie?"

"I do. I think you feel helpless in her house and you're always in charge everywhere else. Those officers were in the house because Mattie let them in. You're upset because the detective's comment about Mattie letting them in the house bothers you. You don't have control over who comes into the house, as seen by the fact that she's taken in your brother without your consent. This sense of powerlessness makes you angry. The last time you were this powerless, your father controlled your life. Now Mattie does. You reacted in the same pattern, with violence."

I said nothing.

"Luc, you will continue to put yourself in compromising situations unless you focus on your issues and deal with them. You can't help Mattie or anyone else if you ignore the underlying problem."

"Do you think all homeless people need therapy? That we're all fucked up and crazy?"

"I believe living on the street is a stressful and emotional environment. There are more stresses put on children living on the street. To ignore it only perpetuates your belief that you're being ignored much like you were when you were living on the streets. I know you don't want people to see who you really are, but you're not invisible to me. I see you, and I want to help you."

"What if I don't want your help?"

"You wouldn't be here if you didn't want help. You're starting to see that your way of living isn't working out like you thought. You've fought so hard to get the life you wanted, and you've continued to fight everyone who gets close to you in fear that it will fall apart. But it's fallen apart despite your fighting. Your new life is crumbling, but not because of everyone else. It's because of you."

"What did I do wrong?" I asked.

"You've been fighting for yourself a long time. But there are others around you that you care about. You think of them as your enemies or people who can take away that life, but they're your friends, your family. They care about you. You need to start fighting for them. Start caring about them. The perfect life you want starts with them."

"So what should I do?"

"I'd start by changing your environment. Give yourself time to adjust to the changes in your life. You need to see a psychologist on a regular basis to learn to calm yourself and refocus your anger in a healthy way. Otherwise, you may just snap and hurt someone unintentionally."

I heard a car pull up out front. Dr. Holstein straightened. I leaned back and waited. When the door opened, I waved to Detective Carter. "Thanks for coming."

He looked confused, and his eyes went to Mary. "Are you okay?"

She nodded.

"Get up, Luc," he said.

I smiled. "She invited me in. I was just waiting for you, anyway."

"Wait outside."

I didn't fight him. I walked outside and waited for him to make sure his sister was okay.

His face was red when he walked out a few minutes later. "This is her home. She doesn't see patients here."

I nodded. "Now you know how I felt when you walked into Mattie's house looking for me. I was actually hoping to talk to you."

He thought about this. "You could have called me."

"Then your partner would have shown up, too, and that would have been awkward. Anyway, I know you're probably not working the Ramirez burglary anymore, but I have something to trade."

He crossed his arms on his chest. "What do you have?"

I thought it very interesting that he was more interested in what I had to offer than what I wanted. "The files that were stolen from Ramirez's office will lead you to his killer."

"Are you in possession of said stolen property?"

I smiled. "Of course not. That would be a crime, but I can deliver them to you. Not the actual files, though. My father stole the files for someone. My guess is that whoever he delivered the files to wanted a specific file, and the others were just stolen to confuse everyone. I'm not sure you'll ever see any of the files again. But my father isn't a thief for hire. If my father stole those files for someone, then he got something much more valuable for himself."

"And that is?"

"An electronic file of all the records. My father delivered all the files as promised, but he held onto a laptop with copies of everything. My guess is he was probably going to blackmail someone with the information."

"And you know where the laptop is?"

I nodded. "I can deliver it to you. And for the record, it isn't coming from Chris Actar. Which brings me to what I want in return."

"Go on."

"I want the charges dropped. I want him returned to Mattie's house with no record. As soon as he's released and safe, I'll give you the laptop."

He nodded. "Okay. You have a deal, but you deliver the laptop only to me. No one else."

I agreed and gave him my cell phone number. He promised to call me as soon as Chris was released. Now I just needed to find the laptop. I was pretty sure I knew who had it.

"You care enough about that kid to do all this?" he asked.

"The kid belongs with Mattie. It's the right thing to do. And I need Detective Ward's name cleared. He had nothing to do with this and doesn't deserve what you guys are doing to him."

He nodded. "I'll help you clear Ward's name as long as you stay away from my sister. Your therapy is over, and your record is clean with me."

I smiled. "Deal."

My phone interrupted our goodbyes. I considered ignoring it, but saw that it was a text message. It read: *Club. Now.* I knew Big Jim wouldn't make a demand like this without cause.

I took one more long look at the Jaguar in the driveway, knowing my desire to return to Mattie was more powerful than my urge to steal it.

Chapter 34

The Paradise Club parking lot was empty when I pulled in, but I knew Jim would be there. Ignoring the *Closed* sign on the door, I knocked. A bartender I knew unlocked the door and let me in. He pointed to a corner booth where Jim was sitting with his security guy. Pioa was already eyeing me. He wasn't happy to see me.

I walked to the booth, and Pioa stood up in front of me. He cursed under his breath and then walked away, leaving us alone. I sat down across from Jim.

"He really likes me," I said. I didn't care about Pioa. I was just glad to have a friendly face to talk to. Unfortunately, I didn't find Jim all too friendly at the moment.

"The police were here for you," he said. "You put me in a bad situation. I don't appreciate it." He lit a cigarette but didn't offer me one. That was a bad sign. His eyes had turned hard as stone. I looked around the bar and found it had emptied. The bartender who had let me in had disappeared, as had Pioa.

"I'm sorry, Jim. I didn't mean to drag anyone else into this. I'll keep my distance until this is wrapped up. Tell Genie I'm sorry for the trouble." I stood.

"Sit down. I'm involved now. A girl by the name of Georgia came by yesterday."

"She came?" I asked, relieved. Maybe I wasn't here to be killed by Jim.

"Yes. She said she knew you. She was looking for a place to hide out."

"How'd she look?"

"Like someone beat the shit out of her."

"Did she tell you who did it?"

"She didn't want to, but I have a way of persuading when I need to know." He pushed the remnants of the cigarette out on the table.

"Tell me."

"A guy came by your father's apartment. He spent an hour or so searching the place. He wasn't a cop. She was sure of that. She thought he was some tweaker looking for drugs. She thinks he may have seen her spying on him through the window. When he was done searching the apartment, he knocked on her door. She was going to give him the brush-off, but he didn't give her the chance. He beat the shit out of her and strangled her until she gave him what he wanted."

"What did she give him?"

"A laptop your father had entrusted to her for safekeeping. She has no idea what's so valuable on the laptop, but it was stamped with the name of some medical facility. She thought the guy would stop when she gave him everything, but he continued to attack her. When she saw the knife, she passed out. When she woke up he was gone, but she was barely alive. She grabbed her gun and was hiding out in your father's apartment in case he came back. That's when you found her."

"He thought he'd killed her." I was thankful she was alive, but I realized I was no better off. I really needed the laptop. Without it, I had nothing to trade with Carter. I had to get it back. "Can she identify him?"

He leaned back. "Not sure, but she said he smelled of cigarettes and apparently knew you. Oh, and he had a tattoo of a spider on his hand."

I nodded. I knew I should have thought of Jeffrey Donovan as a possible suspect since I had last seen him going to talk to Ernesto Ramirez, but the guy just seemed like a whack job. I didn't picture him as a calculated killer. And yet, he'd killed three people and almost killed Georgia.

Worse, she had handed over the last piece of evidence I could use against the guy. The last piece of leverage I had to get Chris back and clear Ward's name.

I leaned back in the chair. "Jeffrey Donovan. He's a patient at the Torrance Treatment Center. One of Dr. Stedman's patients." It bothered me that I had actually liked the guy. I hadn't pictured him hurting anyone. But I trusted Georgia more than my opinions now. My opinions were just getting me in trouble.

Jim pushed over a thumb drive. "She copied the computer files a day earlier. Will this help find him?"

I smiled and grabbed the drive. All was not lost. "This is perfect," I said to Jim, but he didn't seem to find the same joy in it.

I was thinking I was finally ahead of the game. I had pieces to the puzzle; I just needed to fit them together before I could write the article. But I also realized I had started the ball rolling. Jeffrey probably had no idea where my father lived until I stopped by the Torrance Treatment Center and offered his home address. He must have realized that my father hadn't turned over all the files. Maybe he didn't know about the laptop, but when he went searching for his missing file, he'd found Georgia and beaten her severely. I knew it was my fault, and I wanted to make it up to her, but first I needed to find out why Jeffrey Donovan needed his file back so badly. Why was he willing to kill three people?

Before I could figure out my next step, the ground jerked and a loud explosion rocked me from my seat. I grabbed the floor before my face smashed into it. I saw Jim duck down as a billow of smoke engulfed us. I'd been in my share of earthquakes before, so I was certain this was a man-made disaster.

"What the fuck was that?" I yelled.

I realized I could barely hear the words I had shouted. Jim stood up, and I followed his gaze toward the bar. Pioa came running in through the smoke with two men right behind him.

Pioa said something to Jim, but my ears were still ringing.

I yelled, "What?"

Jim stood staring as the cloud of smoke diminished and revealed a gaping hole where the bar had once stood. A beam fell down and shattered the remains of the alcohol bottles. A small fire grabbed at the spilt liquor and ran all along the bar. More flames and smoke rushed in through the hole in the wall that had once been the doorway.

"Let's go," someone said to Jim.

I stood in shock as I realized how close we had been to the explosion.

"Who did this?" Jim asked Pioa.

"It's not you they're after," Pioa said, pointing at me. "He brought this."

"What the hell are you talking about?" I yelled.

"Someone blew your car." He turned to Jim again. "The police will be here any minute. Let's go, boss."

Jim turned to stare at me. I couldn't read the look on his face, but I suddenly felt scared. I was about to tell him I would fix it, but Pioa pulled him away. I could see the smirk on Pioa's face before all four men disappeared out the back door.

I heard sirens. I crouched low and walked through the smoke to get outside to the fresh air. The acrid smell was overpowering as I moved away from the ball of red-hot flames that was once my car. I sat on the curb and tried to figure out what had happened as a fire truck pulled into the lot.

My phone rang. I recognized the voice.

"I thought that might get your attention."

"That was a ninety-thousand-dollar Porsche you just blew up! You could have just called me, Jeffrey. I wouldn't have ignored you."

"I'm impressed."

"You should be. It took me three fucking months to find that car. That Porsche was a work of art, you crazy asshole."

"Not the car. I didn't know you'd recognize my voice. I hadn't realized you had gotten that far in your investigation. That complicates things. I told you that all you had to do was leave me alone. Stay out of my way and I would stay out of yours, but I saw the pictures on Ramirez's desk. You helped the girl."

"So you had me arrested?"

"I'm sorry for that. It wasn't my idea, but Mr. Ramirez refused to help me."

"What do you want?" I asked. A paramedic drove into the lot and glanced from me to the vehicle. Instead of asking if I needed help, he watched the firefighters as they moved slowly to put out the flames of my burning car.

"You have something I want back," Jeffrey was saying.

"Well, I have to tell you, blowing up my car isn't the best way to ask for a favor."

"I didn't realize the hooker was alive when I left her."

I closed my eyes and pictured myself killing him. "I want her—"

"Yeah, you're not the only one," he said, "and seeing as I'm her new pimp, her rates just went up." He laughed. "If you don't hand her over, I'll just add you to my list of items to clean up. I don't like loose ends."

"Why didn't you come for me first and leave her out of it. She gave you what you wanted. I have the rest of it."

He was quiet. I moved further away from the sirens so I could hear him better. I was tired of the games. I was tired of people getting hurt because of me. It was time to push the crazy guy off the edge. If I could have him focused on me for a while, maybe Orin could get enough on him to get him behind bars.

"You still there, Jeffrey?"

"What do you have?" he asked.

"I have a copy of all the files on that laptop you stole from my girl. I have 'your papers' copied on a jump drive. Buy me a new Porsche and I'll be more than happy to make the trade. Otherwise, I deliver the jump drive to the police, and you can go back to jail where you belong." I hung up the phone.

I looked at what was left of my smoldering car and realized it was all I had left of that perfect life. I had nothing but a flash drive to get it back.

~~~

I called Orin and told him everything I knew, including the conversation with Jeffrey Donovan. He agreed to pick me up. As I waited, I called Dr. Brown. I was surprised when I actually got him on the phone.

"Tell me about Jeffrey Donovan."

"I can't tell you anything on a current patient," the doctor said.

"Your patient just blew up my car."

He sighed, and I knew the pause was a good sign.

"Since Dr. Stedman's notes were in the official file that is now missing, I can't speak to that. And I won't divulge any information the patient told me during our sessions, but I can tell you why he was here."

"Stop calling him the patient. I have a feeling he's not sick."

"Mr. Donovan was arrested for assault and battery. He threatened to kill his cousin when she asked him to pay rent. He did quite a bit of damage to her arms before her husband interrupted him. He is fond of knives and explosives."

"No shit. How did he end up in Dr. Stedman's care and not stand trial?"

"He was evaluated by the jail doctor and determined to be unstable. The judge agreed with the doctor's findings and found him mentally incompetent to stand trial. Dr. Stedman agreed to treat him and report his findings to the judge."

"And I'm guessing Dr. Stedman put something very interesting in his file. Something that will probably send him back to jail. He's doing whatever it takes not to go back."

Dr. Brown would say nothing more.

Twenty minutes later, Orin pulled into the parking lot. The police cars were thinning, but four officers were in the process of putting yellow police tape around the entire building. They had already taken
~~~

my statement. I had been as honest as possible. I was here to talk with a friend and did not see the explosion. The fire personnel were focused on the still smoking car.

Orin shook his head at the mass of metal that remained of my car.

"A bomb?" he asked.

"Not the first time someone's tried to kill me. Probably not the last."

"We should call John Carliss. This guy is seriously deranged. If he comes after you . . ."

"Do you really want to hand over the jump drive so soon?"

He looked at it, smiled, and snatched it from my hand. "Give me two hours. I'll find something usable off of it."

I smiled and smacked him on the back. "I'm glad you're part of this team again. You have two hours. Then I have to hand it over to Carter in exchange for the kid."

Orin wasn't happy about the time limit, but he agreed we should help Ward clear his name and get the kid away from the cops. I also had to agree that only his name would appear on the byline of any story printed in the *Crime Reporter*. I was pretty sure Callahan wouldn't have allowed my name, anyway.

"What are you going to do?" Orin asked.

"Considering there's a deranged serial killer after me, I think it's best to stay hidden for a while."

"Where?"

I realized I had nowhere to go. I had lost it all: my job, my car, my family. I couldn't go to Spencer's without having a drag-out fight over Mattie. I couldn't go to Mattie's house without another fight. I considered going to my old apartment in Torrance, but I didn't want to admit defeat.

I asked Orin to drive me to LB Motors. It was the last job I'd held before becoming a journalist, the last job I'd held before turning legit. When I was finally making some real money, I'd bought the place to ensure it would always be there. It was a crutch for me, and although I had left it behind years ago, I always knew I'd be back. If I had nothing else, I had this. If I lost everything, it would always be there. My life of crime would always be there.

~~~

When Orin pulled into LB Motors, Mac walked from the office, eyed us both, and waved me in rather reluctantly. I said goodbye to Orin and promised to call once I heard from Carter.

Mac waited until Orin had driven off before approaching me.

"Where's the Porsche?" he asked.

"Don't ask."

"What are you doing here?" Mac turned and walked back toward his office. I looked around and saw that the place was empty before I followed him.

"What happened yesterday?" I asked.

"Police served a search warrant. They were looking for stolen files, so it gave them access to steal all of my files." He pointed to a folded metal chair. I took it, figuring the metal chair was better than the floor. He took the comfortable one behind the desk.

"Sorry about that. What will they find in the files?"

He studied me for a minute, then shrugged. "They'll see you've been running in the red for a while now. You buy a lot of shit, expensive parts, the best tools. But they'll see business has been slow. We didn't get that many legit customers. Since I had some warning, there was nothing onsite to hang either of us."

"Good. I got enough heat already. I need a vehicle."

Mac shifted in his seat. A phone rang on the desk, but he ignored it. He waited for it to stop.

"Look, Luc, I've known you a long time, so this isn't easy for me. Hell, I taught you and Joey how to steal cars when you were just kids."

Hearing Joey's name had me looking away. I knew what was coming. Another door was closing on me. John was right. I had no one left in my corner.

I said, "This is my place, Mac."
~~~

"You're right. You being the boss makes this even more difficult. I appreciated the money, and it kept us afloat when we needed it the most, but you haven't stolen a car for us in a while. I have boys that bring in ten a week. You don't have the relationship with the Mexicans. They don't even know you."

"My name is on the records."

"That's the problem. The only thing you bring to this business is heat. I can't keep us out of trouble and keep us profitable if you piss off the *po-po*. It's dangerous working here."

I said nothing.

"I can write you a check today, and you can have your lawyer friend do the paperwork. I want the business back in my name." Mac pulled out his checkbook.

Before he started writing, I said, "Make it out to UCLA Medical Center. I owe them a donation, and after what you've taught me, I don't want your money."

I got up and walked out. I started walking down the street when a black BMW pulled up alongside me.

John rolled down the window. "Get in."

"How'd you find me?" I asked.

"It's now my one and only job."

John explained he was taking me back to Mattie's house. He had learned of my deal with Detective Carter and was insistent on being there during the exchange. He confirmed what Orin had suspected. The two bodies found in PV, Henry Dillon and Dr. Jack Stedman, had been identified. The wounds on both were similar to the wounds found on Ernesto Ramirez's body, and all three were being investigated jointly by detectives at the LA Sheriff's Lomita Station and LAPD Homicide Division. Several suspects were being investigated.

I told him to narrow the search and explained my call with Jeffrey Donovan and the resulting death of my car. I did not tell him about Georgia. I felt she was better protected if no one knew she was involved.

"Tell me what you know about Donovan."

"I don't know much. I met him in the waiting room of the Torrance

Treatment Center. He was waiting to see Dr. Brown. I believe he was a patient of Stedman."

"Why would he kill his doctor?"

"Because he's crazy?"

He shrugged. "And you think he killed your father's friend Henry Dillon, too?"

I nodded and described Henry Dillon's experience in the Torrance Treatment Center. "I think he met Jeffrey Donovan, and Jeffrey approached him about stealing the files. After my father received the files, he gave them to Jeffrey. Henry must have been a loose end that would lead him to the files."

"So he kills Dr. Stedman and steals his files. Then he kills Henry Dillon because he can link him to the files. We need to see the files on that drive. When can Orin get us the drive?"

"As soon as I see Chris, I'll have Orin bring the drive."

John nodded. "Detective Carter got him released with no charges on his record. They interviewed him about the burglary, but he refused to talk to them. If you provide us with the stolen items, there's no need to further involve the boy. He's being driven to Mattie's house as we speak. Call Orin and get him to meet us there."

I was in a pretty good mood as we drove up PCH. I was expecting to see Chris with Mattie. I was expecting to see a smile on Mattie's face. I was expecting a reunion and a second chance. It was the start of my return. I might even be able to get my job back at the *Crime Reporter*.

But like most of my life, I was rudely awakened by reality.

As John turned the corner onto Mattie's Street, a Malibu sheriff's deputy car sped past us with lights and sirens blaring. John pulled over, but I saw that his expression had changed from annoyance to concern. He pointed ahead to an ambulance rushing past us in the opposite direction.

John pulled out quickly after the ambulance passed and rushed up the street. My gut twisted, and I suddenly felt claustrophobic in the car.

Several cruisers sat in the driveway, and two uniformed officers were putting up crime scene tape. Before the car came to a complete stop, I jumped out and rushed to the closest uniform. I heard Charlie howling over the screaming sirens.

"What happened?" I asked.

"Get back. *Now,*" the deputy yelled at me, jabbing a finger at my chest.

John grabbed me from behind and yanked me away from the deputy before I could do something stupid.

"Where's Mattie Hardwin?" John asked. The tone told the deputy he needed a straight answer. I was thankful he was asking the questions, because I suddenly couldn't find the words.

"She just left in the ambulance."

I saw Spencer walk out of the house with another officer. He had blood on his right arm, a black spot on his pants. I heard the officer talking to John about a shooter on foot, and something about police searching the area. But my focus was on Spencer as he approached. A cop tried to stop him, but Spencer brushed him off and kept walking toward me. He was shaking his head.

"What the hell happened?" I asked.

He looked up at the sound of my voice. I saw the emptiness in his eyes, and tears rushed out. The sirens seemed to get louder as I tried to make sense of the scene. I suddenly couldn't breathe.

I felt I was going to be sick and pulled away from John and dropped to my knees. Despair had me gripping the ground as my head spun out of control. I heard someone wailing, and then realized the sound was coming from me. A second later, Spencer was sitting beside me.

"She's okay, Luc. It was Chris."

Chapter 35

John stayed at Mattie's house and promised to give me updates on the investigation as long as I promised to stay away from the house. I had no problem with the arrangement. I hitched a ride to the hospital with Spencer. He was smart enough not to talk to me as I stared out the window, thinking of Chris. I focused on him because I knew if I thought of anything else, my mind would snap.

The hospital wouldn't give me any information when we arrived. Spencer told me it was because I was screaming at everyone, so I agreed to let him take over as I sat on the floor of the emergency room. Waiting. With nothing to do.

Frightened women and children moved to the other side of the waiting room. I listened to the noise of the room and watched everyone, expecting Jeffrey to come rushing in and start shooting. I imagined myself killing him.

After an hour, the automatic doors opened, and Sheriff Maclay and John walked in. I jumped up, thankful for something to do, no matter how useless.

I pointed a finger at both of them. "I agreed to tell you everything I knew about Ramirez and Ward," I said. "All you had to do was protect Mattie."

John put his hands up to stop me. Then he pointed at Mattie, who had emerged from another door. Both men continued past me toward her, and I shrank back to my corner and watched. She held onto a sweatshirt I didn't recognize. It was covered in blood, but her face was clean and pale, as if she'd spent the last hour washing it. She spoke to Maclay first before looking around the room. She glanced right past me as if I wasn't there. The three of them walked over to the desk to join Spencer, who was still waiting on an update.

Spencer shook hands with John and put his arm around Mattie. I stayed in my corner, alone. I was easy to ignore.

I watched as Mattie's mother walked in. She saw me first.

"This is your fault, isn't it?" Virginia asked.

I said nothing. I had always felt that the woman didn't like me much, but she had put up with me because of Mattie. Now I could see the disgust all over her face.

"I always knew you'd find a way to bring violence into our family." She turned and walked toward her daughter. I wondered where Bill was as I stared at the family gathering I was not a part of.

Finally John broke away and made his way to me. "Luc, I'm sorry about Chris," he said. "We've got numerous detectives and officers on the scene right now. We'll figure out what happened. Spencer tells me Chris is in surgery and will be there at least a couple of hours."

"She won't even look at me."

"Give her some time. This can't be easy for her."

"I know. You have to catch this asshole, John. You want to do that before I do."

I heard the doors open again and looked past John. Big Jim and Pioa walked in, and then stopped. I smiled at the prospect that I was no longer alone here.

John turned to see what had grabbed my attention. "Jesus, Luc. Please tell me they have licenses to carry."

Big Jim cocked his head at me, waiting. He said something briefly to Pioa before disappearing down a hallway. Pioa remained standing next to the doors.

I felt some of the heaviness in me lift. Things weren't as hopeless as I thought.

"I'll do whatever it takes to keep her safe," I said to John. "You know that."

John sighed. "We have a few detectives on their way here. They need to speak to Spencer. He saw the gunman. We need to confirm that the shooter was Jeffrey Donovan."

"I'm sure it was. It's only a matter of time before he reaches out to me again."

I looked over at Mattie, who was pacing now, her shirt covered in blood. A nurse had taken the sweatshirt from her, and now she looked like she didn't know what to do with her hands.

"We'll find him, Luc," John said before rejoining Maclay and Spencer at the desk.

Pioa approached when I was alone again.

"Where's Jim?" I asked.

"Securing the floor. We heard what happened at the house." He looked like he was struggling to find the right words. Instead he just closed his mouth.

"I don't want a pissing match between the two of us. I want Mattie safe."

"I may not like you much, but I know who pays me. If Jim wants her protected, she'll be protected. I guarantee it."

I offered my hand, and he shook it. "Thank you," I said. "Here's the deal. I don't want anyone talking to her. Not even the doctors. No one comes close to her. The only people allowed to approach her are me, Spencer, and you."

He studied me. "Me? Not Jim?"

"Jim specializes in killing. You specialize in safety. Who do you think I want next to her? In fact, I don't want her to even see Jim."

"Okay, but this hospital is going to be a bitch to secure."

"I can't move her. Even a bomb scare wouldn't drag her away from that boy."

He nodded. "Maybe we can find a secure room away from the busy entrance and hallways. The boy will probably be in surgery a while, anyway."

Detective Ward walked in with another man in a suit and made their way to the group forming by the desk. I wondered how he'd been invited to the party. The patients waiting in the room could see the buzz around the sheriff and were excited at the prospect of hearing breaking news. Everyone was focused on the group, and I was alone in the corner. No one even looked at me now. I sank back to the floor and put my head in my hands.

My phone rang, and I knew who it was before I answered it.

"See now, this is why I don't like guns—no accuracy, and they're so damn loud. Knives are so much easier to handle."

I didn't have the strength to yell at him. I looked at Ward, who was now watching me. He said something to Mattie and then walked toward me.

"If you made a copy of the files, I want them. I won't go to jail," Jeffrey was saying.

"You think I'm going to deal now, asshole?"

"I didn't mean to shoot the boy. I wanted your girl. He got in the way."

"Yeah, that makes me feel better." I closed the phone just as Ward approached.

"Was that him?" he asked.

I said nothing.

"Let me put a tap on your phone, Luc."

"You're not a cop anymore, Ward. Your friends turned their backs on you, remember?"

"We need to talk about earlier."

"I have nothing else to say."

Orin walked in and was the only one to completely ignore the growing group of cops near the reception desk. He made a beeline to me.

"What are you doing here?" I asked.

"I heard it on the police scanner. What happened?"

"The asshole shot Chris. He's in surgery now."

He shook his head. "How are you?"

"I wasn't the one shot."

"And because of that, I know you're beating yourself up over it." He continued without pushing, "I got something." He handed me a folder.

"What's this?" I asked.

"The treatment file on Jeffrey Donovan. I printed it out and highlighted the interesting parts for you."

I skimmed the first page. Dr. Stedman had submitted to the court a report stating that Jeffrey was mentally ill, by California law, and he could not understand the charges against him, but would be able to attain mental competency after undergoing treatment.

Jeffrey was prescribed medication for schizophrenia, combativeness, and manic depression. After a week of medication and therapy, Dr. Stedman issued a report stating that Jeffrey was a sociopath, but he was not an escape risk. He suggested further outpatient treatment prior to trial. The last note in the file suggested Jeffrey was fit to stand trial for his crimes, and Dr. Stedman would continue treatment and medication during the process.

I was right. Dr. Stedman was sending him back to jail.

"The court was awaiting Dr. Stedman's report," Orin said. "But Dr. Stedman states Jeffrey wasn't crazy and he was only faking to stay out of jail and to get pills he could sell on the street. Dr. Stedman was sending him back to jail to stand trial."

"He must have told Jeffrey," I said. "Jeffrey told me he wasn't going to jail. He killed Dr. Stedman to prevent him from giving this report to the judge."

"And he had to steal the files to be sure all copies of the reports were destroyed." Ward took the file from me and read through it.

"All of this is so he doesn't have to go to jail?" I asked. "It seems excessive."

"Some people will do anything to stay out of jail. The reason doesn't have to be a good one."

Ward closed the file. "Good work, Orin." He turned toward the group, taking the folder with him.

Orin watched him and raised his hands. "I just lost my story."

"Let him have it. It might be a way to get his badge back. We still have the jump drive." I thought about my deal with Carter and wished I had never made it. Chris had been better off protected by cops.

"You don't need to stay," I told Orin.

"And I don't need your permission, either."

"Go write the story, Orin. Get it on the front page and make sure everyone knows his name. If the cops don't get him, you can make sure they don't stop looking. This one is yours. I'm counting on you."

He nodded once. "You have a good heart, Luc. I don't know why you're scared to show people that. You don't always have to be the tough guy."

"Get out of here before I kick your ass."

He smiled and slapped me on the shoulder before rushing out the door.

Pioa waved me over to Spencer, who was standing at the door. "He wants to leave."

"No," I said, turning to Spencer. "You stay where I can protect you."

"Luc, I need to change clothes. Mattie needs clothes. We can't sit in bloody clothes all night."

I turned to Pioa. "Can you send someone with him?"

He nodded and punched buttons on his phone.

"Do exactly what he says," I told Spencer. "Grab your clothes and grab something Mattie can wear and come right back. I don't want you going near her house."

Pioa looked up. "They're set."

I watched Spencer walk out with two large men wearing all black. I hoped they could keep him safe. I worried that everyone close to me was in danger from a sociopath who just didn't want to go to jail.

To keep myself occupied, and to avoid going stir-crazy waiting for news about Chris, I set about finding a safe and secure location for Mattie to wait. I was amazed to find the nurses unwilling to close off an empty room for Mattie, but I did find one room they didn't bother me about. I was expecting the chapel room to be larger, grander. More like a church. It was empty, so it would work. I stared at a large stained-glass window as I walked in. The small shards of colored glass illuminated a scene, but I couldn't decipher it. My eyes watered, so I turned away.

"Can I help you?"

An old man stood at the door. Gray hair, full beard, and small hands clutching a black book. He was dressed in black and had sad eyes.

"Father," I said.

He smiled. "Chaplain," he corrected.

"Is there any other way into this room?" I asked.

He looked confused. "Just this one." He indicated the door he had walked through. "Please sit. I don't mean to disturb you."

"I don't need to pray."

He smiled again. "I find the ones who say that are often the ones who need it the most."

I didn't want to talk to this man. For some reason, he made me nervous.

"I want to close this room off."

"You can't do that." He sat, patted the chair next to him. "Tell me what the problem is."

I felt the anger boil up. "The problem is, a child is upstairs dying and a woman is in danger, and you want me to sit and pray with you."

"You have something against prayer, or just God in general?"

"I have a problem with you wasting my time."

He nodded, his eyes still staring at me.

I sat. "Look, I don't mean to be rude, but praying isn't going to help that kid. Praying isn't going to take the bullet from his chest or stop the bleeding. And since I'm not a doctor, nothing I do is going to help."

"You feel guilty." He patted my arm. "It's not your fault."

"It is."

"Did you pull the trigger?"

"No, but—"

"Did you ask the shooter to pull the trigger?"

"No. But the bullets were meant for me."

"How do you know what's meant for you?"

I looked at him, but he had turned to look at the stained-glass window.

"Only He knows what's meant for you," the chaplain added.

"I was supposed to take care of him. He's my responsibility."

"And now you feel guilty and helpless. Let someone else take care of him right now. Let God take care of him. Let God take your guilt and helplessness. There is nothing you can do but take care of you."

"And if he dies?"

"Do you believe in heaven?"

I thought of Mattie's house. "No."

"I've found those that don't believe in heaven often create hell on Earth. You've been doing things your way a long time, haven't you?"

I nodded. "Yeah."

"Maybe this time, try doing things His way. Get on your knees and pray."

I was saved by my ringing phone. It was Pioa.

"We need to take Mattie out of this hallway," he said. "The crowd is getting too big."

I stood and turned toward the door. "Bring her to the first floor, the chapel. We can secure her here." I turned back toward the chaplain. "And she can pray here."

Chapter 36

"Spencer's back. You want him in here?" Pioa asked.

Mattie was still sitting with the chaplain, her mother kneeling and praying beside them. Mattie hadn't looked at me since Pioa brought her to the chapel. She hadn't spoken to me, either. They spoke too softly for me to hear, but I could see the tears on her face, the comfort on his.

"Yeah, he can come in."

As the door opened, I got up to pace.

Spencer asked, "Have you heard anything?" He had changed clothes.

I shook my head. "He's still in surgery."

"You can't blame yourself, Luc."

"I was supposed to protect him. I was his guardian. What the hell do I know about being a father? The only thing my father did to protect me was teach me to fight. What am I supposed to do now? Sit here and wait?"

"Yes."

My frustration was getting too big for the room. I needed to walk. I needed to do something. I stared at Mattie and the chaplain sitting quietly, probably praying. I watched Spencer as he approached them. He kneeled and made the sign of the cross.

I stared at the stained glass and tried to piece together the picture. "Just make sure he's okay," I whispered to myself. I felt stupid talking to no one yet hoping someone was listening.

Then my phone rang. I shouldn't have answered it. I probably should have thrown it through the damned stained-glass window, but I didn't. I looked at the screen and saw it wasn't Ward. A restricted number.

I answered it, and for the first time, Mattie looked back at me.

"What do you want?" I asked. There was silence on the other end. "I told you not to call back. All deals are off the table. I've turned the jump drive over to the cops."

"Lying will make you burn in hell," Jeffrey said.

"I'm not lying. Detective Ward is reviewing your medical records now. You're one sick asshole, but you ain't crazy enough to stay out of jail this time."

"You bastard. I will not go back there."

"Too late. You didn't play nice and shot at Mattie. All deals are off."

"No, the stakes just went higher. Bring the drive, or more people you care about will die."

"You got nothing I want, Jeffrey. It's time to give up. The game is over."

"Your father insists. Meet us at your old apartment."

"My father's dead. The voices you hear are all in your head." I hung up the phone.

I turned and walked out of the chapel. Spencer followed me. When the phone rang again, I let it ring. Just before it clicked to voicemail, I answered.

"You don't believe me?" Jeffrey asked. "Your father needs you, and you're going to ignore him?"

"My father is burning in hell right now."

"That's not nice. He practically raised you. I'll let him plead his case." The phone crackled, and it sounded like he was going into a wind tunnel.

"Luc—don't—st—"

I felt my heart being wrenched from my body. My knees buckled. Anger turned back to fear.

Spencer caught me. "What?" he asked.

"He has Bill."

Although I kept the phone to my ear, I couldn't hear anything but a syllable or two. I couldn't make out what Bill was saying, but I knew the voice. I heard the pain in it and felt it rip through me.

Seconds ticked by, and then Jeffrey was back on the phone. "It appears I don't have great cell coverage in there. You want to speak to him further, bring me what I want. The Torrance Apartments, fifteen minutes. I won't wait."

I straightened. "I'll be there in ten."

I turned and saw Mattie at the door. Pioa blocked her exit, but she was about to push him out of the way, despite his size. I couldn't look at her. The fear on her face was too much, the fear in me too great.

"Pioa, I need Jim."

He nodded and grabbed his cell phone.

I walked to Mattie and pushed her back into the room.

"Luc—"

"Stay here. Don't ask me not to go, Mattie. It's the only thing I can do."

"I need you here. With me." Her arms wrapped around me as if she could hold me there forever. I knew then that she hadn't heard what I'd said to Spencer. I hoped I wouldn't have to be the one to tell her a killer was holding her father.

"I can't. I belong out there. I need to stop him."

"This isn't about him, and you know it. Stay here, with me."

I pulled away from her, knowing I should tell her the truth, but unable to say it. "Spencer will be with you. He does this part better than I do. I know you want me to tell you everything, but I can't. Not because I'm afraid it'll hurt you. I know you're strong enough, but I'm not." I wiped the tears from her face, and then I walked away from her.

I could hear her crying, but I didn't stop. Spencer met me at the door.

"Be careful," he said.

"Don't worry, you'll see me again."

"Yeah, I know. I just don't want you to be wearing shackles."

Pioa returned. "Jim's waiting outside for you."

"Keep an eye on both of them."

I found Jim waiting in the parking lot, with the engine of a black Hummer running.

"You found him?" Jim asked me through the window.

"He called me," I said as I jumped into the passenger seat. I saw he had brought company. The same two large men who had escorted Spencer sat in the back seat. They wore black, with sunglasses hiding their eyes. They stared straight ahead, no expression on their faces. They could have been twins.

"Who are they?" I asked as Jim pulled out of the parking lot.

"Not your concern." He didn't look like he wanted to elaborate, so I let it go. I gave him directions to my old apartment.

"We have ten minutes," I said. "Drive fast."

"Do you have a plan?" he asked.

"You got a gun somewhere in here?"

He looked at me for a second then returned his glare back to the road. "You sure you want to go that route?"

"No choice. He has Bill."

"We all have choices, Luc." When I said nothing, he offered, "There's a nine under the seat."

I found the pistol, as well as a large blade. I knew it could come in handy, so I grabbed both. I ordered Jim to park down the alley a block from the apartment. I saw his brow crinkle, but he did what I asked.

"I'm going alone," I said when he parked ten minutes later.

"No, that's not the deal, Luc."

"There is no deal here, Jim. He's got Bill. I take him alone. I'm not risking anyone else."

"There's no risk. I'm good at what I do."

I opened the door. "Stay here. I'll be back in a few minutes."

Jim sat still, but as I got out of the car, the two back doors opened. I leaned back into the car.

"If I'm not back in ten minutes, come and get Bill out of there. Don't worry about me."

Jim said nothing. He held up his hand, and the two men closed their doors.

~~~

As I approached the apartment building, I spotted the homeless man I had seen a few days earlier. I walked over in hopes he could give me information, but as I stepped closer, I saw that he was slumped over. Blood pooled on his stomach and feet. His throat had been slit.

Apparently Jeffrey had no problem killing anyone he encountered. As I crossed the street, I wondered how someone could turn into such a cold-blooded killer.

I knew exactly where Bill would be. I didn't waste time searching each apartment or room. I walked straight to my old apartment, not concerned whether Jeffrey was watching me or not.

Jeffrey wanted the jump drive. He had no idea if I had it. I had considered getting it back from Orin, but I also knew a blank drive would work just as well. I wasn't dealing with a criminal mastermind here. I didn't worry that Jeffrey would shoot me in the back. At some point, he would realize that we'd made copies, but I hoped he wasn't sane enough to figure it out before he was back behind bars.

For now, I knew I was safe as long as I could deliver what he wanted. But I wasn't so sure about Bill's welfare. He was just a way to get me there, and I had no idea if I would find him alive or dead.

As I reached the front door of the apartment, I stopped. I could smell gasoline. I knew there was no way to walk into my old room without giving Jeffrey the advantage of the faceoff, but the gasoline had me very worried.

I couldn't smell smoke, but I felt the door just in case. It was cold.
~~~

I called out to Jeffrey. When there was no response, I turned the knob and walked into my old apartment. It looked the same, but the air was different. I recognized more than just the gasoline fumes. I smelled fear. I smelled pain. I smelled suffering.

My stomach clenched, but I pushed on. I listened for Jeffrey but heard nothing. The old floorboards were wet with gasoline. Suddenly a new scent hit me. Blood. I walked through the kitchen and into my old bedroom.

Bill was alone in the empty room, slumped in a corner with blood dripping from his nose and mouth. His eyes were swollen closed. I knew Jeffrey had to be close, but I reached Bill quickly. I tucked the gun in my back and crouched to check him for other wounds and found he was still breathing. I pulled out the knife and slid it under his arm. I wiped the blood from his mouth. He was bruised and beaten, and I felt another piece of me fall away. This was my fault, and I knew there was no way I'd let Jeffrey walk out of there alive.

"Where is it?" Jeffrey was in the doorway, a gun in one hand and a cigarette in the other. I wasn't sure which I was more worried about.

"Relax. You're not going to jail, Jeffrey," I said. I stayed crouched so I could shield Bill.

"You're right. Give me the files."

"You didn't have to hurt him." I said.

"I did. Dr. Stedman promised I could trust him. He told me he wanted to help me, but he lied. He said I could tell him anything and it would stay between us. I believed him, but he was going to send me back to jail."

I realized I was prepared to deal with a criminal, but I should have prepared for dealing with a psycho. He hadn't asked for my gun. He hadn't even thought to search me. With Bill in the room, I wasn't willing to count on my ability to draw my gun and kill Jeffrey before he could get a shot off, but at least I knew of his dislike of guns and his bad aim.

"Dr. Stedman believed you weren't sick." I shifted and kept talking to distract him. "He thought you should pay for your crime, so you killed him."

"He lied to me."

"Why did you have to kill Henry Dillon?" I asked. "He helped you. He gave you the files you wanted."

"But he knew. He told me there was a laptop. I had to kill him. If I hadn't cut him up, he would never have told me Tony had stolen the files and he was holding on to the laptop for safekeeping. I heard he had died and had to hope the laptop wouldn't be found. I had no idea where to look for it." He smiled now. "Until you gave me his address."

"And you hurt Georgia to get the laptop."

He didn't answer, but I saw something cross his face. "I'm not crazy. Everyone keeps saying I'm crazy, but I'm not. It's everyone else acting crazy." He shook the gun, and I stayed quiet. "Dr. Stedman thought I wouldn't kill him because of what he wrote about me. After all, he thought his death wouldn't stop me from going to prison, but he didn't think it through. If I killed him and destroyed the file, I wasn't going anywhere."

"You can't stop what he put in motion by destroying him and what he wrote. Eventually it would come back to you."

"You're talking about Henry Dillon? Or the slut your father gave the laptop to? They both thought they were safe as long as they told another person. As if I wouldn't bother just adding another to my list. You bought into that, too, didn't you? I bet you told your friends and that detective. You're all so stupid. Talking to other people doesn't save your life, it just endangers theirs. So you add more work for me. I don't mind. I actually enjoy the killing."

"And yet you stand there telling me you're not crazy?"

"All you did by telling everyone was to ensure your death and the deaths of everyone you know." I saw the look in his eyes and knew he planned on killing me.

"You can kill me," I said. "I don't care. I walked in here expecting you to try. You've taken everything from me. I thought I had nothing left to give you but my life—"

He interrupted me. "Where's the jump drive?"

I slowly pulled out my tape recorder and hoped he would think it was the jump drive. My plan was to throw it at him and then pull my gun as he tried to catch it or moved to avoid it. I had seen it happen in the movies and hoped I could pull it off.

But before I could throw it, I heard a sound behind Jeffrey. He heard it, too. He turned his head to look over his left shoulder. His mouth opened slightly, and his eyes opened even wider. His right hand, the one holding the gun pointed at me, dipped. I heard a snap somewhere and it jolted through my muscles, making me jump.

I launched at Jeffrey, smacking him into the wall. He screamed, and I punched him once in the face. I heard the gun drop and scrambled to grab it. Once I had it securely away from him, I put my other hand around his throat.

He squirmed, and I was so focused on choking him that I didn't see the blade. I felt it slice my shoulder just as I punched Jeffery again. The knife dropped, and I threw it in the corner.

I sat on his chest and shoved the barrel of his gun into his mouth. He stopped moving, and I glanced at my shoulder to see blood dripping down my arm toward my wrist.

He kicked his legs, trying to get me off of him, but I squeezed harder on his throat.

"You took my job, my friends, and my family from me," I hissed. "It took years to get this life, and in less than a week, you demolished it, you sick fuck. You took everything; you might as well take my freedom, too. I have no problem going to prison knowing I rid the world of you. I'd do anything to keep my family and friends safe."

I saw his eyes turn glassy, my words no longer getting to him. He was no longer struggling.

"Put the gun down, Luc."

I looked up and saw Big Jim standing over me, his own gun pointed at my face. He looked at me as if I were a stranger. I couldn't read his face. I wondered if I was looking back at someone completely different from the man I knew.

He looked down at the tape recorder at his feet and smashed it.

"What the fuck?" I asked. The look in his eyes scared me. It was the same look I had seen in Jeffrey's eyes minutes earlier. I knew someone was going to die.

"Drop it. Now."

"No." Confused, I looked behind him. His two men had also followed him in. I noticed that the smell of gasoline had been replaced by the smell of smoke.

The two men dressed in black walked into the room. One held an Uzi and a black bag over one shoulder. The other walked quickly over to me and reached for the gun in my hand. I pulled it away, and he punched me in the face.

"Shit!" I felt Jeffrey squirm underneath me.

"Don't hurt him," Jim said. His voice sounded cold, distant.

The man easily pulled the gun from me as I reached for my face. I felt blood as I touched my nose.

"Too late," I said, wiping my face. "What the hell is going on, Jim?"

"Take Bill to the hospital. I'll take care of this."

Smoke was now entering the room above Jim. It circled around him, hiding the grime on the walls and ceiling. I could taste the smoke in the back of my throat and tried not to gag.

"No way. This is my mess to clean up."

Ignoring my conversation with Jim, the two men in black pulled me up and searched me. One took the nine millimeter I had gotten from Jim. The other shook his head. With nothing holding Jeffrey down, he started to squirm away toward the door.

Jim tilted his head, his eyes quickly scanning the room. "The knife will be on Bill."

It didn't take long for the men to have me unarmed. Jim kept his eyes on me.

"You're an amateur here, Luc," he said. "Go."

"Georgia hired you, didn't she?" I asked. "You told her what you do, and you used me to get to him."

He said nothing. No longer worried about me, the twins turned their attention to Jeffrey, who had made it halfway to the door. They pulled him up and opened their bag as he struggled against them. They made quick work of wrapping duct tape around his face and hands.

Jeffrey was crying now, but he was no longer fighting.

I watched the twins carry Jeffrey out of the room and saw that the fire was spreading quickly toward us. When they were gone, Jim finally lowered his weapon and looked at Bill.

My eyes were starting to burn from the smoke as tears ran down my face. Thick black smoke now surrounded us, sucking the last available air from the room.

"I can help you," I said. "I need to do this. It's who I am. I know that now."

"You didn't come here to kill Jeffrey. You came to save Bill. You made a mistake years ago, and you've deluded yourself into thinking you can do it again. This isn't you. Take Bill and get out of here. Do what you need to get your life back. You don't belong here."

"I sure as hell don't belong there, Jim. I don't fit in there."

"Luc, you need to stop trying to fit into someone else's life. Get the fuck out of here. I have a job to do. I won't ask again."

I turned to grab Bill and fell to the floor. The smoke had thickened, making it hard to see and breathe. I pulled at Bill and stumbled through the room, dragging him behind me. I had to stop twice to catch my breath and cough out the thick black smoke I was inhaling.

By the time I dragged Bill out to the stairs, Jim was gone. Someone had already reported the fire, and I could hear the fire trucks racing toward us. I lifted Bill onto my shoulders and dragged him down the stairs. The intense heat made me move faster as I ran across the street and away from the fire.

Laying Bill down, I turned to watch the fire tear apart my old home. One firefighter rushed over and asked me something. I ignored the question and pushed him toward Bill. He handed me a bandage for my shoulder before moving on to Bill.

Detective Ward pulled up a few minutes later. We both watched as Bill was lifted into the ambulance, an oxygen mask on his face and a new bandage on his head. His eyes were opening, and I felt just a bit relieved as the doors closed.

"How'd you find me?" I asked Ward.

"It wasn't too hard. I just had to follow the sirens." He shook his head. "What happened in there?"

"Jeffrey got away. I had to make a decision. I decided it was more important to save Bill than to do your job."

"Is Bill okay?"

"He'll survive. It's the best I could do."

Ward nodded and turned to watch the firefighters spraying water on the building. He pointed to my shoulder. "You okay?"

"I'll live." I wiped away the blood.

"I'm sorry about earlier. You were right. I'm not good at this friend thing. I've been a cop too long to trust people."

"You mean to trust people like me. I understand. You'll always see me as a criminal, but I'm not, Ward. I may push the lines and make mistakes, but I was just trying to do what's right. For everyone."

"I appreciate you trying to protect me. I screwed up. I'm glad I have someone to watch my back." He helped me up. "Chris is out of surgery. Let's get you back before Mattie takes out her bodyguards looking for you."

Chapter 37

Pioa was on the phone when I stepped from the elevator into the intensive care unit. He pointed down the hall. Spencer sat in a plastic folding chair that looked entirely too used. He jumped up when he saw me.

"How's Bill?" Spencer asked. "Carliss took Virginia away in a rush. He wouldn't tell me anything."

"He's okay. Ward just went to check on him." I wondered how angry Mattie's mother was going to be with me once she saw her husband in the hospital. "Where's Mattie?"

"She's with Chris. He's in stable condition. Came out of surgery like he's done this before."

I looked at the door.

"They only let one person in at a time."

"Call Ward," I told him. "I'm sure Bill's going to want an update on the boy as soon as he's released."

Spencer nodded and patted me on the shoulder. I winced at the pain. I stood by the doorway to Chris's room and waited for Pioa. He glanced at me, nodded, and hung up the phone.

"You look like shit," he said. "And you smell like an ashtray."

"Thanks."

"I understand everything has been taken care of. She's yours now. You don't deserve her, and I should protect her from you, but my services have been recalled."

"Was that Jim?"

He nodded. I had more questions, but knew I would never find the answers. He turned for the elevators.

~~~

I found them both asleep when I walked in. Chris looked peaceful despite the oxygen mask over his face. Mattie lay awkwardly in a small metal chair next to Chris's bed. I was reaching over to push the hair from her face when I heard Chris move.

"She's sleeping. Let her sleep," Chris whispered.

"I will. How are you?"

"I got shot in the stomach. They said I'll be fine." He pulled the mask from his face.

I nodded. "Sorry."

"You're covered in ash."

I said nothing, just stared at the boy and listened to the machines humming.

"Did you find him?" Chris asked.

I nodded. I didn't give the details. He was better off not knowing. "I need you to tell me something, Chris. No bullshit this time. It will determine your future."

He nodded, but closed his eyes. I knew he was tired from the drugs, and I knew the pain that comes with being shot. He would live with the pain every day, just like I did.

"Why'd you send me the file?"

He opened his eyes and looked at me.

"I thought you had the laptop," I said, "and when the detectives told me you mailed something, I assumed you mailed it to Georgia, but Georgia said Tony gave it to her before he died."

He pulled the mask from his face again. "I told you I gave the laptop to Tony. You didn't believe me."
~~~

"I do now. But you mailed something, and I didn't remember until today that Carl Palfy's file was mailed on Friday, the day you were taken into Child Services. I want to know how you got the police file and why, but more importantly, why did you send it to me? Was it a threat? What were you trying to tell me?"

He moved his head back and forth slowly. "No, it wasn't a threat. I knew you'd want it. And don't ask me how your father got it out of the police department. I have no idea. He had it a long time before I met up with him. He told me if anything ever happened to him, I was to send it to you. He said you'd know what to do with it." He coughed and gasped for air.

I waited for him to catch his breath and looked back at Mattie.

"What happens now?" Chris asked.

"When you're done healing, you'll go home with Mattie."

He nodded. "Spencer said he arranged for me to stay with her temporarily, but . . ." He looked away.

"What?" I asked.

"Spencer said you can't be there. He said Child and Family Services wouldn't agree to give you custody without further investigation."

I rubbed the back of my neck. "Don't worry about that right now. We'll figure it out. I won't be around for a while, anyway. I have some things I need to take care of first."

"You're leaving?" he asked. He suddenly looked very young. His eyes dropped.

"I'll be back. In the meantime, you need to keep her safe. You need to keep her happy. Do you understand me?" He nodded. I put the oxygen mask back on his face. "Get some rest."

I sat watching over them for another half hour. I listened to the monitors and watched the two of them sleeping soundly.

Spencer met me outside.

"How's Bill?" I asked.

"He's already arguing with the doctors to be released. I give him another five minutes before he's hounding Chris's doctors."

I nodded. "I need a favor."

I saw him shut off again and knew our friendship wasn't back. He sighed. "What?"

"I need to leave town for a little while."

Spencer sat down on the folding chair. "You're really going to move out? Mattie's not going to like that."

"I never really moved in, Spencer. I need some time to figure things out. To find out who I am. Besides, she needs Chris. We both can't be there."

He looked at me.

"Chris told me."

Spencer shook his head. "Nothing's set in stone. We have to work the details out. We'll make it work. If you leave her again, it will kill her, Luc. Don't do this to her."

"It's best for all of us. We all need time. I shouldn't have rushed this."

The elevator door opened and Ward stepped out.

"When Mattie wakes, make sure she doesn't find out about Bill."

"Yeah, you wouldn't want her to know you saved his life."

"I don't want her to know I chose him over her."

Spencer laughed. "Yeah, that's the way she'll see it."

I shook his hand and wondered if we'd ever be friends like we were before. I watched him walk back toward Chris's room. Then I walked over to meet Ward. He didn't look happy.

"They haven't found him yet, but we will. I promise you, we'll find him."

I knew they wouldn't.

Made in the USA
Monee, IL
05 June 2021

70235656R00152